MERCY!

Switched Series

Book III

Kay Chandler

A multi-award-winning author

This novel is a work of fiction. Names, characters, and incidents are products of the author's imagination or used fictitiously.

Scripture taken from the King James Version of the Holy Bible

Cover Design by Chase Chandler

ISBN:0692675485
ISBN-13:9780692675489

DEDICATED TO
Sergeant Hubert Raymond Denny

This novel is dedicated to the memory of a brave young soldier, Sergeant Hubert Raymond Denny, who served with A Company, 137th Infantry in St. Lo, France during WWII.

Hubert and his beautiful bride, Nealie, met and fell in love at Lake Geneva, while he was stationed at Fort Rucker, Alabama. The happy couple had dreams for a long and wonderful future, but due to the war, those well-laid plans would have to be put on hold until he returned home again.

Then came the dreaded telegram, which began "The Secretary of War deeply regrets . . . "

Sergeant Denny was killed in a foxhole in St. Lo, France, July 17, 1944, leaving to mourn, his sixteen-year-old pregnant widow. Baby girl Huberta Rae was born twenty-one weeks after her father's death.

May God Bless all the brave men and women who have given so much for their country.

Sergeant Denny gave his all.

PROLOGUE

February 8, 1945

My Dearest Garth,

By this time next month, you'll be addressing your letters to Mrs. Garth Graham, instead of Miss Gracie Jackson. All my dreams are about to come true. If only I could hasten the time.

Nine Gables Orphanage will officially open three days after we're married, leaving you twenty-one glorious days on your furlough to become acquainted with "our" kids before being shipped overseas. I visited the foster home today and instantly fell in love with them.

Ludie, the oldest, is thirteen, and according to her records, she's been in five foster homes and is said to exhibit unacceptable behavior. I can't imagine that to be true. She seems very sweet. Then there are the sisters, Belle and Maddie Claire. Belle is eight, and doesn't talk, though no one seems to know why. Six-year-old Maddie has taken it upon herself to become her older sister's caretaker. The towhead twins, Toby and Tanner are eleven and according to Mrs. Ward, they're all good kids, though Ludie is had she asked the same questions and waited for answers that didn't come? Now, everything Gracie believed in was being scrambled like eggs in an omelet.

She buried her head in the pillow, hoping to erase the dreadful telegram from her memory. Yet the words in random order filled every waking moment, as if seared on her brain with a soldering iron. "Killed in action . . . Secretary of War, deeply regrets . . . killed . . . Private Garth Graham . . . in the service of his country . . . Garth . . . April 16, 1945. . . killed." She clasped her hands over her ears. The nightmares had not lessened one iota in the past five weeks nor had the hot tears dried on her face.

She raised up in bed and squinted at the bright sunlight glaring through the open shutters. If she needed one more reason to crawl back under the covers, the noise coming from downstairs was reason enough. Whatever gave her the idea running an orphanage would be easy? The children, who brought Gracie such joy before the telegram, had become a snare, requiring she live when all she wanted to do was die. She'd begun to blame them for her misery.

Before the telegram—when she still had something to live for—she arose every morning at five-thirty, ready to start the day with a song. She laid out school clothes, braided the younger girls' hair, packed sack lunches and had them out the door in time to make it to class without being tardy a single day. Taking care of a big house, cooking for six, doing laundry, and allowing time at the end of the day to spend with each child was exhausting, but she loved every minute. Life was swell. But that was then.

Nothing or no one could remove the agonizing loneliness she now felt, knowing she'd never again feel her beloved husband's loving arms around her. Or his lips caressing hers. Or open her eyes in the mornings to see him lying next to her. If only she could go to sleep and never wake up. She rubbed her temples, hoping to blot out the horrid thoughts racing through her head.

Without bothering to brush her hair, she trudged down to the kitchen in her nightgown. *Ten-thirty?* Surely, the clock above the stove was wrong. Guilt, anger, and heartbreak all meshed together until she could no longer separate the three emotions. Gawking at the chaos in the kitchen, Gracie fought the urge to smash everything in sight. Flour dusted the linoleum tile floor around the Hoosier Cabinet and footprints of varying sizes tracked from one end of the room to the other. Her instinct was to scream at the children for making such a mess. Was it their fault? Or hers, for not getting out of bed to make their breakfast? She forced her lips together to keep from saying something she'd later regret.

The milk pitcher sat on the kitchen table beside something in a pan she could only guess were meant to be biscuits, evidence the eleven-year-old twins, Toby and Tanner had made breakfast. Again. School had let out for the summer and whether good or bad, she had mixed feelings. Now, she wouldn't have to worry about the truant officer showing up at her door to find out why the kids continued to be late for school, but there was the downside. Five active kids would be under foot all day. No longer would she be free to go back to bed in the mornings and hide under the covers until school let out at three o'clock.

Tanner blew upward, sending long strands of white-blonde hair away from his wide blue eyes. Gracie tried to remember the last time she took the twins to the barbershop.

He shuffled his feet and mumbled, "I tried to make biscuits, but I think I left something out. They don't taste like yours, Gigi."

Gigi? She loved the pet name when her husband first suggested it, but hearing it this morning cut to the bone. Garth had thought it inappropriate for the children to call her by her given name, and insisted Mrs. Graham sounded too formal. He'd said, "Your initials are G.G. Why not Gigi?"

Her lip quivered. The morning he left home, she'd stood in the same spot she was now standing when he tenderly pushed her hair back, kissed her on the neck and whispered, "My little Gigi."

Her gaze shifted to the corner of the room, where eight-year-old Belle sat on the flour-drenched floor, sucking her thumb. Gracie swallowed the lump in her throat, seeing the beautiful mute child, rock back and forth in her own little world, while twirling a long shock of blonde hair around her tiny finger. Belle's six-year-old sister, Maddie Claire had stepped up and become her older sister's protector from cruel children in the community, but the biggest bully was living under the same roof—thirteen-year-old Eliza Clementine Doe, or Ludie as she was called.

Maddie Claire stood on a milk stool singing *Ten Little Indians* to the top of her lungs, as she washed the breakfast dishes. Bright rays of light streamed through the kitchen window and reflected off the child's copper-colored hair, causing it to glisten like a shiny new penny. Soap suds dripped from tiny elbows to the floor, creating a white paste around the edges of her stepstool. "Five little, four little, three little Indians . . ."

Gracie shuddered. "*Please*, Maddie Claire. No more little Indians."

"Sorry, Gigi. I'll be quiet."

The sudden silence was more maddening than the off-key singing. With her hands plunked on her hips, Gracie surveyed the havoc in the kitchen—exasperated, yet not riled enough to muster the energy to clean it. Why bother? It was a hopeless cycle. No one warned her kids were so messy. Tears seeped from the corners of her swollen eyes. In the only letter she'd received from Garth before he died, he talked of being proud of her and confident she'd be able to help poor Belle learn to cope with life—and all Ludie needed was lots of love to combat the anger boiling inside her. It sounded well and good at the time. Not anymore. How could she be of help to Belle or Ludie when her own internal boiler was set to explode?

Gracie plopped down at the kitchen table and rested her elbows on the tabletop. When the tacky, syrup-covered oilcloth stuck to her skin, she jumped up, flailed sticky arms in the air and screamed. "I can't do this. I can't! I want out."

The screen door slammed. She didn't have to look around to know the twins had run out the door. The boys were good at taking charge and doing their chores, but when things became stressful, they vanished. Lately, she saw less and less of them.

Gracie winced, feeling damp little arms wrapping around her neck. Maddie Claire's voice quivered. "I'm sorry you're so sad, Gigi. Me and Belle will go pick you a pretty bouquet of daisies. That'll make you all better. Right?"

She lifted her head and swabbed the wetness from her cheeks. "Flowers . . . yes, thank you," she muttered. Glancing about the room, Gracie said, "Where's Ludie?" But Maddie Claire and Belle were heading out the door to pick flowers.

She heaved a sigh. Better she didn't know, she supposed. Lately, there'd been nothing but sparks flying between her and Ludie and Gracie didn't feel like dealing with the rebellious teen's backtalk this morning. What was she thinking when she agreed to take on someone else's problem? After all, if five foster homes had found the girl impossible to deal with, what made her think she was better equipped to handle a disobedient, spiteful kid? For the first few weeks after she arrived, Gracie thought they were making progress, but lately Ludie had become impossible.

Just when she thought things couldn't get worse, the familiar grating sound of an old truck pulling into the yard brought a shudder. *Not him again.* She grabbed a broom and attempted to sweep the flour from the floor, only to send it flying in the air, making it worse. She stiffened when the screen door cracked opened. Why did he always insist on coming to the back door?

"Good morning, Miz Graham. It's a beautiful day, ain't it?" With his left hand, he fumbled with the strap buckle on his worn bib overalls and blushed. "'Scuse my English, ma'am. I meant to say *Isn't* it a beautiful day."

Not wanting to delve into a lengthy conversation with the uncouth dirt farmer, she simply nodded, though she saw nothing beautiful from her vantage point.

Ezekiel Thorne, the twins' father, had a habit of showing up at the most inopportune times. Not surprising since there were no opportune times. She'd begun to suspect he was checking up, making sure she was capable of raising his boys. If he decided she wasn't, he'd be right. So why didn't he take them away, making it easier on everyone? However, as much as she loathed his unannounced visits, she couldn't deny his devotion to his kids was admirable. Her throat constricted, imagining the kind of doting father Garth would've been.

With one foot stuck in the door and one out, Mr. Thorne continued to hold the door partially open. "Mind if I come in?"

"You'll find the boys playing outside."

"Oh, I've seen 'em already. I'm surprised you didn't hear the little rascals squealing like a couple o' stuck pigs, when they saw my truck drive up." He pulled off his straw hat and ran his hands through sun-streaked greasy hair. "I'm sorry if I've been a nuisance. I've tried to stay away to keep from troubling you, but I sure miss those young'uns. I hope they're behaving themselves, ma'am."

"They're doing fine. Have a good day, sir." Once more, she attempted to jerk the door from his grasp.

"Miz Graham, could we talk? Please?"

She glanced down at the worn brogan blocking the door. "Forgive me, but I'm quite busy and I'm sure you came to see your children. If you'll kindly move your foot—"

"You're right, ma'am in thinking I want to see my kids, but I have another reason for needin' to talk to you. I was hoping you and I could have a little chat. I'll make it snappy."

Gracie turned and rolled her eyes. Or did she roll her eyes, then turn? She wasn't sure. Why should she care? He'd formed his opinion of her already and the chaos in the kitchen served only to confirm to them both that his boys would be better off in another environment. She let go of the door and stepped aside. "Fine. Go on into the parlor and have a seat."

"Beggin' yo' pardon, ma'am, but I'm not a parlor-kind of man, so I'd prefer stayin' in the kitchen, if you don't mind."

Well, she did mind. But now that he'd seen the mess, did it really matter? She grabbed a wet rag from the sink and made a vain attempt to wipe the sticky syrup from the tablecloth.

Then, sucking in a lungful of air, she let out a loud gasp and threw the cloth down. Clasping her arms around her midsection, she stuttered. "Oh, my word. I forgot. I'm not dressed . . ."

"Shucks, no need to apologize. I've seen worse."

"Huh?" Surely, he didn't mean it the way it sounded. She clutched the gown tightly at the neck. "I wasn't feeling well this morning and slept in. I need to run upstairs and change. Perhaps you'd like to come back tomorrow?"

"Why, thank you for the invitation. Yes'm, I'd sure like that. Now, take your time getting dressed. I ain't in no rush." He flinched, but this time didn't bother to correct his grammar. "The boys are playing baseball in the pasture, and I promised the little dickens I wouldn't leave until the game's over. I figure that'll be time enough to finish what I aim to say."

Gracie scampered toward the stairs, mumbling, though in her frenzied state, she was less than coherent and concluded it was probably for the best. *He's seen worse? Invitation?* Rushing into her bedroom, she grabbed the skirt and blouse thrown across a chair—the same outfit she wore yesterday. Then, gazing at her frightful image in the armoire, she let out a soft gasp. The oil in her matted hair made it appear dull and lifeless. She picked up a brush from off the dresser and raked it through the tangled mass, yet it looked none the better when she finished. She slid her hand across her sallow face and moaned. "Oh, Lord, I want my life back."

When she returned to the kitchen, the farmer gawked with a silly grin that made Gracie want to turn around and run back up the stairs. Perfectly aligned white teeth sparkled against his tan face when his lips parted.

"Well, now, don't you look spiffy."

Was he asking or making a statement? Her face heated. "I look awful, and you know it." She expected him to contradict her, but he didn't. He was a kind man—but not kind enough to continue stretching the truth. "You said we needed to chat. So what's on your mind? Got someone else to take care of the boys?"

She wasn't sure if she was afraid he'd take them away, or afraid he'd leave them.

He gave a slight nod. "Sump'n like that."

"Fine! I hope they'll be happy." Why it irritated her, she couldn't understand. Unless she was angry at facing the truth. After dreaming of running an orphanage for years, she was a failure. The kids didn't need her and she sure didn't need them. The muscles in her face twitched. "I'll pack their bags."

"Why? They ain't . . . *aren't* going nowhere."

"But you said . . ."

"I said I have somebody else to take care of 'em."

"Mr. Thorne, I'm sorry, but I don't feel like chasing rabbits with you this morning. As you can see, I have things to do that require my immediate attention." She waved her hand across the mess in the kitchen.

"Please. The name's Ezekiel, but my friends call me Zeke. And I'm sorry if I sounded like I was giving you the runaround." He gestured toward the table. "Mind if we sit down?"

She shrugged. "Make it quick. I don't have time to dawdle."

With his elbows resting on the table, he laced his calloused hands in front of him. "I won't beat around the bush. Truth is, I'm desperate, Miz Graham. I need a place to stay, and since you ain't got no . . . I'm sorry, about my English, ma'am, but I ain't got time to keep stopping. I hope you won't hold it agin me."

"Please. Just say what you came here for. I have things to do."

"Yes'm. As I was about to say, since you ain't got a man

around the house, I was hoping you'd allow me to move in until I can make other arrangements. I've given it a lot of thought, and I truly believe it'll be a good thing for both of us."

Chapter Two

"What? You're suggesting you stay here? At Nine Gables?"

The knot in Gracie's stomach twisted. "Mr. Thorne, you caught me at a low point this morning, but in spite of any conclusions you may have drawn about me, I'm still in control of my faculties. The fact you'd even let such an absurd notion occupy your thoughts is not only preposterous, but highly insulting. Now, if you'll excuse me, I'll show you to the door. I have things to do."

He slapped his palm against his forehead. "Good grief, I'm such a nitwit. I'm sorry, Miz Graham, I reckon it sounded like I was hinting at a little hanky-panky—you being without a husband and me being without a wife. Shucks, I may not be real smart, but I ain't plumb loco. Any man can look at you and tell a ritzy dame like you ain't no match for a dirt farmer. Please, just allow me fifteen minutes of your time to explain myself. That's all I ask. Fifteen minutes?"

Gracie made a point of glancing up at the clock. "Fifteen minutes. Start talking."

"Yes'm. Thank you ma'am." He popped his knuckles, then

pointed to the stove. "Got hot coffee in that pot over yonder?"

"No."

He pushed his chair back, strolled across the room, then picked up the percolator. "You mind?"

Did he really care if she minded? He was spooning coffee into the pot while asking permission. Eyeing him from the back, she'd never noticed what broad shoulders and narrow hips the man had, but then she'd never really looked at him closely.

He strutted back to the table, turned the cane-bottom chair backward and straddled the seat. When their gaze locked, Gracie employed her most prudish voice. "Mr. Thorne, I don't wish to be rude, but you said fifteen minutes. Time's wasting."

"Gotcha." His cheeks billowed out, then slowly he exhaled the pent-up air. "Here's the thing, ma'am. My beloved wife died six months ago."

"Yes, I know. Please stop dilly-dallying." She winced at the coldness in her voice, but if he'd come seeking sympathy, he'd come to the wrong place. He wasn't the only one who'd suffered a loss.

"Yes'm. I'm hurrying. You see, my Lucy, she was laid up the last two years of her life with consumption. And though I ain't blaming her, the truth is, she wadn't able to be a mother to them boys—or a wife to me, as far as that goes—for a long spell before then. A mighty long spell."

Gracie squirmed in her chair. She didn't like the direction this was heading.

"Not that I'm complaining. No sirree. I loved my wife and I ain't never regretted a single minute I spent lookin' after her. Truth is, though, I couldn't work the farm, take care of Lucy around the clock, and do right by my boys." His voice quaked. "Then she upped and died on me."

Gracie nodded with all the sympathy she could muster. "Go on . . ."

"Well, Mr. Henry at the bank, he gave me 'til the fifteenth to make back payments or lose the farm. I tried ever' way I knew how to get the money. Lord knows, I tried, but wadn't no way. I just couldn't do it. The bank gave me a week to get out."

"I'm sorry, Mr. Thorne, I really am. But surely you understand your suggestion is ludicrous. You're wasting your time. No way could I ever—"

He glanced up at the clock above the stove. "Wait. I ain't done, yet."

She lifted her shoulder in a dismissive shrug. "I think the coffee's brewed." Shoving her chair back, she grabbed two cups and saucers from the cupboard. "Cream and sugar?"

"Black's fine, thank you."

Gracie sat back down and watched as he poured a small amount of the steaming coffee in his saucer, then blew in it to cool.

He gave a hearty slurp and smacked his lips. "That's mighty good. Just enough chicory. Now, where was I?"

"You couldn't save the farm."

"Yes'm, I recall now. Well, I shoulda seen it coming last fall.

The peanuts didn't make doodlum and all I had in the fields was cotton, but with the bank note due and funeral expenses to pay, I couldn't afford to hire enough pickers. I put the twins in foster care, and thought if I worked night and day without stopping, me and four paid hands could pick enough to keep my head above water." He took another sip of coffee. "Just when I thought things couldn't get no worse, they did. Boll weevils got to my cotton, and I lost the whole crop."

"That's a sad story and I'm truly sorry, but—"

"You said fifteen minutes. I still got time left." He raked his hands through his hair. "Somebody told me Mrs. Ward at the foster home was fixin' to leave town after her husband died, and the state would come in and put my boys up for adoption." With his thumb and forefinger he dabbed the moisture from his tear ducts. "I tell you the truth, Miz Graham, I might have to kill somebody if they wuz to ever try to take my young'uns away from me." Wringing his hands, he glanced at the clock. "Please bear with me. I can't talk no faster."

"You're doing fine."

"Thank you, ma'am." He blew out a light puff of air. "So, hearing the news that my boys could be jerked out from under me, money wadn't my main concern no more. I ain't ashamed to tell ya, I was worried slap crazy. Knowin' I could use all the prayers I could get, I drove over to El Bethel Church to talk with the preacher there."

"Your pastor?"

"Nah, I been too busy to go to church. Besides, I figure religion's for women folk and young'uns. I told him my troubles and he said he'd pray about it, but I left feeling no better'n when I got there. But lo and behold, the next day he called and said you'd be opening a private orphanage here at Nine Gables where the young'uns wouldn't be adopted out. I figured that preacher had a direct line to God, since I was sure it was his prayers what done it."

Gracie felt the ice melting from her heart. "They're good kids. You and your wife have done a great job raising them. Can I pour you another cup of coffee?"

"Thank you. I appreciate you bearing with me, Miz Graham. I'm talking fast as I can, to pack in two long years in fifteen short minutes."

Gracie couldn't help feeling sorry for the fellow. He had troubles for sure. And if it helped him to have someone to talk to, surely she could allow him a few extra minutes of her time. Nevertheless, he wasn't thinking straight if he thought she'd consider his outlandish suggestion to move in. She took in strays, but not full grown ones.

He poured coffee in the saucer and tilting it toward his mouth, made a loud slurp. "My plan was to place the kids here in the orphanage, get 'em settled, and then volunteer for the infantry."

Gracie picked up a napkin and blotted her lips. "Well, I'm glad you came to your senses in time. Of all the idiotic ideas, joining the infantry would take first place. Your sons have already lost one parent. It'd be cruel for you to purposely put yourself in a position where they could lose the only one they have left."

"Well, that ain't exactly how I see it. But whether right or wrong, makes no difference at this point, and I'll tell you why. I had until today to move off the farm and I went straight to the recruiting office and signed up. I felt good about the boys, knowing they'd be in good hands until I returned."

The muscles in her face twitched. Why did every soldier think he wouldn't be one of the ones coming back in a pine box? "*If* you returned." Gracie mumbled.

"I beg your pardon?"

"Never mind. But since you've joined the army, I suppose you were only suggesting you need a place to stay until your papers are in order?"

"I wish that's how it was."

"I don't understand."

"Army turned me down. Seems I have a hernia." He glanced down and wrung his hands. "Sorry, ma'am. I see I embarrassed you. I reckon maybe it ain't proper to discuss such in mixed company. I do apologize."

"It's quite alright. I blush easily. Please continue."

"You a good woman, Miz Graham." His eyes twinkled when he smiled.

Gracie lowered her head and hoped she hadn't blushed again.

"Like I was sayin', for them to turn me down because of a . . . because of *that*, was the stupidest thing I ever heard tell of. Shucks, I didn't even know it was there. I tried to tell 'em I can lift anything any man my size can lift. I'm strong. I've farmed all my life. But it weren't no use. Nothing I could say or do would change their minds." He sucked in a lungful of air and blew out slowly. "Now, ma'am, I reckon I've come to the point I been leadin' up to. Fact is, I had to leave everything behind except my clothes, which are now stuffed in a gunny sack inside my car."

Gracie stiffened. Regardless of how pitiful the story, she had to be firm.

He rubbed the back of his neck, then leaned in. "The way I figure it, ma'am, you need a man to help out around this big place, and I need somewhere to stay until I can get a job and make enough money to rent a place. As an added bonus, I'll get to be near my kids. Don't you see my point? It'll benefit us both. How about it?"

"I understand what you're saying, but surely, there are jobs available with so many of our men away fighting this dreadful war. It shouldn't take long for you to find suitable employment and a room in a nice boarding house, Mr. Thorne."

He cocked his head to the side. "I don't reckon you were listening. Lady, I need a place now and I don't have money for a room in a boarding house. I'll work harder than any caretaker you could hire. And please call me Zeke."

"*Zeke,* it won't work."

"Beggin' your pardon, ma'am, but why not?"

She couldn't believe she was allowing this dirt farmer to put her on the defensive. "Are you crazy? Can you imagine what people will say about the young widow at Nine Gables who allowed a handsome widower to move in only five weeks after her husband was killed serving his country? The idea is absurd."

"Handsome?" His lip curled.

She stared at him, muscles in her face twitching. *Heavenly days. Did I really say handsome?* Now, sizing him up, she supposed he was, in a rugged sort of way. His lips were a bit thinner than Garth's and his square jaw slightly resembled her deceased husband's, but there was no cleft in his chin. His eyes were hazel with yellow flecks—not brown, and the sun-bleached streaks in his chestnut hair made the greasy shocks appear much lighter against his tanned face. Her gaze shifted to his stubby, calloused hands with dirt under his nails and she instinctively compared them to her husband's, recalling the day she slid a wedding band on his long, slender finger. She couldn't even imagine Garth wearing faded overalls. He was very particular about his attire. Her pulse raced. What was she doing, comparing the two? No man could ever measure up to her darling Garth. Especially not a redneck dirt farmer out begging for a place to lay his head.

"Well?" His raised brow hadn't lowered.

The awkward moment caused blood to rush to her head. "I'm sorry. I lost my train of thought. You were saying . . ."

His eyes flickered as if he'd been reading her mind. "It ain't as if I'd be living with you, Mrs. Graham. It'd be the ideal set-up for both of us and it's not like a lifetime commitment. It'll only be until I find a job and can make enough money to rent a place. I'd be staying in the basement and shucks, nobody could fault you for hiring a caretaker. There was bound to be one here in the past. It's plain to see from the overgrown rose garden this place was once tended. Whatcha say, Mrs. Graham?"

It sounded appealing. Gracie could use the help. Though Nine Gables was beautiful, it was old and in need of repairs. Was she crazy? Shoving it from her mind, she shook her head vehemently. "No! It's out of the question."

"May I ask why?"

"I can't afford you."

"Have I set a price?"

"No, but before you do, I can assure you it's more than I can afford."

"What about a place to sleep and three meals a day until I get on my feet?"

"You aren't serious."

"I'm dead serious. I need this, lady. I need you as much as you need me. Say you'll do it. Just give it a chance, that's all I ask."

Gracie covered her face with her hands and let out a soft sigh. "I must be losing my mind."

"So you're saying you'll do it?"

"I'm saying I'll give it a try."

He jumped up and rubbed beads of sweat from his forehead. "Thank you, Miz Graham. Shucks, I'm so happy I could hug yo' neck."

"Excuse me?"

He blushed from his chin to the top of his head. "Good gravy, I didn't mean nothing by that remark. Why, I'd never hug . . ." He stopped and stammered. "What I mean is, not without your approv—"

She interrupted to prevent him from sticking his foot further into his mouth. "Wouldn't you like to take a look at the room in the basement before you agree to such an arrangement?"

"No ma'am. I'll take it."

"When would you like to move in?"

"Immediately. My stuff's in the car."

"You were pretty sure I'd say, 'yes,' weren't you?"

"No'm, but I'm mighty grateful you did. I packed the car this morning and rode around trying to figure out a plan, when the idea came to me." He picked up his hat and stood with his hand outstretched. "Thank you, Miz Graham. You won't be sorry. I promise."

That's what *he* thought. She was sorry already. Not only did she now have five kids to care for, she'd have a man in the house who'd expect her to be up early every morning to prepare the first of three decent meals a day. What had she done?

"Before I bring my stuff in, why don't we get this kitchen cleaned up? Looks like you might've had some help fixin' breakfast this morning."

"No, I'm afraid the kids made breakfast all by themselves." She picked up a biscuit and tossed to him. "Toby made the biscuits."

His eyes twinkled with the unmistakable look of a proud father. Then laughing, he threw it in the air and caught it. "Shucks, I wonder why the kids are playing with a ball of yarn when these biscuits would make a better baseball?"

His light-hearted laughter brought a smile to her lips. How long had it been since she'd smiled? She knew the answer. Five very long weeks, which seemed more like five horrible years. A sudden wave of guilt shrouded her, as if she'd somehow defamed her husband's memory by momentarily forgetting her pain.

"I'll need a mop and a bucket of water," he said. "And I'm figurin' you'll need to go to the store and get a ten pound bag of flour, because I'm guessing the flour bin's empty. There must be eight or nine pounds on the floor."

"No need for you to clean the kitchen. That won't be part of your duties."

"My duty is to make life easier for you. Now, where did you say I'd find a mop?"

She went in the broom closet and brought out a mop and bucket, then hesitated. "Are you sure?"

He reached out and took them from her hands. "Hey, this will be a cinch. I mopped plenty of floors during the two years my wife was ill."

"I'm sorry. You must miss her, terribly." Her voice quaked.

"Yeah, I miss her. But we don't have time to get all weepy here. We've got work to do."

His words caught her off-guard, but she supposed he was right. Grabbing a soapy rag, she began scrubbing the sticky globs of syrup from the oilcloth, then stopped and threw up her hands. “This isn’t working.”

His eyes pleaded. “Give it time. We’ve just started.”

“No, I mean trying to clean this tablecloth with a rag. It isn’t working. Not only is the top sticky, but the syrup has dripped down the sides. I think I’ll take it outside and scrub it in a washtub.”

“Good idea. I see already me and you gonna make a swell team.”

Though she bristled at the idea of being linked as ‘a team’ with someone so uncouth, she couldn’t deny his gentle voice and warm smile made her feel like a human being again. Accountability. That’s what had been lacking in her life. And now that an adult would be in and out, maybe she’d find the energy to face each new day. She relived the humiliation when he walked in at mid-morning and found her slouched in her gown and the kitchen a total disaster. Yet, he hadn’t judged her. The last thing she needed was a judge. Gracie had become her own judge and jury and condemned herself already. She supposed in a snobbish way, she’d judged Zeke as well. True, he was rough around the edges, but he meant well.

The kitchen was soon cleaner than she’d seen it in weeks, and she had more energy now than when they started.

Zeke carried the mop to the back yard and hung it across the clothes line to dry.

Gracie brushed a lock of hair back of her ear. "I need to run to the store and pick up a few things for lunch." She knew exactly what she wanted to prepare. Having a cow was certainly a blessing, since milk and fats were now rationed because of the war. But sweet iced tea was the one thing she missed more than anything. With sugar being rationed, she used her allotment to make treats for the children. She'd even stopped making ice in the metal trays. But today, there'd be sweet tea on the table. For the first time in weeks, she'd begun to feel alive again, though she dismissed the ridiculous idea the dirt farmer had anything to do with it. On her way home, she stopped by the ice house for a block of ice to go in the tea.

When she drove down the long driveway at Nine Gables and saw poor Belle squatting on the ground with Zeke standing over her holding a chicken by the legs as it flopped back and forth, her heart pounded like a jackhammer. The children were hollering to the top of their lungs. The car made a loud grinding noise when she stomped the clutch and jerked it in neutral. Had she lost her mind, leaving them with a total stranger? "Stop it! What are you doing to her," she screamed.

Maddie yelled, "It's okay, Gigi, Belle's got chicken pox and Mr. Zeke's gonna make her all better."

He reared back and grinned as if expecting thanks for his efforts. "That's right, ma'am. Look at them spots on her arms. Ever'body knows ain't no better way to get shed of the chicken pox than to lie the young'un on the ground and let a chicken fly over 'em. I was just fixin' to turn it loose when you drove up. Wanna watch?"

"Are you crazy? Get up off the ground, Belle." Gracie rushed over and brushed dirt from the child's curly-blonde hair. Her breathing slowed when she realized the kids weren't in danger. The man might be steeped in ridiculous folklore, but he was harmless.

"It works like this, ma'am—when a chicken flies over the infected, it causes the young'un to break out quicker, and scab over." His long face revealed his disappointment. "I can see you don't believe me, but it ain't no lie. I had eight brothers and sisters, and my granny swore by it. And not nary one of us ever had a bad case."

"I know you meant well, Zeke, but that's nothing more than an old wives' tale. Besides, Belle doesn't have chicken pox. She and Maddie went blueberry picking and she got a case of redbugs."

"Redbugs? Well, I Suwannee."

"No harm done, I don't suppose. As soon as I catch that chicken and maybe one more, we'll have it for lunch."

"You go on about your business, ma'am. Me and the boys'll be glad to fetch them chickens and ring the necks for you."

"Thank you, I'll go scald the water." No way would she turn down such an offer. She'd rung quite a few chickens' necks, but never quite got the hang of it.

Tanner brought in two headless chickens. Gracie quickly dunked them in scalding water and watched out the window as she plucked the feathers. What a difference a man on the place had made. She could hear the children screaming a little ditty, "Ain't no boogers out tonight, Grandpa killed 'em all last night," as they ran from Zeke. The joy on the faces of the children and the gleeful sound of laughter had been missing for weeks. Had she been so consumed with her own hurts, she'd failed to see the pain she was inflicting on the children? Earlier, she'd debated her decision to let the farmer stay, but the debate was over. He'd brought life to a dead house. Even if she didn't need him, it was evident the children did.

Spotting her at the window, he stopped and yelled. "I plan to repair the stair railing after lunch, but if there's something you'd like me to do now, I'll be glad to take care of it."

"No. What you're doing is very needful. Thank you."

He'd even managed to get Belle to play. Everyone except Ludie, who still wasn't home. Since school let out, she'd been leaving the house every morning, staying gone for hours. She'd often leave again in the afternoons. "Going for a walk," was all the explanation she ever offered. It hadn't been long since Gracie was a teenager and she recalled having anger issues after losing her mother, but nothing to compare with Ludie's hostile behavior.

Gracie cut up two fryers and made a bowl of potato salad. The tablecloth was still on the line, so she pulled out a lace cloth from the sideboard and draped it over the dining table. She surveyed the bounty to make sure she'd done everything. Fried chicken, potato salad, collard greens, sliced tomatoes, corn bread and sweet tea. She opened the back door and rang the dinner bell.

The stunned look on the children's faces made her realize how lax she'd become over the last few weeks. She breathed easier when not a single child made reference to the shoddy meals she'd been guilty of putting before them.

Toby said, "You're a good cook, Gigi."

"She's the best in the whole wide world," Maddie Claire responded, gnawing on a drumstick.

Belle nodded in agreement.

But it wasn't only the children's approval she'd won. Zeke Thorne filled his plate and couldn't stop bragging on the chicken.

"Best I've ever had, and I've had some finger-licking good chicken in my day. The kids are right. You're a fine cook, Miz. Graham." He took a bite of cornbread, then wiped the back of his hand across his mouth. "Yes'm it's all mighty good, Miz Graham."

She picked up her napkin from her lap and blotted her lips. Without looking his way, she said, "I suppose there's no harm in your calling me by my given name."

He shrugged and crammed another corn pone in his mouth. "Sure thing, Gracie."

His flippant attitude, as if he expected it, caused her to flinch. Had she lost her mind? He was the hired help, for goodness sake, and as such should be kept in line. "*Mrs.* Gracie, if you please." She drew a long breath. *That sounded snooty.* No need to make herself miserable over it. What was done, was done. Besides, he'd be gone shortly.

"Whatever you say, Miz Gracie. Pass the 'tater salad, please." Half-way through the meal, Zeke said, "Ain't we missing somebody?"

Tanner spoke up. "You mean Ludie? Aw, she never eats with us."

Zeke looked at Gracie, as if expecting an explanation.

"Tanner's right. She'll come dragging in mid-afternoon and scramble around the kitchen searching for something to eat. I've learned it's easier to leave her alone than to try to get her to conform."

"You ain't serious. She's a kid, for cryin' out loud. You can't let her make up her own rules. It just ain't right."

Up until now, things had been going rather good. Up until *now*! Gracie slammed her fist on the table. "Who are you to come here and tell me what *is* and what *isn't* acceptable? Just because I said you could stay here doesn't mean you have a license to tell me how to run this household."

"You're staying, Daddy?" Tanner squealed. "For real?"

Zeke blotted his mouth with his napkin. "I reckon you'll have to ask Miz Gracie. I thought so, but now I ain't so sure."

Gracie slumped in her chair. Peering into four little waiting eyes, she nodded slowly. "Yes, boys, your father will be doing some work for me and staying in the basement." She lowered her head. "I'm sorry I lost my temper. I apologize."

Her jaw ached from gritting her teeth. Just because she

apologized was no sign she was ready to let Zeke Thorne or any other man come in and start telling her how to run the orphanage.

Chapter Three

Wednesday, June 3rd . . .

Gracie jerked the iron skillet off the stove and ran out of the kitchen, leaving sizzling bacon, half-cooked.

If Zeke hadn't been sure before, his doubts were now confirmed. He pulled the fry pan back on the eye and finished cooking breakfast. Poor girl. He winced at the sounds of gagging coming from the hall bathroom. He recalled his visit with the preacher at El Bethel, and concluded with a certainty God had led him to this place. After caring for his sweet Lucy for two years, he felt lost when she died. He fooled himself into believing the twins didn't need him, but he'd been wrong. They needed him even more than they did before their mother died. And now, Gracie desperately needed him, although she'd never admit it. But he wasn't sure who needed who the most.

Tanner lumbered in, sloshing a full milk pail. With a look of jealousy in his eyes, he glared at Toby who sat in the corner, pushing the dasher up and down on the churn, while gleefully quoting the little ditty their mother taught them. "Come butter come, come butter come, St. Peter waiting at the gate, hopin' for a butter cake, come butter come."

Tanner poured the milk into a gallon jug and put it in the refrigerator. "Why are you cooking, Daddy? Where's Gigi?"

His father forked up the fried bacon on a sheet of newspaper. "She'll be in d'rectly."

Toby said, "She ran out of the kitchen like the house was on fire. What's wrong with her, Daddy?"

"She'll be fine. Are the girls up?"

"Yessir. They were getting up when I went to milk. All except Ludie. Daddy, tell Toby it's his turn to milk tomorrow. I'd rather churn than milk."

"Go tell her to come to breakfast."

"Who?"

"Who are we talking about? Ludie, of course." Tanner shrugged. "She won't come. Never does. She eats after we finish."

"Not anymore, she don't," he muttered under his breath.

Maddie and Belle walked into the kitchen. Maddie pulled out a chair for her older sister and tucked a napkin corner inside the collar of her blouse, before taking her seat. "Where's . . . "

Zeke didn't let her finish. "Gigi's a little under the weather, so I expect you kids to be extra good today. Think you can do that?"

Heads nodded. "She's not gonna die, is she?" Maddie asked.

"Of course not!"

"Mama did." Toby responded without looking up.

"People do die, you know." Tanner seemed to feel the need to remind his father of something Zeke only wished he could forget.

"Yes, they do, son. But Gigi ain't that sick."

"Wanna bet?" Gracie, stood in the doorway mumbling and holding her stomach.

Zeke pulled out her chair, but Gracie shook her head. "I don't feel like eating. I think I'll go sit on the veranda and get some fresh air. Y'all go ahead without me." She wanted to admonish Zeke for calling her "Gigi," but she supposed he did it because he was speaking to the children, since that's how they referred to her. No need in getting herself riled. If she had it to do over again, he'd still be calling her Mrs. Graham.

After putting the food on the table, Zeke trekked upstairs and knocked on Ludie's door.

"Go away!" She screamed.

"Ludie, breakfast is ready and we're waiting for you to come to the table."

"You deaf? I said go away."

"If you ain't decent, wrap up, 'cause I'm fixin' to come in."

"Suit yourself."

Zeke pushed the door open. "Get outta bed, Ludie. Now!"

She stretched and turned over. With her eyes still shut, she mumbled, "I ain't gotta do what you say. You ain't my boss."

"Young lady, at the moment, I'm the only boss you have, and I'm telling you to get up and come eat breakfast with the others." When she failed to budge, he jerked the chenille spread back. Her nightshirt was pulled up to her thighs and Zeke's breath left him, seeing countless huge scars covering her legs. He quickly turned his back. "Good gracious, shug, who done that to you?"

"What does it matter? You planning to add your own signature? Go ahead and take off your belt. I'm used to it."

"I ain't up here to beat you, sugar. I just want you to do things with the rest of us. We never see you. You don't eat with us, you stay gone all day, to who knows where, and you go to your room at night. That ain't no life."

"Then why you trying to run my life, if I don't have one? Just leave me be. And don't ever call me sugar again. I'm not your sugar."

He turned and walked out the door. She'd won. But what else could he do?

The kids took their breakfast plates to the sink and Maddie pulled up her stool to wash the dishes. After gentle coaxing, she convinced Belle to dry them. If Zeke could've had a little girl, he would've wanted her to be just like Maddie. Cute as a calico kitten, sweeter than honey and with more stamina than many adults he'd come in contact with. But it was the compassion she showed for her big sister that touched his heart.

He poured a cup of coffee and walked out on the veranda. Pushing the cup toward her, he said, "Sip it slowly, Miz Gracie, and see if it won't settle your stomach."

With her hand covering her mouth, she groaned and shook her head.

Did he dare tell her he knew? Though it'd been almost twelve years since he watched his darling Lucy go through the same symptoms, it was as fresh on his mind as if it were yesterday. "Gigi, why don't you go upstairs and lie down until you feel better?"

She screamed, "Don't *ever* do that again? Do you understand? Not ever!"

His shoulders lifted. "Beggin' yo' pardon, but exactly what did I do?"

"My name is Gracie. Mrs. Gracie, to you."

He rubbed his chin. "Sorry. I reckon I picked it up from the kids. Didn't mean to rub you the wrong way, Miz Gracie. Won't never happen again."

Gracie's chest rose when she sucked in a heavy breath. "No, it's I who should apologize. I overreacted. I'm afraid my nerves are on edge. Gigi was my husband's pet name for me." Her voice quivered. "To hear another man use it . . . well, it just doesn't set right."

"Yes'm. I understand. Now, why don't you go rest and I'll keep an eye on the kids. I'll be putting up extra shelves in the butler's pantry this morning, so I'll be around if you need me."

"Thank you. I'm sure it's a stomach bug and will pass shortly. If you'll excuse me, I'm going to my room.

Zeke had an urge to take her by the elbow and help her upstairs, but recalling her recent outburst, he declined. He hadn't forgotten how the least little incident could cause Lucy to burst into tears, when she carried the twins. He had a feeling in her condition, Miz Gracie would be needing him even more than he needed her.

****

At the sound of the refrigerator door opening, Zeke peeked out from the butler's pantry in time to spy Ludie in the kitchen, sneaking food. She pulled out a round package wrapped in white meat-packers' paper. He watched as she sliced off an inch or more of bologna, then set the package back on the shelf. Next, she opened the lid on the wooden cheese box and cut a large wedge. Then, removing a dish rag from a drawer, she carefully wrapped her bounty. Zeke's patience ran thin when he realized the little thief wasn't through. Instead of surprising her, he'd watch and see exactly what she was up to.

She glanced around, then reaching for the soda cracker tin, filled a penny sack with saltines. When she started toward the butler's pantry, Zeke quickly slipped out the door leading into the dining room and hid, peering through the crack. He'd made a real effort to like the girl, but she'd made it impossible for him to get close to her.

Reaching up on the top shelf in the pantry, she pulled down a pint mason jar, then tiptoed back to the kitchen. The refrigerator opened, then closed. Zeke stepped back into the pantry and watched as she filled the jar with fresh buttermilk. Then spying a left-over biscuit on the iron griddle, she poked it in her pocket. When the kitchen screen door slammed, he ran to the window and saw her heading toward the backwoods.

She might fool Gracie, but she didn't fool him. She was meeting a boy in the woods and feeding the low-life from Gracie's table. What other explanation could there be? She was only thirteen but could easily pass for fifteen or sixteen. He tried to erase the graphic pictures racing through his mind. The kid was too pretty for her own good. For Miz Gracie's sake, it was up to him to put an end to the shady shenanigans, and let Ludie know in no uncertain terms, such behavior would not be tolerated. Not only did she have no business stealing food and sneaking off, she was a bad influence on the other children. Miz Gracie had made it plain he wasn't in charge of the household, but she didn't need one more thing to worry about, in her delicate condition. He'd handle this himself, and once she learned the truth, she'd thank him.

Zeke checked on the younger kids, who were playing in the field, then decided to follow and see exactly what the little thief was up to. He wandered through the woods, but she'd disappeared in the heavy brush. He soon gave up the search and headed back to Nine Gables. Miz Gracie was in the yard building a fire under the washpot when he returned.

She wiped her forehead with the tail of her apron. "There you are. I wondered where you went."

"Miz Gracie, you ain't got no business standing over a hot fire in this heat. I thought you was fixin' to take a rest."

"Oh, I did and now I feel much better. Besides, a little heat doesn't aggravate a stomach virus and I'm behind on the washing."

If only he could get her to admit her condition, but he'd known plenty of married women in his own family who were too embarrassed to admit they were pregnant and would go to all lengths to hide the fact until the baby was born.

"Please, Miz Gracie, let me do the wash. It's too hot for you to be out here scrubbing them heavy dungarees. I can watch the young'uns play while I—"

She dismissed him with a wave of her hand. "There are plenty of jobs around the place without you having to do a woman's work."

He held his tongue, though her comment pricked his nerves. He'd washed more loads than he could count during the years his wife was bedridden. It was good no one told him he was doing woman's work back then, or it might've been the last time they said anything to anyone.

"Didn't you say you planned to put up shelves in the butler's pantry today?"

"Yes'm and I done got one up. Why? You thinking I ain't earning my keep?"

"That's not what I was inferring. I was simply asking. Why are you so edgy?"

Maybe he was. But until she chose to share the news of her condition, he couldn't admit he'd watched one woman die and he wasn't ready to watch another one. Didn't she realize she needed to take care of herself, not only for *her* sake but for the sake of the children? Stubborn woman!

He scratched his head and questioned how he should bring up the subject of Ludie. "Miz Gracie, where ya' reckon Ludie goes when she takes off and stays gone half-a-day at the time?"

"The woods." Her answer was quick and to the point as if it was perfectly natural.

"I don't reckon it's none of my business, ma'am, but don't that seem a bit peculiar to ya'—her being a girl and roaming around in the woods?"

"What does being a girl have to do with it? I think she enjoys the solitude. Poor kid has so much warring inside her, I suspect it does her good. Being alone with nature can have a calming effect, and heaven knows, the child needs something to calm her."

Zeke sucked in a deep breath and hoped he could make his point without sending her on a tangent. "Half-a-day seems to me like a heap of solitude for a girl her age. Ever wonder what she might be doing out there in them woods?"

"Probably climbing trees, wading in the creek or just lying on the grass and watching the squirrels. For some unknown reason, Ludie doesn't seem comfortable taking meals with the other children, but I've caught her packing a picnic lunch to carry with her, so I don't worry about her not eating. The way food disappears around here, I'd say she's getting more than enough nourishment."

"Yeah, like maybe enough for two people, wouldn't you say? He pulled off his straw hat and scratched his head.

"There's nothing she can get in to, if that's what's worrying you, Zeke."

"So, you sayin' you got no idea what's going on in them woods and yet you ain't worried? Hadn't it ever crossed your mind she might be up to no-good?"

From the look on her face, he'd gone one step too far. She dropped the scrub board and it sank to the bottom of the washpot. "There you go, again, Zeke, questioning the way I run this orphanage. I thought maybe this arrangement would work, but now I'm not so sure. I keep getting the feeling you question every decision I make."

"It ain't that, Miz Gracie. I reckon I was raised to obey my elders and it just gets my goat, seeing that kid run all over you."

"Zeke—"

"You ain't gotta say it. I need to keep my big mouth shut. Now, if you'll excuse me, I'll get started mending the fence." There were things that needed mending a lot worse than the fence, but if he didn't learn to keep quiet, he'd soon be out of a place to stay and ruin his chances of being near his boys. He couldn't risk it. He'd grit his teeth and put up with whatever he had to, for as long as necessary.

****

Gracie mulled over Zeke's warnings. Maybe he had a point. She recalled the day she and her father went fishing together. "Give the fish some line and let him run with it, before you reel him in," he'd said. She hoped the same held true with Ludie. She'd certainly given her enough line. Would Gracie be able to reel her in, or would the pigheaded teenager use the slack to hang herself?

Raising children was a big responsibility. What made her ever think she was qualified?

Chapter Four

Ludie sprinted through the woods, stopping only long enough to pull the sandspurs from her socks. The old servants' cabin was practically hid behind the brush. The door was open and she could see the old man lying on the makeshift cot, straw poking out from the faded blue tick mattress.

Her lip quivered. "Uncle George, you don't look so good."

He opened his eyes and squinted. "Zat you, Ludie?"

"Of course, it's me. Nobody else knows you're down here. Not now, no how. But I gotta tell somebody. I just gotta. You gonna die, sure as the world, hiding out in this ol' dirt-floor shack. You need a doctor."

The old man's brown wrinkled face twisted in a frown. His hand shook as he reached out and took her by the hand. "No, sugar. Don't you breathe a word to nobody. This cabin was good enough for my pappy and it's good enough for me."

When tears seeped from his clouded eyes, Ludie leaned over the bed and kissed him on the forehead. "Don't get yourself in a dither, Uncle George. It ain't doing you no good. No good a'tall." She loosened the ring on the pint jar and took off the lid. "Looky what I brung you. I got you some fresh buttermilk, a biscuit, a chunk o' bologna, a hunk o' cheese and a few sodie crackers. I woulda brought you breakfast, but it was all gone, 'cept for the biscuit. Maybe tomorrow."

He shook his head. "Sugar, you done real good, but your ol' Uncle George ain't got no appetite no more. Can't eat nary a thing."

"Oh, no you don't ol' man. You gonna eat if I have to push it down yo' throat. You ain't gonna lie here and die on me."

He gave a slight chuckle. "Land sakes, chile, you couldn't sound more like Beulah if she'd a raised you. I recall her saying them exact same words to Veezie one time. Law, how I miss that woman."

"I wish I coulda met Beulah. I betcha we woulda got along jest fine."

Uncle George's gold tooth sparkled when he smiled. "No doubt about it. My Beulah was a fine woman. A fine woman, indeed."

"Enough talk. It's time to eat. I'll take a bite, and then you take one."

"Sugar, you can't keep slipping food down here. You need to sit down at the table at the Big House and eat with the other young'uns while the food's hot."

"No. I want to eat with you. I may be only thirteen, but I'm closer to being a woman than I am to being a young'un. They don't none like me, no how."

"That ain't the case, sweetheart. You don't like yo'self. You gotta learn to like yo'self, before you can git other folks to take a liking to you. I learned that lesson from Beulah and it's the truth." He attempted to push her hand away when she held the cold biscuit to his mouth, but Ludie shook her head, and with her thumb and forefinger, she gave his chin a gentle tug, opening his mouth. "Eat! Gigi makes good biscuits."

He took a small bite and chewed slowly. "Promise ol' Uncle George you'll start sittin' down at the table and eating with the others. Do it for me, and I'll eat every bite of that biscuit."

"I'll make a deal. I'll sit down at the table with 'em if you'll eat what I bring you every morning."

"I reckon I could abide by that."

"Fine. Now. Move yo' hand and eat."

"Law, chile, I do wish yo' grand mammie coulda seen you. Oh, how I wish that."

Ludie had so many unanswered questions, but now was not the time to bring them up. Once he was stronger, she'd get him to tell her everything.

It took almost an hour to get enough food into him to satisfy her, but Ludie managed to get him to eat enough to sustain him. She sat in the rocker, and picked up a book—The Scarlet Letter—and began reading where she left off yesterday. Why it was so important to Uncle George that she read the red book, was beyond her, but he'd insisted. Said something about it being a book Beulah claimed had changed Veezie's life. Uncle George spoke of the woman named Veezie, as if she were his own daughter. According to him, she wound up being a fine lady, highly respected among the folks in her husband's church. Ludie knew Uncle George hoped for such an outcome for her, but if only he knew the truth. Nobody gave a flip about her. Nobody but him. And she didn't care. She had no use for nobody but Uncle George.

"Uncle George?"

"Yeah, sugar."

"Why didja tell me to call you 'uncle' when you ain't no kin?"

"'At's what all the white folks call me, sugar. Been Uncle George long as I can recollect."

His face writhed with pain when he coughed. He looked so frail. If only he'd let her get help. She laid the book down and swiped the tear cruising down her cheek. He couldn't die on her. He just couldn't. Not now. Not before he answered all her questions.

Chapter Five

Gracie had been wrong about Zeke. True, he had a habit of taking over, but he meant no harm. It was his way of attempting to make things easier for her. As much as she appreciated his efforts, he'd put her in an awkward situation.

The day he moved in, he indicated he'd be actively searching for a job, and would be staying only long enough to make a payday and get on his feet. There were bound to be plenty of jobs available, with so many men off fighting, but as far as she knew, after almost six weeks, he hadn't been on a single interview. She hesitated to bring up the subject for fear she'd hurt his feelings. He'd been a big help with the kids and he'd worked hard getting the house in shape and working the garden, so what did it hurt for him to stay? It wasn't as if they were doing anything immoral. The children benefitted from his presence and though she'd never get over losing Garth, having Zeke around had helped her feel human again. She wrung her hands. Then why did it feel so wrong, having him around?

At lunch, Gracie said, "Tomorrow is the fourth-of-July, and I happen to have a little money stashed away for fireworks. If you kids can talk Zeke into going over to Bell's Seed & Feed, maybe he'll pick out some really good bottle rockets for us. They're my favorite."

Zeke cut his eyes toward her and winked. "I think I can handle that. Who wants to go help pick 'em out?" Every hand went up except Ludie's.

"Fine. As soon as you finish lunch and get the kitchen cleaned, go pile in the bed of the pickup and we'll go see what we can find. We might even find a creek to go wading in while we're out. Ask Gigi . . . I mean, Miz Gracie, if she'd like to go with us."

Gracie shook her head. "Thank you, but I have a ton of things to do."

"Come on, Miz Gracie. You've never ridden in my truck. We'll turn the radio up and have a sing-along. It'll be fun."

Fun? Zeke was a nice man, but he didn't understand. She had fun when Garth was alive. Her fun days were over. Survival was now the goal. If she could make it through a day at the time without shedding a dishpan full of tears, she'd consider it a fair day. Fair was all she could hope for, and those fair days were few and far between.

In spite of Gracie's encouragement, Ludie balked. "I ain't going."

Zeke and the kids stayed gone longer than Gracie anticipated, but she managed to get a lot done. She brought in the dried clothes from off the line, sprinkled and bundled them, then sat them in the refrigerator so they'd be easier to iron later. She couldn't remember when she'd had so much energy. Certainly a big change from early morning, when she was confident she was dying a slow death. She fried squirrel the twins brought home, made mashed potatoes and gravy and a pear salad for supper, then hurried upstairs to brush her hair and freshen up, before the kids returned.

Who was she trying to fool? It wasn't the kids she was primping for. Overwhelmed with guilt as she glared at the shameful woman in the mirror, Gracie quickly washed the rouge from her face and blotted away the lipstick. Had she lost all sense of respect? He was a dirt farmer, for crying out loud, and she was acting like a trollop. What was she thinking? Garth was her one and only love. Always would be.

She laid her hand on her knees, in an effort to stop the shaking. What would her father say if he knew she allowed a man to be living under the same roof? Gracie could almost hear him saying, "The Bible warns to avoid all appearances of evil." He'd learned that lesson the hard way. Did she really want to set herself up for scorn by the same town gossips who were responsible for her father leaving Flat Creek Fellowship?

She made her way down the stairs and found Ludie in the kitchen. "Gigi, I saw some wieners in the refrigerator. Looked mighty good."

"You still hungry?"

"If there ain't enough . . ."

"Go ahead. Take a couple. I bought them for tomorrow night

when we celebrate, but I think we have more than enough."

"Thanks." Ludie grabbed two wieners and hurried out the door.

****

Zeke walked in holding up a bulging paper sack. "If the kids have as much fun tomorrow night as they had picking out these fireworks, it'll be a humdinger of a night. We've got firecrackers, bottle rockets and a dozen boxes of sparklers. I'm feeling like a kid again, myself."

It was difficult not to return his smile, but he was the caretaker, she was the employer, and it was her responsibility to make certain neither of them ever forgot their position. "Would you mind telling the children to come in and wash up for supper? I'll be taking the cornbread out of the oven shortly."

The children ran in, all babbling at the same time. All but Ludie. Gracie watched out the window. Just as she concluded Zeke was right and she was too lenient on the girl, Ludie came bursting in the house, and flopped down at the table. Relieved, Gracie glanced in Zeke's direction and bit her lip to hide her smile.

Everyone was seated when Toby stomped in the dining room, holding up clean hands to prove to Gigi he washed them. He walked over and pulled on Ludie's arm. "Get up. That's my place."

Zeke trekked over and gave his son a whack on the backside. "Not anymore, it ain't, buddy. That's now Ludie's place. So how about if you sit on the other end of the table in the empty chair."

Toby formed a pout, but did as his father instructed.

Ludie spooned a generous helping of mashed potatoes on her plate. When the cornbread was passed her way, she brushed a long ringlet from her eyes and glanced up at Gracie. "How many corn pones are we allowed to get?"

Zeke spoke up quickly. "Why not take—" The stunned expression on his face reminded Gracie of a whipped puppy.

"Ludie, I think Mr. Zeke was about to say, 'Why don't you take one, and after everyone is served, if you've finished eating your bread, then you may ask to have the tray passed to you again.'"

Zeke massaged the back of his neck. "Well, I'll be, if you ain't a mind reader. That's exactly what I was about to say."

Gracie gave him an approving look. He was a nice man. He just needed to learn which one of them was in charge.

After supper, Ludie started up the stairs. Maddie hollered, "Ludie, if you want to help me, you can."

She stopped, then slowly turned around and ambled back down the stairs. "Sure, kid."

When Maddie reached for the stool, Ludie stepped up to the sink and said, "We won't need that. I'll wash, and you dry."

Maddie giggled as if it were Christmas and Santa had found her at last. She said, "Belle's good at drying. I'll put the dishes away."

Whatever caused such a change in Ludie's disposition was a mystery to Gracie, but she hoped it was not a passing fancy. It hadn't seemed fair for the other kids to do their share of the chores and let her get by with doing nothing, but then Gracie hadn't felt up to the task of going toe-to-toe with a rebellious teenager.

Zeke went into the butler's pantry to adjust the shelves. His eyes widened when he walked back into the kitchen. "Wow, you girls did a bang-up good job. It's spotless."

"Ludie did most of it," Maddie said, then grabbed Ludie around the waist and gave her a squeeze.

"Stop it kid. I ain't yo' momma."

Maddie's hands dropped. "I know. I don't have a momma."

Gracie looked up from the rocker in the corner, where she sat darning socks. She couldn't decide which she'd rather do. Hug sweet Maddie or give Ludie a licking she wouldn't soon forget for being so rude. Instead, she did nothing. *Patience, Lord. I need a double dose.*

Chapter Six

September 2nd

Gracie went upstairs after breakfast and pulled off the stained, pink chenille robe. For weeks after Zeke first came, she was embarrassed for him to see her in the tattered house coat, but in these past couple of months she'd become much more comfortable around him.

If she'd had a brother, she supposed this is how she would've felt about him. *Safe.* Yes. He made her feel safe. When depression set in, Zeke could always do or say something to help lift her out of the valley.

The weather was beginning to cool off, and she reached in the closet and pulled out last year's fall skirt. She moaned when it lacked a good two inches being able to reach around her waist. As a last resort, she slipped on the loose cotton dress she'd worn all summer. She couldn't afford to buy a new wardrobe. It was definitely time to push away from the table. She'd enjoyed baking for the children, but apparently she was eating more of the sweets than they were.

She gathered up the dirty clothes and took them outside to wash. Zeke had the fire going under the washpot and she could feel the heat as soon as she rounded the back of the house. She'd resented his insistence to let him do the wash—yet, today, she was almost willing to give in to his pleas and hand him the scrub board.

Maybe it was the extra weight she'd put on that made her feel so exhausted. After ringing out the last garment, she picked up the hamper of wet clothes and plodded across the freshly-swept yard toward the clothesline. A sudden rush of nausea left her feeling lightheaded. The basket dropped from her hands.

Lying in her bed with Zeke standing over her, she batted her eyes. "How did I get up here? What happened?"

"You fainted. I was in the garden and saw you when you went down. How do you feel now?"

"Not sure what happened, but I feel fine. My goodness, what's going on outside? Why are all the horns blowing? I've never heard such a racket. Sounds like a parade."

He nodded. "Gracie, maybe you should stay in bed."

She gave a dismissive shrug. "I'm afraid that's a luxury I can't afford. Too much to do. Zeke look out the window and see if you can tell what's happening. Today isn't a holiday, is it?"

Hem hawing, he twisted his hat in his hands and muttered, "I reckon you might say it is. President Roosevelt just announced on the radio that Japan has surrendered—the war has ended."

"Oh." She slid her feet off the bed.

Zeke's eyes squinted. "I'll have to say, that wasn't the reaction I expected from you."

"And what did you expect me to do, Zeke? Ride in the parade? I'm proud for the women who have their men coming home. Really, I am. But if you expect me to do cartwheels on the day my husband should have returned and didn't, then you don't know me well."

"Pardon me for saying so, Miz Gracie, but you need to—"

"Stop it, Zeke. You have no right to tell me what I need to do. I'll handle my grief in my own way. Now, if you'll excuse me, I have chores to do. The laundry needs to get on the line while the sun's out." She slid her feet off the bed.

"Please, Miz Gracie. I'll hang the clothes. Please. For me. Stay up here and rest."

"Zeke, you worry too much. I've never fainted before, and it'll likely never happen again." She stood and shook the wrinkles from her skirt.

He ran his fingers through his hair and groaned. "Don't be so stubborn, woman. I know you're pregnant, so stop pretending."

Her heart palpitated. "What did you say?"

"Really, Miz Gracie. You must consider me awfully naïve if you thought I wouldn't know."

"Pregnant?" Her throat closed. "But that's impossible."

A look of disgust painted his face. "Surely, you aren't saying you didn't know."

"It can't be true. You're wrong. Garth has been gone—"

"About five months."

"Pregnant." She repeated.

"For crying out loud, Miz Gracie, didn't you suspect something when you were throwing up every morning?"

Her thoughts scrambled. He was right. The morning sickness. The tight clothes. There were other signs she'd ignored, contributing each one to depression. Everything except the peculiar rumbling in her stomach, which she attributed to gas. She laid her hand on her abdomen. *A baby?* She felt a slight movement beneath her hand. "Please, Zeke. I'd like to be alone. Would you mind closing the door as you leave?"

"Of course." He pulled a quilt from off the rocker and gently laid it over her legs. "I'll be outside hanging clothes. I'll check on you shortly."

Gracie lay in bed trying to absorb the shock. *Garth's baby.* It was a miracle. God was giving her back a piece of her heart she lost. Never had she missed her mother as much as she missed her now. If only she could lay her head on her shoulder once again while hearing her mother's sweet voice. "Oh, Mama, I'm gonna have a baby. Alone. I need you. Why did you have to leave me?"

Gracie had bitterly resented Veezie when her father first began dating. Not only was Veezie half his age, but she was ignorant and uncouth. What would people say about the Reverend Shep Jackson marrying a backwoodsy girl from Goose Hollow? Gracie supposed that was what troubled her most at the time. Talk. And talk, they did. But only because they didn't get to know what a wonderful person her father had fallen in love with.

She was glad her daddy was able to love again after her mother died. But sometimes she wondered if he really loved her mother as much as he'd pretended. If so, how could he love another woman with the same passion? She could certainly never love another man the way she loved Garth. Never. Especially an ignorant dirt farmer. Not that she had any such inclinations, so she had no idea why he came to mind.

Stirred by a convicting thought, Gracie realized she was defining Zeke with the same high-and-mighty attitude she took with Veezie in the beginning. As someone beneath her. She squirmed. Who set her up to be his judge? Was she no better than the do-gooders in her daddy's former church?

It was understandable why her father felt the need to leave Flat Creek Fellowship Church and take a pastorate in Mt. Pleasant, near Coffee Springs. She couldn't blame him, but if only she had family closer by, what a comfort it would be at such a time as this.

"Oh, Garth, we're gonna have a baby."

Chapter Seven

Zeke sucked in the cool autumn air, and marveled at how quickly summer had come and gone. When he first arrived at Nine Gables he had great intentions of getting outside work, but there was so much to do to get the orphanage and grounds in shape, he failed to find the time to interview. As time passed, he purposely hesitated, fearful he'd be forced to leave, once he landed a job.

However, in the past few months, he'd sensed a change in Gracie. The tender way she looked at him was proof enough that she enjoyed his company as much as he enjoyed hers. His lips parted in a smile. Now, that he was confident she didn't want him to leave any more than he wanted to go—it was time to start bringing in a paycheck. That's why he called Mr. Daniels at the cotton mill and set up an interview for nine o'clock. He wouldn't feel like much of a man asking Gracie to marry him if he wasn't doing his part to support her and the kids.

With just enough time to gather vegetables before getting dressed, Zeke hurried to the garden. He could hardly wait for Gracie to see him in his new trousers, shirt and shoes he charged at

Mr. Watson's Dry Goods Store. It was time to throw away the ragged overalls. He leaned against the hoe, reflecting on the change that had taken place in his life in such a short period of time. The sun seemed brighter than usual. He sucked in a deep breath. Even the air smelled sweeter than ever before. It was as if the whole world was rejoicing in his good fortune.

The back door opened and chattering children ran out, ready to begin their first day of school. Seeing Tanner limping, he yelled. "Hurt your foot, didja?"

"No sir. Got me a risin on the back of my leg."

"Well, come here boy. Pull up your britches leg and let me take a look." He nodded. "Yep, it's a beaut."

"I gotta go, Daddy."

"Not yet, you don't." He leaned down, dug an Irish potato from a hill, and cut off a thin white slice. Then pulling a handkerchief from his hip pocket, he placed the potato against the risin and tied it around his son's leg. "Keep this on it and it'll draw out the boil."

Toby had his brogans tied together and slung over his shoulder.

Zeke yelled, "Toby, stop right where you are and put on them shoes."

"Aww, Daddy. I watch out for rusty nails. I'm not gonna get lockjaw if that's what's worrying ya.'"

"You heard me boy. Ain't no son of mine gonna go to school barefooted like a throwed-away scalawag. Besides, it rained last night and you'll get ground itch, wadin' in them mud puddles."

Toby stooped to put on his shoes. "Wait for me, y'all."

Zeke held a mess of turnips in one hand and waved with the other. "You kids be good now, and mind your manners. And remember, if I hear tell of a teacher needing to paddle one of ya', you'll get a second whoopin' when you get home. Got it?"

"Yes sir. We'll be good."

"Sure, you will. Now, get going before you're late."

Watching them scurry off brought a lump to his throat. The twins would be fine. They were good boys. And smart. But Ludie . . . he rolled his eyes. She was a different story. It'd be a miracle if she didn't find someone to pick a fight with on her first day. What she needed was a firm hand and as soon as he could convince Gracie, he'd straighten little miss Ludie out and let her know who was in control.

His thoughts drifted to sweet little Maddie, heading off for first grade. What a doll baby, yet far too serious for her own good. It had taken persuasion for the Principal to agree to let Belle go to school and start first grade with Maddie. Zeke convinced him that although Belle couldn't speak, she was as bright as any child her age. Now, he wondered if he'd done the right thing. Had he put too much responsibility on Maddie's tiny shoulders? She needed to be a child and not feel such a burden to take care of everyone. Funny, how quickly he'd attached himself to these children.

But something else happened he hadn't seen coming. He'd fallen wrong-side-out, upside-down, right-side-up, and head-over-heels in love with Gracie Graham.

****

Gracie picked up the bundle of greens Zeke laid on the counter and placed them in a large porcelain dishpan in the sink.

Zeke nudged her. “Move over, beautiful. I’ll wash them turnips. It’ll take several soakings to rid the grit.”

A blush heated her cheeks. “No need. I’ll take care of it.”

“I don’t mind.”

Chills ran down her spine when she felt his hand on her shoulder. “Zeke, stop it.” She dried her hands and plopped them on her hips. “I’m quite capable of washing turnips.”

“I’m sorry, Miz Gracie. Didn’t mean to rile you. But is it so wrong for me to want to make life as easy for you as I can?” Not waiting for an answer, he walked toward the basement door. “I reckon I better get dressed for the interview. I’d sure appreciate it if you’d say a little prayer for me while I’m gone.” He rubbed the nape of his neck. “Mr. Daniels said there are two empty slots, but six men being interviewed. Miz Gracie, do you think it’s wrong to pray that someone else doesn’t get a job, in order that I can?”

Gracie had no answer. She supposed he was counting on her to pray, since she was a preacher’s daughter. If only he knew. She couldn’t remember how to pray. It had been too long. Her prayers ended the day two uniformed men walked up to her door.

When Zeke walked into the kitchen before leaving for the interview, Gracie’s breath shortened. The sun streaks in his freshly washed hair looked as if golden threads had been intricately woven into his chestnut locks. She wanted to tell him how nice he looked in his crisp white shirt and dark trousers, but fearing he'd read more into it than was intended, she refrained. "Good luck. I hope you get one of the jobs."

"Thank you. So do I. I don't like knowing that you're footing the bills alone. I'm beginning to feel like a kept man."

Seeing the somber expression on his face, she rolled her eyes. "That's ridiculous. I could never afford to hire a handyman to do all you do for three meals a day and a clammy room in the basement."

"Is that how you see me, Miz Gracie? As just a handyman?"

She wouldn't allow him to manipulate her. "There's no shame in being a handyman." The dejected look on his face, confirmed it wasn't the answer he sought.

****

The hours drug by. Gracie could hardly wait for the kids to get home to tell her about their first day at school, and for Zeke to return from his interview. She expected him back hours ago.

Hearing the children's laughter, she ran to the window. Maddie, Belle, Toby and Tanner were walking through the gate, but where was Ludie? *Fighting again?* What type punishment would it take to alter her bad behavior? It was no secret Ludie didn't like staying at the orphanage. What if she'd run away? But where would she go? Gracie had resented it when Zeke tried to warn her she was being too lenient with Ludie. He seemed to know much more about child rearing than she did. In fact, lately she'd begun to feel he knew much more about everything than she did. Though ignorant in book learning, he was wise in so many other ways.

Perhaps the fact he was still gone was an indication he got the job. On the other hand, was it possible he might be out looking for another place to stay, as per their agreement when he first arrived? She couldn't blame him for wanting to leave. She'd been hard to deal with lately. Zeke excused her antagonistic attitude to the pregnancy, but she knew the truth. The superior act was a cover-up for feelings he stirred within her. It was her way of fighting back—not at him, but at the unwelcome thoughts that had flitted through her head, since the morning she looked out the window and saw him working in the garden without a shirt. Never had she seen a man with such bulging muscles. Though she only looked for a second, it took much longer to rid her mind of the picture in her head. Her throat tightened.

He was leaving. She was sure of it. Maybe she could manage without his help, but did she really want to?

Gracie ushered the children into the kitchen, where she had two Pork Cakes, fresh out of the oven, waiting for them. She tried to dismiss the anxious thoughts of the missing child and focus on the four who did return. "So, who all had a great day?"

Three hands shot in the air, and they all chattered at once. All except Belle, who seemed bewildered by the excitement.

Tanner said, "Guess what, Gigi. The teacher can't tell me and

Toby apart."

Toby broke off a large chunk of his cake and stuffed it in his mouth. "Yeah, so we tricked her."

Gracie feigned a smile. She glanced out the window, hoping to see Ludie coming down the road. "Chew your food before trying to speak Toby. Then tell me how you tricked your teacher."

Tanner said, "It was my idea, so I wanna tell."

Toby, who seemed more interested in eating his cake than talking, shrugged.

"I answered roll call for Toby and he answered for me."

Gracie didn't know whether to laugh or scold. "Well, I'm sure it won't take the teacher long to catch on to your little tricks. So, how was your day, Maddie?"

"Scrumptious," Maddie picked up two slices of Pork Cake, put one on her plate and the other on Belle's.

"Scrumptious? That's a mighty big word for a first grader. Was it really that good?"

"Good? No ma'am. It was bad. Really, really scrumptious."

Toby hee-hawed. You don't mean—"

He stopped abruptly when Gracie wagged a finger in his direction, while giving him a stern look. She said, "Tell me, Maddie, what made it such a bad day?"

"A boy at recess said Belle was deaf and dumb. She's not deaf and she's not dumb. She just don't feel like talking."

Gracie tried to tell Zeke this would happen. Belle had no business going to school, when she wasn't even capable of answering the teacher's questions. It wasn't fair to either her or Maddie. Especially Maddie. Maybe he was wise in some things, but the man didn't have all the answers. "I'm sorry you had a bad day, Maddie. It won't be happening again, sweetheart."

Tanner said, "You got that right. You should've seen Maddie clobber him. She looked like Joe Palooka when she threw that punch."

Gracie's mouth flew open. "You hit him?"

Maddie's nose crinkled. "Right in the snout."

"And what did the teacher say?"

"He didn't tell. Tanner told him he'd punch his lights out if he told on me."

Gracie tried to hide her smile. Who would've believed sweet little Maddie would've been the one getting into a playground brawl?

The back door opened and Ludie stomped into the kitchen and threw her books on the cabinet.

"Ludie! I was beginning to worry. I'm glad you're home."

She walked over to the refrigerator and opened the door. "Home? This ain't my home."

Why argue. She was right. "I baked a fresh Pork Cake. Could I cut you a piece and pour you a glass of milk?"

"Cake? You used your sugar-rationing stamps to make a Pork cake?"

"It calls for brown sugar, which is easier to come by. Veezie sent me the recipe. She shoved a plate toward Ludie. Here, try it."

"Ain't you got nothing heartier than cake? Something that'll stick to the bones?"

"What did you have in mind?"

"Is supper cooked?"

"Zeke requested chitterlings, and they're outside boiling, but I cooked a mess of turnip greens and boiled some corn already. But I could fix you a bologna sandwich."

"No thanks. I'd rather have the turnips and corn."

The only consistent thing about Ludie was the fact she was never consistent. "Zeke's been concerned about your poor eating habits. He'll be pleased to hear you chose vegetables over dessert. Have a seat and tell me about your day at school."

Ludie slumped down in a kitchen chair. "So whatcha wanna know?"

"Tell me about your teacher."

"She's okay, I reckon."

"Did you make any friends?"

"Nope. Don't need no friends."

Gracie dipped out turnips and put an ear of corn and a corn pone on the plate.

"Corn looks good. Okay if I take two?"

"My, you *are* hungry. Help yourself. There's plenty."

"Thanks." She arose, turned and walked toward the door with the plate in her hand.

"Aren't you gonna sit down and eat?"

"Not here. I'll bring the plate back. You ain't got a problem with it, do ya?"

"I don't suppose so." Ludie was being civil and her appetite was increasing. Gracie felt she was finally making progress. This was no time to cross her.

****

Zeke pulled the truck into the yard at six-thirty. He didn't remember when he'd felt so exhausted. Physical work was much less strenuous than mental work, and his brain had certainly been taxed in the past eight hours. But the worst was over. Or so he hoped.

"Sorry, I'm late," he said.

"I went ahead and fed the children. I hope you don't mind. They're upstairs doing their homework."

"Good. How did their day go?"

"I'll let them tell you. But how was yours? Did you get the job?"

"Yeah, I got it." She sounded quite eager for the details. Maybe he was right and she did resent him for waiting so long.

He walked over to the sink and stood beside her to wash up. The scent of lilac perfume filled his nostrils and caused his pulse to race. Never in his life had he had such an urge to hold a woman in his arms as he had at this very moment. If Ludie hadn't barreled into the house when she did, he wasn't sure he could've resisted. The thought frightened him.

Ludie let her empty plate slide into the dishpan. "I'll wash the dishes."

Zeke said, "Where have you been until this hour, young lady? I thought you were upstairs with the other children. Don't you have homework?"

Gracie interrupted. "Thank you, Ludie, but I'll finish in the kitchen. Do your homework, then see if Maddie might need help with her numbers."

"Sure thing. Uh. . . I'll take a slice of cake if you have any left over."

"Help yourself. It's in the pie safe."

She cut a hefty slice and was up the stairs before Zeke could offer protest.

Gracie poured two cups of coffee, and sat down at the table with Zeke.

"Chit'lin's! My favorite." He filled his plate, and after forking a large portion into his mouth, he closed his eyes and groaned in satisfaction as he chewed. "I declare, Miz Gracie, these are good as Mama used to make. Seasoned with just the right amount of red pepper." He wiped his mouth on his shirt sleeve and then gave a little snort. "My Lucy tried to cook, bless her heart, but I Suwannee, that woman couldn't boil water without scorching it. "

"I'm glad you like them. The kids all turned up their noses, after Toby explained what they are, so I opened a can of Tripe and fried it for them." Toby was the first to ask for seconds." She giggled. "But enough about the kids. Tell me about the job."

"Nothing much to tell, Miz Gracie. I got the second shift. I'll have the mornings free to work around the place. There's still much to be done here. That is, if you don't mind me staying a tad longer. I know we agreed I'd leave when I found work, but—" He took a bite of cornbread and waited for her response.

"I'll admit I was concerned at first, but if you'd like to stay, I have no problem with it." Her voice was slightly above a whisper. "And perhaps it's time we dispensed with the Mrs. . . please call me Gracie."

"I'd like that."

She sipped her coffee slowly, then held her head up. "I witnessed a real breakthrough with Ludie today. I sense the storm raging inside the poor child is finally leveling off."

He fought the urge to roll his eyes. He and Gracie would never agree on anything concerning Ludie. Still, he knew better than to show disinterest. "A breakthrough, you say? That's great. Tell me about it."

"She stayed at school all day, and didn't get into trouble."

"Well, that's surprising, for sure. But is that all?"

"There's more. When she came home, I offered her cake, but she opted for turnips and corn. I suppose you noticed she even offered to do the dishes without being asked. There's definitely been a change in her attitude."

"Turnips? That don't make a lick o' sense. She hates turnips." The way the little conniver hoodwinked Gracie was more than he could swallow. "Tell me, Gracie . . . did Ludie sit down and eat the vegetables at the table?"

"No, but—"

"Just as I figured. And you don't think that's peculiar? I'll guarantee you she's meeting somebody back there in them woods."

Gracie cackled. "You're not serious. Who would she be meeting?"

"I don't know. Maybe you're right." But she *wasn't* right and Zeke knew it. Ludie had conned Gracie, but the girl wasn't slick enough to fool him.

"She's coming around, Zeke. I definitely see a positive change in her attitude."

He clamped his mouth shut. Fighting with Gracie was never wise. It wouldn't take long before he'd catch Ludie and prove the girl was up to no good. "I'll check on the kids after I finish eating, then head downstairs and hit the sack. It's been a rough day. See you in the morning."

****

Though he worried needlessly, Gracie knew Zeke was only concerned for Ludie's welfare. She appreciated the way he took such a keen interest in the children. They needed a man's influence and she couldn't have found a better mentor for them. Or a better medicine for her. She needed a caretaker, and he seemed eager to meet her needs. She missed Garth so much that at times it seemed her heart would burst open. But having Zeke around to talk to, helped fill her empty hours and gave her less time to grieve. Her initial fears had all been unfounded. Recalling her opinion of him the first weeks he visited his boys, he seemed so . . . so backward. She remembered thinking of him as an ignorant dirt farmer. Funny, how she didn't see him that way now. Had he changed? Or had she?

Chapter Eight

Zeke focused on the clock at work. Never had the minutes ticked by so slowly. Would she still be up when he arrived home? The thought brought a smile. Never had he felt as much "at home," anywhere. Not even in the thirteen years he was married to Lucy.

Now that Gracie's delicate condition was out in the open, he could better take care of her. Surely, she'd see he *couldn't* leave. Not until after the baby was born, for sure. And if things progressed the way he hoped, he'd never have to leave at all.

When the cotton mill whistle signaled the end of the shift, Zeke hurried out the door, ran the length of the parking lot and jumped in his truck.

His hopes plummeted when he rushed in the house and discovered she'd retired to her room. He threw his hat on the rack and moved jars around in the Frigidaire, searching for left-over fried chicken. Gracie had tried to persuade him to take a sack lunch to eat on his break, but he assured her he'd be fine with a bag of peanuts and a Grape Soda from the Snack Bar. Yet now, his stomach felt as if it were sticking to his backbone. Maybe the gnawing in his gut had more to do with shattered nerves than with actual hunger.

He hoped Gracie would have a girl. He'd wanted a boy the first time, and the twins were a double blessing. But a little girl would be nice. *The first time?* Was he crazy? It was the *only* time. Gracie was carrying another man's child. Not his. But Garth was dead and he was alive. The baby would need a father figure and Zeke had already discovered it wasn't difficult to love another man's child. Maddie had won his heart. If the roles were reversed and he'd been the one killed while Gracie carried his child, wouldn't he want another man to love and care for his wife and his baby the way he would have? He dismissed the questions flooding his thoughts. She wasn't his wife and it wasn't his baby, so how could he honestly answer such absurd questions.

At the sound of footsteps, he whirled around. Gracie stood in the doorway, her cheeks as pink as the robe she wore.

"Hi!"

He swallowed hard. Long, shiny locks of auburn hair hung loosely around her shoulders, with a few ringlets bouncing between her eyes like loose springs. Never had he seen such an alluring sight. "You look flushed. How do you feel?"

"I feel fine. Really. I tried to fall sleep, but I'm so excited I can't." Her eyes flickered. "Oh, Zeke. I'm gonna have a baby. Garth's baby."

He knew it was Garth's baby. Why did she have to emphasize it? "I'm glad you're feeling better."

“You hungry?”

“Starving. I was looking for the left-over chicken.”

“Oh, dear. I fried extra, but I’m afraid Ludie raided the refrigerator. I put away two thighs and a breast, but when I came down to get a glass of buttermilk at six-thirty, I noticed the chicken was gone. And so was she.”

“You aren’t serious. Are you saying she took off in the woods again, instead of sitting down at the table and eating with the others? I Suwannee, for the life of me, I don’t know why you put up with that. If I was in charge—”

“But you aren’t in charge, are you, Zeke? I am. And she did eat with us tonight. I’m guessing she wasn’t fed well in some of the foster homes, so when she sees a surplus of food, she can’t resist taking it. But her attitude has greatly improved. She’s much kinder to the other kids, and she’s offering to help without being asked.”

“Is she upstairs now, or still wandering around, who knows where?”

“She wasn’t gone long.”

“Where did she say she’d been?”

“I didn’t ask.”

“I’ll tell you what I think. I think she’s having a rendezvous with some riff-raff down there in those woods. No telling what’s going on between them, and you’re letting her run down there and feed him. Are you so naïve, the thought hasn’t crossed your mind?”

“Maybe I choose to trust her.”

“Why? Has she earned your trust? I don’t think so. You said she sat at the table and ate supper. Then why would she raid the refrigerator and take all the left-over chicken, if she’d already eaten?” He’d gone too far, but he was tired and hungry and in no mood to pretend.

“I can see you’re upset, Zeke, and I understand. I’m sorry there’s no chicken left, but there’s plenty of rice, string beans and collards.”

“It’s not the chicken that upsets me most. There’s nothing I hate worse than a sneak.” He slammed the refrigerator door. “I’ve lost my appetite. I’m going to bed. Good night.”

“Good night, Zeke. See you in the morning.”

His eyes followed her up the stairs. If things went his way, one day in the near future, he’d be walking up those stairs with her. Then, if he became head of the household, there’d be some changes made, starting with Ludie.

Not if, but when.

****

The following day, Ludie counted the minutes for school to let out, eager to check on Uncle George, even though he’d been doing much better lately. He claimed it was because she was such a good nurse. The thought made her smile. Was it possible someone like her might be able to become a real nurse one day? Uncle George said she could be anything she wanted to be, but she’d have to study hard. That’s all it took to make her want to finish her homework every night.

On the way home from school, Maddie babbled non-stop. "Guess what I learned today, Ludie? Listen. Thirty days has September, April, June and November. All the rest have thirty-one except . . . except." She grinned. "I forgot the rest."

"That's real good, kid. I think the answer's February."

"Is this February?"

"Nope. This is October, when the leaves turn colors and drop off the trees. Won't be long before pecans will be all over the ground and we can pick them up and get Gigi to make us a pie."

The twins played kick the can as they raced from one side of the dirt road to the other, trying to be the first to kick it. Belle held tightly to Maddie's hand.

Ludie had grown quite fond of the children. In spite of the hateful way she treated them in the beginning, they all seemed to truly care about her. It was a new feeling. No one had ever cared about her in the past.

Gigi met them at the door, the way she always did. The dream of being a nurse wasn't the only dream Ludie had, though it was too personal to share with anyone. Her secret longing was to be a mother. The kind of mother she'd always wanted. The kind of mother Gigi would be. Sometimes the sting of jealousy would sneak up on her like a pesky mosquito and she'd resent the unborn baby. Not that she wanted to, for she didn't. But life seemed so unfair. Why couldn't her mother have wanted her as much as Gigi wanted *her* baby? Lately, it was all Gigi talked about. She had what she called a layette in a trunk on the porch and she must've opened it a dozen times a day, pulling out tiny clothes and soft flannel blankets, while oohing and ahhing as if it were the first time she'd laid eyes on them.

Gigi had five buttered biscuits, filled with fig preserves and five glasses of milk on the table. "Ludie, how did you do on your math test?"

"Made 97. It was easy."

"That's fantastic, sweetheart. I'm so proud of you. Now, we need to work on your English."

"I made 68 on my English test."

"Really? Well, that's not bad, and I'm sure you can do even better."

"I studied hard. I reckon I need to start learning good English, 'cause I'm gonna be a nurse one day."

"That's a wonderful profession, sweetheart. You'll make a great nurse."

"These preserves are real good, Gigi. It must've taken nearbout all your sugar rations to make 'em."

"Didn't use any. Veezie and I canned these figs the year she and my daddy married. I still have three jars left in the pantry. I'm glad you like it."

Ludie crammed the last bite of biscuit in her mouth and gulped down her milk. She was wasting time, sitting here discussing future plans when she had a very important job to do in the present. Uncle George would be waiting.

When she stood, Gigi handed her a cardboard shoe box. "Here. Take this with you. I packed liver and onions, mashed potatoes, black eyed peas, and a fig biscuit. There's buttermilk in the jar."

"What's it for?"

"For your friend."

"You *know*?"

"No, but I feel when you get ready to tell me, you will. Just remember it gets dark earlier now. Don't let the sun go down before you're back."

"Thanks, Gigi. I wish I could tell you, but I made a promise."

"I understand. Promises are meant to be kept. Now scoot."

Ludie wanted to tell her, but Uncle George would have to agree and he was dead set on no one finding out. Who was he hiding from?

Chapter Nine

Uncle George was sitting in his straight back chair when Ludie arrived at the shanty, and she could hardly wait to give him the news. “Uncle George, you’re sittin’ up, and looking well. How d’ya feel?”

“Fair to middlin’, sugar. I reckon this old body ain’t ready for the grave jest yet. I even managed to walk down to the creek this morning and take a bath. I can thank my nurse for helpin’ to get me back on my feet again.”

“Aw, shucks, I didn’t do nothin’ special.”

“Why, if it hadn’t been for them vittles you brung me, I’d be lying in a grave by now, and that’s the honest truth. But I’m better now, so I don’t want you frettin’ over me no more. In a day or two, I ‘spect I’ll be able to walk down to the Weinberger place and see if Mr. Oliver don’t have some odd jobs for me to do to earn a little cash. I use to do odd jobs for his pappy off and on when I got caught up with my reg’lar job at Nine Gables.” His gaze focused on the box in her lap. “Whatcha got there? Been catching frogs down at the creek?"

She giggled as she reached in and pulled out a bowl. "I don't chase frogs no more, Uncle George. I'm too old for that now. Wait until you see what I brung you. Gigi packed it for ya', and she put enough food in here to last a couple of days. I ain't gotta slip around no more."

His shoulders dropped. "Oh, sugar, I don't mean to sound ungrateful, but we can't have folks a knowin.' How much did you tell her?"

"I didn't tell her nothing. Uncle George. She knows I'm slipping food to somebody, she just don't know who. So out of kindness, she packed this lunch and told me to take it to my friend. Ain't nothing wrong with that, is there?"

"So you didn't tell her who you wuz coming to see?"

"Course not. She ain't got no inklin'. But Uncle George, truth is, I don't know nothing much to tell. That day I wandered back here and found you lyin' on the ground like a dead person, you called me Ludie when you came to. How didja know my name?"

"Maybe I heard somebody call you that."

"You said to call you Uncle George. It's plain to see, we ain't no kin."

He reared back and chuckled. "It's what all the white folks call me. Been called Uncle George since I was old enough to hold a plow behind a mule."

"Is the law after you? That's it, ain't it? That's why you don't want me telling nobody where you are."

"Don't fret over the why's and wherefore's, child. Just promise me you won't tell."

"Cross my heart and hope to die. But the day I found you, you kept sayin', 'Delia, I found her.' Over and over you said it, like you'd been looking for me. Who's Delia and why did you say you found me, when it was the other way around? I found you."

"I was talkin' outta my head, sugar."

"But you looked straight in my eyes and said, "You look jest like yo' granny, Miz Delia." That's exactly what you said, plain as day. What is it you're holding back from me, Uncle George? I ain't never known who I was, so if I've got a granny and you know where she is, you gotta tell me. You jest gotta. Is she alive?"

He closed his eyes tight, like he was trying to shut out the world.

Maybe she should've waited. The last thing she wanted was to worry him, and cause a set-back. Did it really matter who her granny was? Why should she care if the woman was alive? If she was, it was obvious she didn't care a flip about her, or she wouldn't let her be tossed from one foster home to another like an alley cat that folks wanted just long enough to rid the barn of rats. "Forget it. Eat your food and we'll talk about it later."

He nodded. "Yeah, sugar. Later." He pulled the napkin back and looked at the plate full of food. "Liver and onions! My stars, I can't remember when I last had liver and onions. I reckon not since Beulah died. She could make the best onion gravy." He took a bite, closed his eyes and the sound coming from his throat confirmed the food was as good as he remembered. "Yo' Miz Gigi sho' is a fine cook."

He ate half the food, then put the plate back in the box. "I reckon I'll save the rest. That's the most I've et in a good while. But sugar, don't bring no more vittles down here."

"Why not? Gigi always makes more'n enough."

His face twisted into a frown. "I don't want you bringing nothing else down here, you hear me, girl? I took care of myself before I got sick and I can do it again, now that I'm all better. So listen to what I'm saying."

"I hear you, Uncle George, but I don't understand. I don't understand nothin'."

"You gotta trust me, Ludie. They is just some things best left unsaid. You asked if yo' granny is dead. She is. But seeing you is almost like seeing her. She'd be so tickled, seeing what a fine looking young'un you turned out to be." His face scrunched up like a prune and his eyes squinted into tiny slits as if he were trying to see for miles down the road through shattered spectacles. "I know you're curious, sugar, but some things ain't meant to be understood."

"Please, Uncle George. I'm thirteen and there ain't nothing you can tell me that'll be worse than what I've already imagined. Or what some folks are saying. One ol' biddy told me I was left on the mayor of Goose Hollow's doorsteps and some folks believe he must've been my pappy and others say it's a lie. What do you say, Uncle George?"

"I say some folks oughtta have their tongues tightened."

"Because you know the truth, don't you? I know you do. So what are you waiting on?"

"Hmm . . . what am I waiting on? Wisdom, sugar. I fear me and you is about to come to a crossroad. One road leads to your deliverance, but taking the wrong road could lead you on the path to destruction."

"You're talking in circles again. Please, Uncle George?"

"If only Beulah wuz here, she'd know the right path to take. She always did. Oh, Lawdy, how I miss that woman."

****

Monday afternoon the children were at school, and Zeke had gone to the Post Office, when Gracie heard a knock on the door. Her eyes widened. "Dr. Flint McCall, what are you doing here?"

"May I come in?"

"But of course. Please excuse the scraps of material on the floor. I've been piecing a quilt and I'm afraid I've made an awful mess. Do you have a patient here in Flat Creek?"

He winked. "As a matter of fact, I do. She happens to be pregnant and I was asked to make a house call. I'll have to say, though, she looks good."

"You mean me? But how did you know?" She giggled and rubbed her belly. "Well, I'm sure it's obvious now that you're here, but you didn't really come all the way from Flat Creek just to check on me, I'm sure."

"That's where you're wrong. Your daddy is concerned about

his little girl. He and I had a lengthy discussion on the phone and I've given him my word that I'll take really good care of you."

"Oh, I'm so sorry. He's a worry-wart, I'm afraid, but he shouldn't have wasted your time by sending you here. You can tell him I'm doing great. The first few months were miserable, but once I found out what was wrong with me, it was almost fun being sick. That doesn't make sense, I know."

"It makes perfect sense. We can endure a lot if we know there's to be a happy outcome. And there's no finer outcome than a newborn baby. Now, if you'll kindly go up to the bedroom and put on a gown, I'll be in shortly to examine you."

"Is it really necessary?"

"You bet! You wouldn't want to see me tarred and feathered, would you? That's likely to happen if I tell the Reverend we simply chit-chatted and I left without giving you a thorough checking over. "

"I understand."

Following the examination, Dr. McCall walked down to the parlor and waited for her to come down. He said, "Well, I suppose you'd like to know what you're having?"

"You mean you can tell?"

"Of course, I can tell. I graduated top in my class. According to my calculations—and I don't mean to brag, but I've been right in every single prediction I've ever made—Gracie Graham, you're gonna have a baby. And there's a fifty/fifty chance it'll be a boy."

"You big tease. I thought you were serious."

Zeke walked in, and Gracie made the introductions and gave a brief reason for the surprise visit.

"I'm glad you came," Zeke said, thrusting out his hand. "I've been trying to get her to let me call a doctor, but the woman is stubborn as a mule—just a whole lot prettier." "So, doc, can you give us a due date?"

Us? Gracie felt her face blush, when he acted as if he were the giddy expectant father.

Dr. McCall glanced toward Gracie, then his gaze quickly darted back to Zeke. "Somewhere around the second week in January. I'd say that's a wonderful way to start a new year." His smile faded. "Gracie, I must tell you, I'm concerned that you haven't gained enough weight to be so far along. Are you not able to keep food down?"

"I couldn't eat for the first few months, but it's much better now."

"What about chores? You've taken on a lot of responsibility, starting this orphanage, and it could be that you're working too hard."

"I try not to overdo."

"It's imperative that you don't."

Zeke stepped forward and laid his hand on her shoulder. "Don't you worry, doc. I plan to take real good care of our little mama."

Gracie stammered, "Doctor, did you say the second week in *January*? Are you *sure* about the date?"

"Well, babies can sometimes be unpredictable. Some get eager to greet the world and come a couple weeks early, and some seem comfy in Mama's womb and come a couple weeks later than expected. But I calculate the little fellow will be ready to greet the world around the ninth day of January."

Zeke extended his hand. "Doc, I appreciate your stopping by to check on her. And when you talk to her ol' man, please assure him I'm taking really good care of his daughter and this little grandbaby of his. I'm sorry to have to rush off, but I need to get to work or I'm gonna be late."

"No problem. I'm on my way out."

Gracie stood at the door to wave them off, when she noticed a car in the driveway. Two elderly women stepped out of a new Packard—the same two ol' goats responsible for Gracie's father leaving Flat Creek Church and moving to Mt. Pleasant. She could only imagine the damage done as they shook hands with Zeke, and exchanged a few words.

They were sashaying up the walk when Zeke rolled the truck window down and yelled, "Gracie, now you do as the doctor ordered, hon. Take it easy and don't wait up for me tonight. You need your rest."

He meant no harm, but why did he have to make such a crackbrained statement? She never waited up for him. Surely, he understood that. If she happened to be in the parlor when he came in, it was because she couldn't sleep. Not because she was waiting up. But there was no doubt in her mind how Mrs. Cora Dobbs and

Mrs. Eunice Watts would be able to twist his words to suit their brand of gossip.

Gracie mumbled through clenched teeth. "Good afternoon, ladies. To what do I owe this visit?"

Mrs. Watts gave her girdle a yank. "My, you look well, Mrs. Graham. Doesn't she look well, Cora?"

"Simply radiant. Uh, it *is* still Mrs. Graham, isn't it?"

This was going to be worse than she'd imagined. "Of course, it is. Why would you ask?"

"I didn't mean to offend you, dear. It's just . . . well, you never know, nowadays, with all the divorces taking place, especially among young women left all alone while their husbands are out on the battlefield. And then, of course, there are the lonely widows left behind. Mrs. Dobbs and I were in the neighborhood and thought we'd pay you a visit. It's a bit nippy out. May we come in?"

"I'm sorry ladies, I'm afraid you caught me at a bad time. I've been working on a quilt and the house is a mess."

"Don't give it a second thought. We're not here to inspect your housekeeping, dear. We'll just scoot in and scoot out."

Gracie sighed heavily as she ushered them into the parlor.

Mrs. Dobbs said, "This is such a beautiful place. Years ago, Mrs. Watts and I often played bridge here with the original owner, Mrs. Ophelia Harrington. It's such a shame how the place has deteriorated, but I'm sure a house this large is too much for a woman to handle alone."

Gracie nodded. “There’s always something to be done, for sure.”

“Well, I know that’s the truth. I suppose that’s why you needed that fellow to move in with you?”

Mrs. Watts gave her crony a sideways glance. “He introduced himself as we got out of the car. I believe he said his name was Thorne? I’m sure he’s a tremendous help.” She smirked. “Doesn’t hurt that he’s so handsome, either, does it?”

Gracie’s teeth meshed together. “If you’re insinuating there’s something immoral going on in this household, let me set your mind at ease. Mr. Thorne has not moved in with me.”

“Oh, I beg your pardon, dear.” She thrust her hand over her heart, feigning indignation. “I certainly meant no harm. I just assumed, since he suggested you not wait up for him—

“Well, he does live here, but not—”

Mrs. Watts clicked her tongue. “For heaven’s sake, don’t say another word. We aren’t here to judge. I happened to overhear talk this morning at the Washateria that you might be in the family way, so I immediately called Cora and we agreed we should come check on you. It must’ve been awful getting the news your husband was killed, and you carrying his child.”

“I didn’t know at the time of his death that I was pregnant, but you’re right. I was devastated when I received the news. I loved my husband very much.”

“Well, bless your heart, I’m sure you did, honey. If I remember correctly, Mr. Graham was killed in late March or early

April. Am I right?"

Gracie twisted in her seat. "April 16th."

"What a cryin' shame. So when are you due?"

Gracie bolted to her feet. "I don't wish to be rude, but it's almost time for the children to get home from school, and I like to have them an afternoon snack set out when they arrive. Thank you for dropping by, but it won't be necessary for you to return. We'll be attending Brother Charlie's church in Goose Hollow." She grimaced as the unrehearsed words poured from her lips. What made her tell such a lie? She had no intention of going to church in Goose Hollow or anywhere else. Was a liar any better than a gossip?

"Goose Hollow? Whatever for? I hear that ol' fire-and-brimstone preacher can hardly stand up long enough to deliver a message, and besides, Flat Creek is your home church. Your father pastored here for many years, and your dear mother played the piano. She was a real lady. We thought the world of her. It must've been devastating to you when your father upped and married that . .. that girl."

Gracie walked to the door and opened it. "Good day, ladies."

Chapter Ten

October 26

Gracie paced the floor Thursday night, waiting for Zeke to get in from work.

The moment the truck drive up, she rushed to the porch to meet him. "Where in the world have you been? You're late."

He grinned. "Aww, that's sweet. I'm sorry if I worried you. I rode across Pea River bridge after work, to see how high the water was, after the big rain yesterday. I told you not to wait up, but I'm glad you did."

"Waiting up? I wasn't waiting . . . well, I suppose I was."

"What's wrong, Gracie?"

"Did I say anything was wrong?"

"You didn't have to. I know you. Tell me what's going on. Is it Ludie?"

"No. Why do you always think if something's wrong, it's Ludie's fault?"

"You don't want me to answer that, Gracie. Why don't we go

brew a pot of coffee, sit down at the table, and you tell me what's got you in such a dither."

"The pot's on already."

His grin stretched from one ear to the other. "That's amazing."

"What?"

"How quickly you and I have come to understand one another. I came in and took one look and knew you were troubled. And you knew I'd come in wanting a hot cup of coffee. Funny, how quickly we've bonded. You know, Gracie, I loved my wife. I really did. But she never understood me the way you do."

"Zeke, I'm afraid you're reading more into this than is there. You like coffee. You've said so, and I've observed your habits. It's no big deal."

He poured two cups of coffee and sat down. "Maybe not to you, hon, but it's a big deal to me."

Gracie's pulse raced. She glanced down at her hands and twisted her wedding band.

He poured a small amount of coffee into his saucer, turned it up and slurped.

It had never bothered Gracie as much in the past, but suddenly she wanted to lash out and demand he learn to drink from a cup.

With the back of his hand, he wiped his mouth. "So, what's on your mind, beautiful?"

She rolled her eyes. "Please, Zeke."

"Sorry. Didn't mean to offend. Now, tell me what's on your mind."

"You know the two women who drove up, as you were leaving for work?"

"Ah, yes. Nice, friendly ladies. I was glad to see friends stopping by to visit. This being your first baby, I can imagine there were lots of questions you had for the ladies, and judging by their ages, they probably had plenty of advice for a new mother-to-be."

She rolled her eyes. "Those two are always full of advice and they dispense much of it at the Washateria."

"I don't understand."

"I'm sorry, Zeke. I thought I could talk about it, but I'm going to bed. I'm tired. Maybe things will look differently tomorrow." She stood and picked up her empty coffee cup and took it to the sink.

He walked over, stood beside her, and with his thumb, gently turned her face toward his. "Hey, are those tears I see?"

She burst into full-blown sobs.

Zeke put his arms around her and held her tightly as she buried her face against his broad chest and cried. He stroked her thick hair. "Shh! Please don't cry. Whatever's troubling you, it's gonna work out. I promise. I'm here for you for as long as you'll let me stay." His voice lowered to a whisper. "I love you, so much it hurts, Gracie Graham."

She stiffened and shoved back with both hands. "No. Don't say that. It isn't true."

"But it *is* true. And if you'll be honest, you'll admit you're falling in love with me too."

"No, Zeke. We're both tired and need to go to bed." She turned and without looking back, headed up the stairs.

Gracie turned and tossed for hours. She thought of a dozen reasons why she needed to ask Zeke to move out of Nine Gables. She'd do so, first thing in the morning, after the kids got off to school. Had she given him reason to believe she was falling in love with him? She certainly hadn't meant to. She could never love him. Never. Her heart raced. Well, maybe if Garth hadn't come along first, she possibly could've fallen for Zeke. But he did come first. And he'd always be first in her heart and in her thoughts. No one could ever take his place. If that were true, why did it feel so good, being in Zeke's arms?

At two a.m. she slipped out of bed and crept downstairs to pour a glass of milk. "Zeke? What are you doing up?"

"I never went to bed. I knew I wouldn't be able to sleep."

She pulled out a chair and sat down. "I'm having a hard time falling asleep also."

"Because of what I said?"

"That's only part of it. Zeke, the doctor said my baby isn't due until the second week in January."

"So?"

"Well, that can't be."

"What d'ya mean?"

"Garth and I married March 17th. Nine months from March 17th would be December 17th."

"Maybe you got pregnant the night before he left and not on your wedding night. When did he leave?"

"April 2nd. But even if I got pregnant the night before he left, the way I figure it, nine months later would be January 2nd."

"I don't understand why you're so upset."

"Don't you get it, Zeke? You heard the doctor say babies often come late. What if I didn't get pregnant until the last day? And what if the baby is two weeks late? Don't you know what people will say? Especially busybodies like Eunice Dobbs and Cora Watts. They'll say the baby is—"

His eyes twinkled. "Mine?" He reached across the table and took hold of her hand. "Let them believe what they want to believe. I wish it *was* my baby."

"Are you crazy? My reputation will be ruined. They'll take the children from me and put them into another foster home. Oh, Zeke, I'm so frightened."

"Hey, take it easy." He stood, walked over and held out his hand. "Come here, and let me hold you."

"No, Zeke. I can't. It isn't right."

"What's not right about it, Gracie? You're not married. I'm not married, and I'm not asking to follow you up the stairs." He winked. "Not tonight, anyway."

He pulled her against him and held her tightly, in spite of her measly attempts to stop him.

He said, "For now, I just need to hold you in my arms and comfort you. You're stressing out and it's not healthy for either you or the baby."

"Zeke. Please, let me go. It's wrong."

His faced brushed against hers. "The only thing wrong is me sleeping downstairs with you two flights above me. You know I'd marry you tomorrow, Gracie Graham, but I'm a patient man. I want you to want me as much as I want you. One day you will. I'll make you love me."

She could feel the beating of his heart. A part of her wanted to shove him away. The weaker part of her wanted him to hold on and never let go.

Then, his lips met hers.

Chapter Eleven

Maddie Claire's lips formed a pout as she stirred her creamed potatoes around and around on her plate.

Gracie said, "Maddie, you've hardly touched your food. Something troubling you?"

"No'm."

Zeke rolled his eyes. "Then stop dawdling and eat." His gaze met Gracie's. "Uh . . . you want to grow up to be a big girl don't you, sweetheart?"

She dropped her fork. "I'm not hungry."

Gracie said, "What's going on, Maddie. This isn't like you. Do you feel bad?"

"Yes'm."

"I thought so. Where does it hurt?"

She patted her chest. "Right here. My heart hurts."

Zeke grinned. "Not surprised. Indigestion, probably. She ate enough last night to last her a week. I don't reckon it'll hurt her to go without a meal."

Gracie reached over and laid her hand on top of Maddie's.

"What's wrong?"

"It's Sunday."

"Yes, it is. But what does it have to do with your not eating?"

"Why don't we go to church?"

Zeke said, "I'll answer that. Gracie's gonna have a baby. She don't need to be around a lot of people who might be sick."

Gracie's eyes squinted. "Please, Zeke. You know why *you* don't go, but that isn't what Maddie is asking. I'm quite sure you aren't aware of the reason I don't go and take the children."

"Sorry." He lowered his head. "I reckon I'm doing it again."

She forced a smile. "I know you mean well, but I beg you to respect my wishes."

He threw up his hands. "You're right. I have no way of knowing why you don't go, so I'd love to hear your answer."

"Maddie, honey, my daddy is a preacher, and I cut my teeth on the back of church pews. Growing up, I was inside the church building more than I was in a house. You might say I was raised in the church, so I'm not sure there's anything a preacher could say that I haven't heard before. And after all those years, since it's obvious God still doesn't seem to know who I am—or care—why bother getting you kids dressed every week? It's a pointless routine."

"But we went when Garth was here."

Gracie's chin quivered. "Yes, we did go when Garth was here. But he isn't here and he won't be coming back. That's proof enough God doesn't care."

"I like going to Sunday School."

"Well, it's a waste of time, so stop pouting and finish your lunch."

"Gigi, you mad with me?"

"No, honey. I'm not mad with you. I'm sorry if I sounded cross."

"You mad with God?"

How should she answer such a question? Make up a lie, the way Zeke did? What about after the baby comes. What would she say then? Wasn't it kinder to tell the truth and save them from believing stories about a God who loves them and will work all things out together for their good? How had that worked for her? "Yes, Maddie. I *am* mad with God."

"Why?"

"Because He didn't answer my prayers."

"Do you still pray?"

"No. I don't."

"Well, maybe if you did—"

Was she going to sit here and let a six-year old heap guilt on her for something Mattie couldn't possibly understand? "I want to hear nothing more about church. We won't be going, so let's leave it at that. Apparently you aren't hungry, so you may be excused. Why don't you and Belle go upstairs and take a nap. I'm sure you'll feel better when you wake up. I'll help Ludie with the dishes."

Ludie picked up her plate and headed to the sink. "No

ma'am."

Zeke's eyes darkened. "Young lady, did you just say 'no' to her?"

Ludie nodded. "I'm gonna do the dishes alone. Gigi looks tired."

Gracie gave her a wink. Ludie understood her better than Zeke. "Thank you, honey. You can leave the food on the table and throw a cloth over it. We'll eat left-overs for supper. Feel free to fix your friend a plate."

"Yes ma'am."

Gracie winced when she saw Zeke eyeing Ludie like a cat eyeing a rat. He loved the kids. They needed a male influence and he was good with them. He played with them, took them fishing, and they loved him. All except Ludie. If only he'd back off and give her a little slack. Gracie understood why the child had problems trusting adults. She'd been let down too many times. If only Zeke could understand and be a little more patient with her.

Instead of going downstairs, he headed for the parlor with the newspaper. She needed to remind him his room was in the basement and folks could get the wrong idea if they should drop in and find him lounging in the parlor, making himself at home. But he'd been a bit testy lately, so now was not the time to bring it up. Maybe it was stress at work, but whatever was bothering him, she hoped would soon be resolved. Midway of the stairs, Gracie stopped and looked back at Ludie, cleaning the kitchen. What a change had been wrought in such a short length of time. Garth would've been proud of her, the way she'd been able to get through to Ludie. Her stomach felt as if she'd swallowed a box of roofing nails. Would he be proud? Or would he be shocked to know he'd only been gone such a short time, and already she was beginning to entertain feelings for another man.

****

Zeke waited for Gracie to go to her room, then lowered the newspaper enough that he could keep an eye on Ludie. He didn't trust the girl. Why Gracie couldn't see what was going on in front of her face was a mystery to him.

The cloth was over the food, as Gracie instructed. After Ludie finished putting away the dishes, she took a clean plate, lifted the corner of the tablecloth and dipped a hefty portion of food from each bowl. She then grabbed a quart jar and filled it with sweet tea. She pulled the cloth back over the leftovers on the table, covered her plate with a napkin and slipped out the back door.

Gracie was too trusting for her own good. He watched out the window until Ludie was in the edge of the woods. He laid the newspaper on the lamp table and hurried outside.

He followed her tracks in the sand along the edge of the creek, as far as he could. Then up ahead, he spotted an old shack. Had she gone inside? Where else? He could rush in and threaten her partner in crime and dare him to eat another morsel taken from Gracie's table. But what if it wasn't a teenage kid? What if it was a big brute, who couldn't be frightened by words? Storming into an unfamiliar situation was not the answer. He'd go back to the orphanage, tell Gracie what he saw and let her handle it. Another bad idea. If he knew Gracie—and he felt he did—she'd approach Ludie, ask her if she was meeting someone in an old deserted servants' quarters in the woods, and the girl would lie. And, of course, Gracie would believe her. Again. Now that he knew where she was going, he'd wait until supper and force her tell the truth in front of everyone.

Chapter Twelve

Gracie lay in bed mulling over the discussion she had with Mattie at lunch. She wasn't proud of the way she handled it, but if she were to do it again, would she know a better way to answer the questions? It was bound to come up sooner or later.

When the doorbell rang, she sat up. Who could be calling on a Sunday afternoon? The bell rang again. And again. Except for Maddie and Belle, the kids were all outside, but where was Zeke?

Maddie came into her room rubbing her eyes. "Somebody's at the door, Gigi. Want me to see who it is?"

"Yes, please. I'm sorry the bell woke you up. If it's the twins, tell them I said to please stop playing with the doorbell. It isn't a toy."

Gracie lay back down and closed her eyes. She roused when she heard Maddie calling.

"Gigi! Somebody's here to see you."

She grabbed a brush and ran it through her hair, before heading down the stairs.

"Brother Charlie! What a surprise."

"Hello, dear. I wasn't sure you'd remember me. The child invited me in. I hope you don't mind."

"I'm glad she did, and yes, I certainly do remember you. With fondness, I might add. Please have a seat."

He propped his cane beside the chair and sat with a stiff leg stretched out in front of him.

"You came to Flat Creek Church a few years ago in support of my father when those busy-bodies were voting to have him kicked out because of idle gossip."

"I did indeed. And what a glorious outcome. God truly works all things together for good, to those who love Him and are called according to His purpose."

She bit her bottom lip. Should she go ahead and let him know upfront he could peddle that bill of goods at someone else's door, because she wasn't buying it? Gracie looked up to see Maddie standing in the doorway. "Honey, would you like to go outside and play, while the preacher and I visit?"

"I'd rather stay here."

Brother Charlie chuckled. "Well, I'd like you to stay, precious. Come over and sit with Brother Charlie." He patted the seat beside him. "You're a mighty pretty little girl. How old are you?"

Maddie held up six fingers.

"Well, I suppose you go to school, do you?"

She nodded.

"You like school?"

Again, she nodded.

Gracie said, "Maddie, I've never known you to be shy. She can talk the ears off a Billy goat, when she feels like it."

The old man patted her on the back. "Why don't you tell Brother Charlie what you did at Sunday School this morning? Did your teacher tell you a Bible story?"

She glanced at Gigi and shook her head. "We aren't allowed to go to Sunday School. Gigi's mad at God."

"I see."

But Gracie was quite certain he *didn't* see. She feigned a smile and said, "Honey, I'd like you to go upstairs and wake Belle. I think she's napped long enough."

After Maddie left the room, Gracie braced for what was sure to come. She didn't feel like arguing with the old man, but neither could she allow him to shame her for teaching the children they make their own destiny. Where was God when she depended on Him for a long and wonderful future with Garth Graham?

"Gracie, I've been meaning to call on you for some time now, to offer my condolences. Your husband's death was a tragedy."

"Yes, it was. Preacher, I suppose my daddy sent you here to check up on me to find out if I'm going to church, but you can tell him I have no plans to go back to Flat Creek Fellowship and sit among that bunch of hypocrites."

"I haven't heard from your father since he and Veezie stopped by Goose Hollow on their way to accept the pastorate at Mount Pleasant. That's a fine church. Good people, the Dalrymples, Redds, Martins, Nichols, Sessions, Baggets—"

Not interested in listening to the old man go through the church roll, naming people she had no way of knowing, she stopped him. “So, if Daddy didn’t send you, who did?” She flinched. “Oh, I hope that didn’t sound rude. But I’m sure you didn’t happen on my doorsteps for no reason.”

His eyes twinkled when he smiled. “Your assumption is correct, my dear. I’m not here by happenstance. I was sent.”

“Veezie?”

“No. But how is Veezie? I’m so proud of that girl. She’s a perfect example of God’s mercy and grace.”

Gracie squirmed in her chair. “She’s fine. But if it wasn’t my father or Veezie who sent you here . . . Zeke?”

“I’m sorry, I’m not familiar with anyone by that name. A relative of yours?”

“No. But do you mind telling me who suggested you come?” She quickly added, “I’m very glad you did, of course. I’m simply curious.”

“I don’t mind at all, dear. The Lord whispered your name in my ear and I knew with a certainty I was supposed to pay you a visit.”

Gracie feigned a smile. The old man was apparently senile. No need in trying to reason with someone who had lost all sense of reason, so why not humor him? “That’s nice. Can I pour you a glass of sweet tea?”

“That would be lovely. Thank you, shug.”

After pouring the tea, Gracie walked over, pulled back the

curtains and peered out the window. “Where did you park? I don’t see your car.”

“Oh, I no longer drive. My eyes aren’t what they used to be, and neither are my responses. The Greyhound bus passes by my house and the driver’s mother is a member of my church. She asked her son to stop and pick me up on his way and drop me off at the bus station here in Flat Creek. I caught a ride here from the station with a very nice fellow.”

Now, she knew he was crazy. Another bus wouldn’t be going back to Goose Hollow until morning. She poured the tea, and walked back into the parlor.

The front door opened and Zeke walked in.

Gracie pulled at the neck of her blouse and tried to think how she’d explain why a strange man would open the door and walk in as if he owned the place.

Zeke’s eyes widened. “Brother Charlie, what are you doing here?”

“I was about to ask you the same thing, Junior.”

Gracie scratched her head . “Brother Charlie, I didn’t think you knew Zeke. You two are acquainted?”

“Zeke? I know him as Junior. That was the only name I ever heard Tobe and Eve Tanner call him.”

Zeke nodded. “I’m quite sure they called me other names, just not to my face. Gracie, my wife’s family was from Goose Hollow, and when we’d visit, they’d always drag us to church.” He gave a nervous-sounding snicker. “No offense, preacher, but I always felt my mother-in-law didn't feel I was good enough for her daughter, so I resented her constant efforts to turn me into the image of Lucy's holier-than-thou father. So if I seem—"

Gracie had questions of her own, but at the moment she needed to gain control of the conversation before the preacher got the wrong idea. "I'm not sure if you're aware, Brother Charlie, but Zeke's boys are living here. He's a very devoted father. Spends as much time as possible with them. Zeke, I'm sure you want to check on the twins. They're outside playing. Could I get you a glass of tea, or are you in a hurry to get back wherever you're headed?" Who was she trying to kid? Brother Charlie? Or herself?

"Did you say, wherever I'm headed?" His gaze met hers. "Oh. Uh, I'm in no particular hurry. A glass of tea sounds good."

Gracie glanced toward the preacher. His expression never changed. If there was nothing immoral with Zeke living at Nine Gables, why did she feel the need to hide the fact? Maybe she didn't tell an outright lie, but wasn't twisting the truth to sound like something else a form of lying? The preacher said God whispered her name in his ear. What if her name wasn't all God whispered? Maybe Brother Charlie was aware that Zeke had moved into her house and was making an effort to move into her life. No. Such thinking was paranoid. The old man didn't *really* mean God whispered to him. Did he?

Gracie came back from the kitchen with the tea. "Zeke, no need to bring the glass back inside. Leave it on the doorstep and the children will bring it in when they come to supper." She glared until he picked up on the cue and headed toward the door.

"No problem. Well, it was nice seeing you again, Brother Charlie."

"And you too, Junior. Where are you living?"

"I live here . . ." He glanced at Gracie, then quickly added, "Uh . . .I mean here in Flat Creek. Well, I'd better go find the boys to tell them bye. Gotta run. Thanks for the tea."

Chapter Thirteen

Ludie shrugged. “Stop being cantankerous, Uncle George. I know you told me not to bring any more food, but Gigi always cooks way too much on Sundays, and there’ll still be food left over after everyone finishes supper tonight. If you don’t eat it, I’ll just have to throw it out.”

“Now, that’d be sinful as all git-out to throw away perfectly good food.”

“Well, ain’t it the truth! So eat, before you force me to sin.”

“Lawsy, child, you as stubborn as Miz Delia ever was. You git more like her ever’ day.”

“You talk about my granny a lot. I want to know all about her, Uncle George. Did you know my mother, too?”

His head dropped. “Yeah, sugar. I knew her.”

“Was she pretty?”

“About as pretty a little gal as I’ve ever laid eyes on. That is, until you come along and I Suwannee if you wadn’t just as pretty.”

“How do you know so much about ‘em? Did you work for my

granny's family?"

Uncle George wrung his hands. "I don't reckon you gonna ever stop pestering me until you know. But sugar, let me warn you. They is times when not knowing is more blessed than knowing. I fear this could be one of them times."

****

Gracie heaved a sigh when the front door closed behind Zeke and a longer sigh when she heard his car leave the yard.

Brother Charlie took another sip of tea. "Mighty good, Gracie."

"Thank you." She tried to think of a nice way of saying what was on her mind. "Pardon me if I sound nosey, Brother Charlie, but I'm not aware of a bus going to Goose Hollow before dawn. Did you make other arrangements to get back home?"

"Other arrangements? No, dear. There are nice long benches at the bus station. They look just like church pews, and from my observation through the years, it appears there's no better place to snooze than on a pew." He threw his head back and chuckled at his little joke.

Gracie forced a smile. "Oh my goodness, I won't hear of it. I can't let you spend the night on a hard, slatted bench in a cold bus station." Her eyes widened at the words coming from her mouth. What was she saying? Did she have another suggestion?

"I'll be fine. It's only for one night and I'll ride the bus back, first thing in the morning." His mouth dropped open, as if he'd come up with a wonderful solution. "Say, I just remembered

George and Beulah had quarters in the basement here, years ago. If the cots are still down there, I'd be very comfortable and you wouldn't be worried. I'm glad I thought of it."

She bit her lip and stalled. "But won't you have to preach tonight?"

"Services have been called off. I felt God had something else for me to do." His face flushed. "I apologize, dear. I shouldn't have invited myself." He stood and lifted his hat from the hat rack on the wall. "I'll be fine at the bus station."

"No." Her stomach churned. "You're more than welcome in this house, but I insist you sleep in the guest room upstairs. It'll be much more comfortable." Surely, the old man would be tired and ready to go to bed before Zeke returned.

The preacher glanced up at the winding staircase and slowly shook his head. "I'm afraid I wouldn't make it up the third step, dearie. The basement will do fine. I'll go around the house tonight and enter through the back door, to avoid the stairs."

Gracie swallowed hard. Why wasn't she upfront with him from the beginning? "Brother Charlie, please sit back down. There's something I haven't told you."

He sat down beside her and took her hand in a firm grip. "I know what you want to talk about, sugar, and I understand."

Sweat prickled the back of her neck. "You do?"

"Yes, dear. And now that I'll be staying over, we'll have plenty of time to talk about the situation."

Gracie wasn't sure she wanted time to talk. The less she

discussed it, the better she'd like it.

"I lost my sweet wife, Bertie, back in the spring, you know." He let go of her hand and pulled a handkerchief from his breast pocket. "The Bible says when God joins a man and wife, they become one, so it stands to reason when a spouse dies, the one left behind feels like half a person. Bertie and I were married fifty-four years. That's a mighty long time." He handed her the handkerchief.

She dabbed the moisture from her eyes, while questioning her next move.

"Sugar, I see the anguish on your face and trust me, I understand. I can't tell you the pain goes away, but I can attest to the fact that God makes it easier to bear, as time goes on."

So he thought he knew how she felt? He couldn't even come close. He got to keep his wife for over half-a-century. "Daddy told me about your wife. I'm sorry." Ignoring the dull ache in her stomach, she forged ahead with the inevitable. "Brother Charlie." She stopped and licked her dry lips. "When I said there was something I hadn't told you, it had nothing to do with Garth's death. I wanted to let you know Zeke will be coming back to Nine Gables tonight." There. She got it out. Gracie glared into his eyes, in an effort to read his expression.

"Oh? He left something, did he?"

"No, he lives . . . he's staying . . . he's working here. It's not how it looks. I hired him as a caretaker. The place is going down fast, and I needed help."

"I gather you feel the need to explain his presence? Why

would that be?"

He knew perfectly well why she felt the need, so why was he acting as if the thought of an impropriety didn't flit through his mind?

"Well, with him being a widower and me being a widow and the two of us living under the same roof, it's possible you might get the wrong impression. But it's strictly a business decision." Tears welled in her eyes and before she knew the reason why, she found herself bawling.

"Why the tears, child?"

"Because I just lied to you, and I'm not sure why I did." Her voice lowered. "Our relationship has progressed further than that of a caretaker and employer. Brother Charlie, I didn't mean for it to go this far and now I don't know how to turn it around."

"And how far has it gone?"

She was surprised how freeing it felt to talk to him, now that she'd opened up. "Zeke came to me when he had nowhere else to go, and I agreed to let him stay in the basement and work here until he could find a job."

"But he has a job, now, doesn't he?"

"He does. But he's fallen in love with me and that changes everything."

"How do you feel about him?"

"He's a good man."

"That's not what I asked. You say he's in love with you. So how do you feel?"

"I don't know, preacher. When he first came here, I saw him as an uncouth, uneducated dirt farmer. But now I can't decide if he changed or if I did. He seems . . . different. When I'm not with him, I tell myself I don't love him and it'd be wrong to marry him. But when I'm with him—I become confused."

"When did the confusion begin?"

She fumbled with her wedding band. "He kissed me." Without forethought, the words blurted out. Yet, it was the truth. The tormenting confusion began the night Zeke's lips caressed hers. Scarcely a minute went by, day or night, she wasn't reliving the feeling of being in his arms. *I love Garth and I always will.* So why couldn't she just forget the kiss ever happened?

Her gaze lifted. "I suppose my little confession shocks you."

"Sugar, I'm almost eighty years old. Not much shocks me. So tell me how you felt when he kissed you."

She lowered her head when a blush heated her face. "The truth? I had to force myself to push him away. But I'm afraid I may not next time and that scares me."

"Gracie, you're very vulnerable at this point in your life. You're lonely and hurting. God didn't send me here to judge you . . . only to give you a warning. Be careful. You say you didn't mean for it to go this far, but sin carries us further than we want to go, keeps us longer than we want to stay and costs more than we want to pay. In all my years of counseling couples, I've yet to hear a single person say, 'I chose to sin in order that I'd lose my spouse, my family and my reputation.' No, it usually begins with an innocent flirtation, followed by a kiss, a desire for more, then come the lies and ultimately heartbreak that ends in shattered lives."

"I suppose I'm at stage four. We've passed the flirtation, the kiss, the desire for more and now I'm lying about it. "I've got a feeling God whispered more than my name in your ear. I don't think it's a coincidence we're having this conversation. You said my daddy didn't send you, but maybe he did, in a round-about way. I know he prays for me. If it wasn't his prayers, it was sweet little Maddie's."

"Ever think it might be your own?"

Her lip trembled. "Brother Charlie, I'm afraid I don't even know how to pray, anymore."

"According to my Bible, sweetheart, those times when we don't know how to pray or what to pray for, the Holy Spirit intercedes for us, with groanings we might not can make heads nor tails of, but God knows exactly what we would've said if we could've found the words."

"Preacher, I've been sitting here trying to get the words out to tell you what's on my mind, so I hope you understand what I'm about to say. Maddie was right when she told you I was angry with God. I was. I thought He allowed Garth to die, but maybe I was wrong."

"Am I understanding you to say you don't think God allowed it? Would you care to explain?"

"I sometimes feel that Garth isn't dead."

Brother Charlie lowered his spectacles. "I beg your pardon?"

"I said sometimes I feel as if Garth isn't dead." Instead of her taking him by surprise, it was he who shocked her when he appeared interested, yet not startled by her statement.

"So when did these suspicions begin?"

"The first time was about a week ago."

"The first time?"

She nodded. "He comes to me in my dreams."

Brother Charlie smiled. "Oh, trust me, I understand. My sweet Bertie visits me in my dreams also. Sometimes I awake from a dream and reach across the bed, thinking she'll be there beside me. Those are sweet times, for sure."

"But it's more than just a dream, Brother Charlie. My heart tells me he isn't dead."

"And your heart would be right, precious. God can speak through his Word, through angels, and even through dreams. I believe the Holy Spirit is reminding you that death has no hold on the Christian. In John 3:16, we are promised everlasting life, and I have no doubt that your Garth is alive forevermore."

"I don't know, preacher—"

The front door opened and Zeke strutted into the parlor as if he owned the place. His eyes widened. "Uh, I didn't expect you to still be here, preacher. I forgot something."

Gracie shook her head. "No, Zeke, I'm the one who forgot something. I forgot to tell the truth. Brother Charlie will be sharing the quarters with you tonight, since a bus won't be leaving until morning."

Zeke said, "If you'd like, preacher, I'll be happy to take you home now. I have nothing else to do."

"Thanks, Junior. I was hoping you'd ask."

Gracie stood and gave Brother Charlie a hug. "Thank you for coming. I needed you and didn't even know it. Now, if you fellows will excuse me, I'm very tired. I think I'll go finish my nap."

Gracie ran outside when Zeke's car pulled up in the yard. "Thank you for taking Brother Charlie home. I'm sure he appreciated it. Did the two of you talk?"

"Talk? Of course we talked."

"About us?"

He put his arm around her and drew her close. "I told him I wanted to marry you, if that's what you mean." He leaned over and kissed her on the forehead. "You look as if the rest did you a world of good."

"It did. I had the most wonderful dream. I was standing in the field and the peanuts had just been plowed. I looked in the distance and there was someone running toward me—"

"That's nice, dear. But first, you won't believe what I saw after lunch while you were upstairs. I'd planned to wait until supper to bring it up, but I might as well tell you now and prepare you. I saw Ludie sneak food from the kitchen and I followed her to see what she was up to."

"You *what?* You followed her? After the discussion we had

earlier? She is not your responsibility, Zeke. I wish you wouldn't undermine me."

"Good grief, how is it undermining you? The girl's up to no good, Gracie, and the sooner you admit she's a bad seed, the less problems you'll face in the future. Don't you want to hear what I saw?"

"No. I don't. Ludie will tell me in her own time. But she'll never tell me anything if she suspects you're checking up on her. Don't you understand? I'm trying to win her trust, but if she knows you're following her, she'll assume I put you up to it. I'll lose her for good."

"Oh, Gracie, why can't you understand? Girls like her are bad news. You can't expect to reform her. It just doesn't happen. It's in her blood."

"You're wrong, Zeke. Ludie reminds me so much of Veezie, my father's wife. She too, was called a bad seed. Even my father caved in to the talk. Veezie said she would've given up on life if it hadn't been for an elderly maid named Beulah who refused to accept other people's assessment, but instead the kind old soul loved Veezie with an unconditional love. I want to be Ludie's Beulah. But before I can expect her to trust me, I have that I trust *her.* If I ever hear of you following her, questioning her or belittling her in any way, I'll have to ask you to leave immediately. Do you understand?"

His jaw flexed. "I'd have to be brain-dead not to understand. You've made yourself quite clear who's in charge."

"I'm sorry, Zeke, I can see you're angry with me. But this happens to be something I feel strongly about."

"I got that. So, why don't we move on? You said something about a dream. What was it about?"

She chewed the inside of her cheek. "Another time."

Chapter Fourteen

November 9th

Two weeks passed and neither Zeke nor Gracie mentioned the incident in the kitchen the night of October 26th. They continued to pretend it never happened, yet she could feel the electricity in the room whenever they were alone together.

She had just finished icing an eight-layer chocolate cake when the children came bursting through the door. "We're home," Toby shouted.

Gracie was glad they'd come to think of it as home.

Ludie said, "Gracie, guess what happened after school today?"

Maddie poked out her bottom lip. "I wanted to tell."

Ludie patted her on the head. "Sure, kid. You tell it."

"Gigi, you know what?" Maddie began ninety-percent of her sentences with the same question.

"Suppose you tell me, Maddie."

"Belle can talk."

Gracie glanced over at Belle, who was sucking her thumb and seemed oblivious to the excitement. "She talked?"

Every head except Belle's bobbed. Tanner said, "Yes ma'am. She surely did."

"Is it true, Belle? Can you talk, sweetheart?"

Maddie said, "She won't do it again. We tried to get her to say something else all the way home, but she won't. But now we know she can talk if she wants to. She doesn't want to."

"What did she say, Maddie?"

"We were walking home and when we got in front of Mr. Oliver's house, we heard a yipping noise and there behind his white fence was a mama dog and some puppies. Gigi, what kind of dog has long brown and white hair? I said it's a bull dog, but Tanner and Toby said it was a cawldy."

Tanner threw up his hands in obvious exasperation. "Not a cawldy. A collie. Tell her, Gigi. Tell her Mr. Oliver's dog is a collie."

"First I'd like to hear more about why you think Belle talked."

Ludie said, "We didn't just think it, Gigi. We all heard her. Plain as day, she said—"

Maddie screamed, "No, no. I get to tell it. You said I could."

"Well, go ahead. Tell it."

"Gigi, Belle said, 'puppy.' And she didn't just say it one time, either."

"Really?"

"For real. Two times she said it and all the way home, we tried to get her to say it again. We all kept saying, 'puppy, puppy.' But she clammed up and wouldn't say it anymore."

Gracie knelt down and hugged Belle. “That’s okay, sweetheart. You don’t have to talk unless you feel like it. Are you ready for some milk and chocolate cake?”

Her eyes lit up and she gave a hefty nod.

After listening to each child tell about their day at school, they all went outside to play. Everyone except Ludie.

“Gigi, do you mind if I go visit my friend?”

“I don’t mind, honey, but we’re having chicken ‘n dumplings for supper, but it isn’t quite ready.”

“Oh, I won’t be taking food. That was just until he got better.”

“I’d say you’re gonna make a fine nurse one day. But what about a slice of layer cake? You think he’d like that?”

“Oh, I’m sure he would.” She carefully wrapped a slice in wax paper and started for the door.

Tanner ran to the table and took a seat. “I can’t remember when I had chocolate cake.”

Gracie pulled a scarf from around her neck, draped it over Ludie’s head and tied it under her chin. “The wind’s beginning to blow. Keep your head tied up or you’re likely to catch cold. And make sure you’re home before dark.”

Gracie couldn’t deny she wondered who Ludie visited so faithfully, but she held to the belief that in time, Ludie would tell her the whole story.

Ludie ran toward the woods, but when she got to the bridge, she crossed the creek and headed straight for Mr. Oliver

Weinberger's fields, where she'd spotted Uncle George baling hay on her way home from school. She was happy he was feeling better and able to work.

"Hey, Uncle George," she shouted. "I brung you something."

He frowned and shooed her away with his hand. "Git away from here, girl. You ain't got no business hanging around me. Now git."

"But Uncle George . . ."

"Ain't you got ears? I said go on home."

Ludie burst into tears. "Home? Where would that be? I know you know, but you a stubborn ol' man and won't tell me. I hate you. I hate ever'body. I'm gonna run so far away you won't never be bothered with me again."

She threw the cake on the plowed up ground and stomped through the woods, winding up at the old man's cabin. If she plundered through his things, maybe she'd find a clue to the hidden secrets.

She came across a picture of a beautiful baby girl dressed in a frilly long gown and a crocheted bonnet and booties. Her pulse raced when she looked up and saw Uncle George standing in the doorway.

"That's my baby you hidin' behind yo' back. Don't wrinkle her picture, sugar."

Ludie slowly brought her hand forward and handed the picture to Uncle George. "She's real purty."

"Yep. She took after her mama."

"Beulah?"

"No. Beulah wadn't her mama."

"So you had two wives?"

He grinned. "Well, not two at the same time. But it's true I had two wives. My first wife died of cholera."

"I thought only hogs got cholera."

"Nope. Ain't the same. My wife, she wadn't no hog, for sure. She was about the most ladylike lady I ever met."

"I'm sorry she died. So where's your little girl, now? Did she die, too?"

He laid the picture on the mantle above the fireplace. "I don't wanna talk about it."

"I'm sorry, Uncle George. I was just looking for—"

His eyes hardened. "I know what you was looking for. But you ain't got no right to pilfer through my stuff. I'll tell you all you need to know in due time."

Ludie's lips poked out. "I reckon you know you hurt my feelings when you was in the fields."

"I'm likely to hurt more'n yo' feelings if I catch you hanging around me while I'm working. You ain't got no idea the trouble you could get me in if folks found out you been hanging around me. Don't you know they likely to lynch me? Is that what you want?"

"Lynch you? That's crazy. Why would they do that?"

"Why? Some folks don't need no reason why. Just knowing a little white gal been hanging around an old darkie would give 'em enough reason to start looking for the nearest hanging tree."

"You making that up to scare me, Uncle George?"

"Nah, sugar, it's the gospel truth, but if it scares you, then I'm glad. Maybe you'll be more careful next time."

"I'm sorry. I'd just die if anything happened to you." She ran over and threw her arms around his waist. "You the best friend I ever had. All white folks ain't like that, Uncle George."

"I know they ain't sugar. I've met some mighty fine white folks in my day. Ain't never been a finer man than Mr. Will Lancaster, the owner of Gladstone."

"Gigi wouldn't care if you was green. I don't reckon there's nobody she don't love. I sure tried her out when I first got to Nine Gables, but she kept loving me no matter what I done. She even loves Zeke. Sometimes I think she loves him more'n she oughta, if you know what I mean."

"What you got agin the man?"

"Can't rightly put my finger on it. I jest don't like him."

"Ain't right to not like somebody for no reason a'tall. You gotta have a reason."

"Well, give me time and I'll come up with one."

****

Gracie pulled a sweater over her arms as she walked outside on the veranda. There were no sounds. Not even the usual hoot owl. The children were asleep, Zeke was at work, and the lump in her throat was growing. Too many memories trying to surface.

She recalled the special time she and her father had, the week they camped out in the Georgia Mountains, several years prior. The trip had been her idea. Gracie had hoped she could help lift his spirits by going with him to the place he and her mother celebrated every anniversary. She hated fishing, but her father wanted to believe she was like her mother. Her throat tightened. If only she could be more like her precious mama. But tonight there was another ache in Gracie's heart. This one had a permanent place in the center, where the crack was. The day she got the message of Garth's death, her heart split down the middle and nothing would ever be the same again. Ever.

She heard the Weinberger's dogs barking, and saw a figure walking down the road. "Zeke? Is that you? Where's your truck?"

"Yeah, it's me. Sorry, if I frightened you. I slid off into the ditch, but I'll get Mr. Ausley to pull it out with his tractor in the morning."

"Why are you getting home so early?"

"Early? It's ten-thirty. I would've been here thirty minutes ago, if I hadn't wasted time trying to get the truck out."

"I had no idea it was that late."

He walked up the marble steps. "Mind if I sit out here with you?"

"It's getting a bit chilly. I'm ready to go inside."

"Please stay. Just a few minutes more." He sat down beside her and cocked his head. "Say, you're wearing your hair different. I like it. Did you do it for me?"

Anger boiled up from deep inside, yet she wasn't sure why.

Was he wrong? "I did it for me. It's the latest fashion and it's called a victory roll. In case you haven't noticed, all the women are wearing their hair this way."

"Well, it looks good on you. I like it."

"Frankly, I don't. Garth wouldn't have liked it, either." She reached up, snatched out the hair pins, one-by-one, letting them fall in her lap. She jerked out the rattail and with a shake of her head, long, thick locks fell loosely around her shoulders. "Garth liked long hair and he always wanted me to wear it down."

Zeke's brow meshed together. "Well, you aren't dressing for a dead man, Gracie, and I happen to think it looks spiffy up. Betty Grable ain't never looked so good." Putting his arm around her he drew her close. His eyes suddenly widened as he pointed to the sky. "Hey, look! A falling star. Make a wish."

Giant tears welled in her eyes. The night she and Garth said their vows, she saw her first shooting star. Her wish was for her husband to come back home from the war. He did. In a flag-draped casket. She thrust her hand over her mouth and ran toward the door. "Excuse me, all of a sudden, I feel sick."

Chapter Fifteen

Zeke was on a ladder repairing a rotten board, when Gracie sprinted from the mailbox, waving an envelope in the air. "It's wonderful news," she yelled. "The best!"

"Whoa. Slow down, girl. A woman in your condition doesn't need to be running. What's going on?"

"I got a letter from Veezie."

"Veezie? That's your step-mother, right?"

"Yes, but she's not much older than me, so I don't think of her as a step-mother. In fact, for a long time, it was hard to think of her as my daddy's wife, even though she is. She's a very dear friend. She and Daddy are coming, Thanksgiving. I haven't seen them since Garth's funeral."

He laid his hammer on the ledge of the second-story window.

"That's a crying shame. It's not as if Mt. Pleasant's on the other side of the world. Seems to me they could've come see you before now."

Disappointed in his negative attitude, yet not willing to let him put a damper on her excitement, she swallowed the pain. "There were circumstances, Zeke. Not only because of the gas rationing, but Veezie helped care for a woman in their church who had the flu and then she came down with it.

"So she got the flu, and now she wants to come here? How do we know she ain't a carrier?"

"Trust me, they wouldn't come if there was any danger. Oh, Garth, I'm so—" *Did I say Garth?* She clamped her hand across her lips. "I'm sorry, Zeke. I'm not thinking straight. It's the excitement."

He shrugged. "No problem," though the pain on his face revealed otherwise. "Step back, Gracie." He jerked at a rotten board and let it fall to the ground.

"My baby sister was barely four months old the day of the funeral. I can hardly believe she'll soon be a year old. I can't wait to see her. Veezie named her after my mama. Mama's name was Jennifer, but everyone called her Jenny. My baby sister's name is Jennifer Emerald. Beautiful, isn't it?"

"Hold on, I'm coming down." He walked her to the veranda. "You're talking a mile-a-minute. It's good to see you happy. I'm glad I'll finally get to meet your folks. I'm sure we'll get along just fine."

Her throat tightened. "Uh . . . Zeke, when they come, it might be better if you just showed up for the Thanksgiving meal, but didn't linger in the parlor with the family after dinner, if you know what I mean."

"No, I'm afraid I don't know what you mean. You 'shamed of

me?"

"Of course not, silly. But Daddy says the Bible warns to avoid all appearances of evil. And even though nothing immoral has taken place under this roof, we must be careful to avoid the appearance."

"That's crazy. What about the verse that says every tub shall sit on its own bottom?"

Gracie stuck her tongue in the side of her cheek. "I can't comment since I'm not familiar with that verse."

"Well, it's in there. Somewhere. My granny said so. I don't mean to offend you, sweetheart, but there's talk around town that your ol' man wasn't too careful about appearances when he met the little firecracker he married. They say the mailman caught him spending the night, then sneaking out in the wee hours of the morning. I don't mean to bad-mouth your ol' man, but do you really think he was going over his sermon notes with her?"

Before she had time to think, her palm made contact with the side of his face. Her eyes widened, and she quickly rubbed her hand across his red cheek. "Zeke, I'm so sorry. I've never slapped anyone in my life. I don't know what came over me."

"My fault. I had no business saying what I did. You want to believe your father's perfect, but you need to grow up, Gracie. He may be a preacher, but he was a man before he started preaching. Face facts. Dogs act like dogs. Pigs act like pigs. Chickens act like chickens. And men act like men. That's just how the Good Lord made us. So I wasn't trying to find fault with your father. I was merely trying to make a point he's a man and will understand a lot more than you think he will."

His brow furrowed. "You ain't heard a word I said."

She muttered, "I can't believe I slapped you. It wasn't like me."

"Don't worry about it. As I said earlier, it's all part of being pregnant. It seems to affect a woman's logic. Like now, for example. What reason would you have for needing to hide me in the basement? Afraid I might embarrass you in front of your preacher daddy?"

"That's not it and you know it. But Daddy might get the idea there's something going on between us if the caretaker joins the family in the parlor."

"Are you saying he'd be wrong? Gracie, you know how I feel. I want to marry you and give the baby my name."

"Zeke, we've gone over this a dozen times. You know I can't agree to that."

"Which part? Marrying me or giving the baby my name?"

"You don't give up, do you?"

"Gracie, you'll have to admit we're good together."

"Zeke, I'm very fond of you, but I've been honest with you. I've told you more than once I don't love you. I know what it feels like to love a man. I loved my husband and I could never love another man the way I loved him."

"I know you feel that way now, but I believe with all my heart in time you'll grow to love me. My mother was a mail-order bride.

She once told me she only married my father to get away from a bad home situation. She didn't even like my daddy when they first married. But their love grew through mutual respect for one another. We're already one step ahead of them. I don't have to learn to love you. I love you already with my whole heart. What a wonderful Thanksgiving it would be if you'd allow me to announce our engagement, just before your father carves the turkey. I'll even ask his—"

Gracie;s eyes widened. "Zeke, quick! Go call Dr. McCall."

"Why? What's wrong?"

"I'm not sure. Just call him. Please hurry. His number is on the slate above the phone. Tell him it's urgent."

"Dr. McCall, this is Zeke Thorne. Gracie said I should call you. She won't tell me what's going on, but she said tell you it's urgent."

"Tell her I'm on my way."

When he hung up, he heard Gracie hit the floor. Zeke picked her up, carried her up the stairs and laid her on her bed. His heart ached, seeing her wedding picture on the mantle. *"I'll make her forget you, Garth Graham. She's in love with me. She just doesn't know it yet."*

He dipped a washrag into the water pitcher beside her bed and rubbed her face with the damp cloth. Gracie opened her eyes and glanced around the room. "How did I get up here?"

"I brought you up the stairs."

"Did you call the doctor?"

"He's on his way. How do you feel now?"

"Scared."

"Don't be afraid. You're gonna be alright."

"But Zeke. Something's wrong. Bad wrong. I'm . . . I'm—never mind." She covered her face.

"What, Gracie. You can tell me anything."

"No. I can't. It's private. You should go back downstairs."

"Good grief, Gracie, are you in pain?"

"No."

"Then what?"

"Please go and leave me alone."

"I can't leave you. I'm staying until the doctor comes."

Zeke watched out the window and ran downstairs as soon as the doctor drove up.

Flint said, "How is she?"

"Scared to death."

He grabbed his bag and rushed in the house. "Is she spotting?"

Zeke nodded. "Yes, I think so, although she hasn't said. I'll show you to her room."

"That's not necessary. I've been here a number of times in the past. I'm sure I can find it."

Zeke followed him into Grace's room.

Flint said, "Sir, I don't wish to be rude, but I'd appreciate it if you'd step outside while I examine Mrs. Graham."

Zeke bit his tongue to keep from blurting what was on his

mind. *If he's trying to annoy me, he's doing a swell job.*

When Flint walked out, Zeke met him at the door. "How is she, doc?"

"Her body's trying to abort. I need her to stay in bed until after this baby arrives."

"I understand. I'll call Mr. Daniels at the mill and let him know I won't be able to work for the next few weeks. I may lose my job, but we'll manage."

"That's not necessary."

"Oh, but it is, doctor. You don't understand. That woman means the world to me. If anything happened to her—"

"Gracie doesn't need for you to quit your job. She needs a *woman* to take care of her. I called my wife from the phone in Gracie's room and asked her to get in touch with Veezie. She called back and said Veezie is packing and will stay until after the baby comes. She'll be here before the kids get home from school."

"Well, that's just dandy. I wish you would've consulted me before making that decision. Doc, are you aware her stepmother had the flu? I don't like the idea of her coming here."

"*Had* is past-tense. There's no danger to either Gracie or the baby, if that's what you're implying."

Zeke rolled his eyes. "Can I see her now?"

"I suppose so. Just don't stay long. She's exhausted. I'd like for her to rest."

Zeke knocked on the door. "Gracie, it's me."

“Come on in.”

“The doc says you’re gonna need complete bedrest for the next six weeks.”

“I know. Oh, Zeke, I can’t lose this baby. I just can’t.”

“And you won’t. Gracie, I want to be able to take care of you twenty-four hours a day, and yet I can’t stay with you unless you’ll agree to marry me right away. What if you should need me in the middle of the night? I’d never hear you with me in the basement. For the sake of the baby, Gracie, we need to do this and not put it off. It could mean life or death for our . . your baby. Your father can marry us Thanksgiving.”

“Zeke, I’ve never lied to you.”

“No, you haven’t. I know you don’t think you love me, but I believe you’re afraid to admit it. In some twisted way, you believe you’re failing Garth. But he’s gone, Gracie. He’s never coming back. And I’m here, and I love you. Please?”

“I don’t feel like discussing it.”

“There’s nothing to discuss. Just say, ’yes.’”

“If I say ‘yes,’ will you let me go to sleep?”

“Yes! You said, yes. You won’t be sorry. I promise you, my darling, you won’t be sorry.”

Chapter Sixteen

After Veezie arrived, she tiptoed up the stairs at Nine Gables, holding her baby girl. It felt strange walking into the bedroom that was once hers. Seemed another lifetime ago. In a way, perhaps it was.

Not wanting to wake Gracie, she quietly pulled a quilt from the closet and made a pallet on the floor for little Jennifer Emerald.

Just as she laid the baby down, she heard footsteps and the door swung open. Her heart beat against her chest, but before she could scream, a tall, good-looking stranger whispered, "Thank you for coming, Veezie."

"I'm sorry. Do I know you?"

Zeke extended his hand. "Forgive me. I'm Zeke Thorne, Gracie's fiancé. I was glad when Flint said you could come help us."

"Her what?"

"I can see I've shocked you. I should've waited and let Gracie break the news, but to tell the truth, I think she's afraid of what people will say, since it happened suddenly. But we've learned love is something you can't put a time limit on. Sometimes it takes years to develop. Other times—as in our case—it happens almost at first sight."

"I must say, this is a shocker. I had no idea."

"Naturally, she's more afraid of what her father will say than anyone else. It's that whole thing of avoiding all appearances of evil that he preaches. We'd hate for him to form the wrong opinion. It might be best if you didn't mention you know until Gracie's ready to tell it. I don't want to put any undue stress on her, especially now. Let it come from her."

"I won't say a word. How did you two meet, if you don't mind me asking?"

"I don't mind at all. It was fate. Or what you and your husband might refer to as Providence. I'm a widower, she's a widow. Although falling in love wasn't on our minds the day I moved in, I'll have to admit, it's the best thing that could've happened to either of us."

Veezie cleared her throat. "I don't know what to say."

"How about congratulations? We consider ourselves lucky to have found one another. I just hope she can carry the baby full term." His eyes lit up. "We're hoping for a girl this time."

"This time?"

"Oh, didn't I mention I have twin boys? They're living with us, along with three precious orphan girls, but I suppose she's told you as much in her letters. I couldn't love the girls any more if they were my own flesh and blood. The oldest tries us at times, but

I suppose all parents of teenagers must feel this way at some point."

Seldom at a loss for words, yet the thoughts whirling in her head were best left unsaid.

"Well, I'd like to stay and visit longer, but I go to work at two o'clock and I have just enough time to get there. The children will be home around three-fifteen. I sat out apples and cheese for their snacks. Gracie usually has something homemade when they get home from school. We allow them to play outside until dark, and after supper, they're to get their baths and do their homework. I hope they don't give you any trouble."

"I'm sure I can handle them." When little Emerald stirred and grunted, Veezie picked her up to keep from waking Gracie, and followed Zeke down the stairs. She made a pallet in the corner of the room and laid the baby down with a bottle.

Zeke walked toward the door, then turned and snapped his fingers. "Oh, one more thing I forgot to mention. Ludie . . . the oldest girl . . . has a friend she visits in the afternoons. She has our permission."

He certainly knew the routine. She waited for him to close the door behind him, then picked up the parlor phone to call her husband. "Operator, I'm calling Mount Pleasant, Alabama. Station to station, number 430." Veezie swallowed hard. Was she doing the right thing? The truth would devastate Shep who thought his daughter could do no wrong—but wouldn't it be unfair not to warn him what to expect, before he arrived?

She mulled Zeke's words in her head. *We* allow them . . . ? *Our* permission? This didn't sound like the Gracie she knew. But then, how well did she really know her?

Shep answered on the second ring. "Veezie? Honey, I've been waiting on pins and needles for your call. How's my little girl?"

Her knees buckled. Stalling, she feigned a chuckle. "Which one?"

"Both of them, but at the moment, I'm concerned about the first born. Is she okay? I called Flint after he examined her, but I'm more concerned with what he left unsaid than what he told me. He's never sounded so evasive."

"Actually, I haven't had an opportunity to speak with her. She was asleep when I arrived, and she's still resting. But don't worry, darling. I'm here and I intend to make sure she doesn't lift a finger."

"How's Emerald? Giving you any trouble?"

"Not a bit. You know how riding always puts her to sleep. I laid her down when I arrived, but she napped about twenty minutes, and now she's on a pallet sucking a bottle."

"I miss you, Veezie."

"I miss you, too, honey."

"Why do I get the feeling there's something you aren't telling me?"

She paused. "Maybe because you know me."

"So there is something wrong?"

Now that she'd begun, there was no turning back. "Wrong? Maybe peculiar is a better word."

"Spit it out. What's going on?"

Veezie pressed her back against the wall. "Sweetheart, your daughter is engaged to be married."

"Is this supposed to be a joke?"

"No joke. I met her fiancé when I arrived."

"Veezie, that's crazy. What are you talking about?"

"Shep, maybe you should sit down while I tell you."

His words came out in spurts. "I'm seated. Now stop stalling. I want to know everything you know."

Hearing the panic in his voice confirmed she was doing the right thing by giving him time to adjust to the news and calm down before meeting Zeke. It took a lot to upset her husband, but when he did get riled, he could be difficult to reason with.

"When I got here, Flint left and I went upstairs to her bedroom. She was asleep, so I made a pallet in the corner of the room and put Emerald down. It was then I heard the sound of a man's footsteps on the stairs. It frightened me, since no one had knocked on the door. Then the bedroom door swung open and I spotted a metal ashtray on a stand, grabbed it and was ready to clobber the intruder. Only, it wasn't an intruder."

"Go on."

Veezie tightened her grip on the receiver. "I discovered he lives here." There was heavy breathing on the other end of the line. "Honey, are you okay?"

"No. I'm *not* okay. I'm confused. It sounded as if you said—" He blew out a faint whistle. "Honey, tell me again what you said. It must be the connection. I'm getting a lot of static."

"He lives here, Shep."

"No. You aren't saying . . . with Gracie?"

"Apparently so." A long silence ensued. "Shep, are you still there?"

"I'm here. I just can't believe what I'm hearing. It doesn't make sense, Veezie. Are you sure you didn't misunderstand? "

"I understood perfectly. He made it very clear. Said he and Gracie fell in love at first sight. All his sentences are sprinkled with words like *we*, *us*, and *our* as if they're already married."

"Well, for crying out loud, I wish they were if he's living in the house with her." His voice quaked. "There's a bus leaving this evening around five. I'm coming."

"No, Shep, there's no need. Your coming isn't going to change a thing."

"Don't tell me it won't. You don't know me well if you think I'm gonna let some man move in and destroy my little girl's reputation? Won't happen."

"You're upset, I understand. But darling, she isn't a little girl, anymore. She's a grown woman and I'm quite sure he didn't move in without her approval. So if you come barging in making demands, I'll assure you, it'll only make things worse. Let's keep our plans. I'll stay here, and you wait and come for Thanksgiving. You'll have time to cool down and can sit and talk rationally with her. We'll learn a lot more about what's going on if you let me spend time with her, than if you come bursting through the door with a shotgun."

His voice lightened. "Well, I wasn't planning to shoot the guy. But I wouldn't mind roughing him up a bit."

"I'm glad you're beginning to calm down. I started not to mention it to you, but decided it'd be better if I gave you time to pray about the situation before getting here and doing or saying something you might later regret."

"Maybe you know me better than I know myself."

"I've got to go, hon. I hear the children coming in from school."

Maddie was the first to walk inside. "Who are you?"

"My name is Mrs. Veezie. I'm married to Gracie's father."

She glanced about the room. "Where is he?"

"He's coming later."

Toby and Tanner appeared unfazed by a new face in the house and headed straight for the kitchen.

A pretty little girl with long curls, grabbed the older girl's hand.

Veezie addressed the teenager. "You must be Ludie."

"Yeah, and this here is Belle." Ludie knelt down on the child's level. "There ain't nothing to be afraid of, kid. She's a friend of Gigi's. She's just here to visit."

Veezie raised a brow. "Gigi?"

"Uh, yeah, it's what Garth told us to call Gracie. Did you

know Garth? He's dead now."

"Yes, I knew him. He was a nice man."

Ludie nodded. "And this is Belle. She don't talk, but don't think she's dumb, 'cause she ain't. Maddie is . . ." she looked around and giggled. "Maddie is the one who beat us all to the table and is stuffing her mouth. She's Belle's sister and Toby and Tanner are the twins."

"Well, I'm proud to finally have an opportunity to meet you kids. Gracie has written wonderful things about all of you."

"Yeah? Well, I ain't a kid. Where's Gigi?"

"She's had a little setback, and the doctor wants her to stay in bed."

Ludie shrieked. "She didn't lose the baby, did she? I wanna see her."

"No, honey. She hasn't lost the baby. And to keep the little rascal from coming too early, the doctor says she'll need to stay off her feet. So I'm here to make sure she's able to follow the doctor's orders. Do you kids think you can help me take care of her?"

Ludie nodded. "Can we see her?"

"Don't you want to eat your snack first?"

"I ain't hungry. I want to see Gigi."

"That's fine. Let her know I'm here and we're all gonna pitch in and take care of things so she can rest easy."

"She doesn't know you're here?"

"Not yet. She was asleep when I arrived. She'll be surprised to see me."

"Then I reckon you want to go up first."

"No, she'll want to know about your day. I plan to be here for a spell, so I'll have plenty of time to visit with her."

"Thanks, you're swell."

"You're pretty swell, yourself, kid."

Maddie spotted Emerald playing in the corner of the room and shrieked, "Gigi had her baby and she's a girl."

Ludie tiptoed up the stairs and peeked her head in the room. "Gigi? You awake?"

"I wasn't, but I am now."

"I'm sorry. Didn't mean to wake you."

"I'm glad you did. How was school?"

"It was okay. But how are you? It scared the living daylights outta me when Veezie said you had a setback. I didn't know what it meant. I thought you lost the baby."

"Veezie? She's here?"

"Yeah. She said she's gonna stay awhile and help us take care of you, 'cause the doc wants you to stay in bed. I like her. She's nice."

"Yes, she is. You're a lot like her, Ludie."

"Me?"

"Yes, you. I think you two will get along just fine."

"Gigi, what's wrong with you? I know you're PG, but why you gotta stay in bed? Did Zeke do something to hurt you?"

"Zeke? Of course not, sweetheart. What would give you such

an idea?"

She lifted her shoulders. "I dunno. I just figured something bad must've happened for you to be fine when we left home this morning, and he was the only one here with you. I wouldn't put nothing past him."

"Ludie, that's not a very nice thing to say. I wish you'd try harder to get along with him. He loves you kids."

"I don't trust him."

"Has he given you reason not to trust him?"

"Maybe not. But he ain't give me no reason why I oughta trust him, neither. I've been around enough scumballs to know one when I see one, and he's a giant scumball."

"Could it be you're a little jealous?"

"Of him? Why would I be jealous of *him*? "

"Maybe you're beginning to feel I'm not spending enough time with you kids and am spending too much time with Zeke. Is that it?"

"You spend plenty of time with us. But if I wuz to say that was the reason I don't like him, would it make you want to tell him to haul buggy?"

"Come here, and sit down on the side of the bed."

When she sat down, Gracie took her by the hand. "I may as well tell you now. Zeke has asked me to marry him."

Ludie jumped up. "Are you crazy? Marry him? You too good for him."

"Sit back down, Ludie. I'm not through."

Ludie slapped at a lone tear trailing down her cheek.

"Sweetheart, there's something else I haven't told you."

"It can't be no worse than what I jest heard."

"I want to adopt you, after Zeke and I marry."

"Adopt me? For real?"

"For real. Would you like that?" There was a long silence. Gracie tried to read her reaction. "What's wrong?"

Ludie's lip quivered. "All my life I've wanted somebody to want me. Nobody never did until you came along. Gigi, there ain't nobody I'd rather have for a mama than you, and that's the honest truth."

"Then what's the problem?"

"The problem? Don't ya get it? Zeke would be my daddy. I thought I wanted a daddy, but I ain't that hard up."

"I'm sorry you feel that way. But it would be a package deal. I hope you'll change your mind, because I'd like very much for you to be my daughter."

Ludie stood. "I reckon I better go and let Veezie come up. She wants to see you, but was nice enough to let me come first."

Chapter Seventeen

November 13, 1945

Veezie picked up Emerald and ushered the four younger children up the stairs to Gracie's room. Gracie oohed and ahhed over little Emerald and took time to give each of the children a hug to reassure them she was okay. "You kids can play outside until suppertime, but ask Ludie to come back upstairs, please."

Ludie came bouncing up the stairs, skipping every other one. "Maddie said you wanted to tell me something. You changed your mind about marrying the scumbag?"

Gracie ignored the question. "You may visit your friend, but please don't stay long. You'll need to help Veezie with supper. One other thing. Would you like to invite him to come for dinner Thanksgiving Day?"

"Jeepers Creepers, you mean it?"

"Of course I mean it. I'd love to meet him."

She wrung her hands. "He's kinda shy, so I don't know if he will or not, but I think you're swell to invite him. He doesn't have any folks."

"I gathered as much, though you haven't told me much about him."

"I reckon he was afraid I couldn't go see him if I told. But you'll like him. He's the best friend I've ever had." She rolled her eyes. "But what about Zeke?"

"What do you mean?"

"What if he doesn't want him to come?"

"Honey, you have Zeke all wrong. He'll be thrilled at the opportunity to meet your mystery friend. Now, run on if you're going. I need you back in time to peel potatoes to go in the soup Veezie will be making for supper."

"Mind if I take him a couple of apples?"

"Sure. Take several."

After Ludie left the room, Veezie had plenty of questions, but the answers she wanted most were to questions she couldn't ask. She regretted making Zeke a promise to let Gracie be the one to bring up the subject of the upcoming marriage. Hoping to find a subtle way to get her to tell, Veezie said, "Gracie, tell me about Zeke. I met him briefly when I arrived, and he seemed quite congenial. But what does Ludie have against him?"

Gracie laughed. "What does Ludie have against the *world* would be a fairer question. Heaven only knows what all that child has been through in her short life. She didn't trust anyone, including me, when she first arrived. I think I've finally won her trust, but she and Zeke still lock horns from time to time."

"Why do you suppose that is?"

"He represents an authority figure, and Ludie hates authority. She's mellowing, but I've tried to help Zeke understand that bossing her around is not the way to win her trust. He's always sure she's up to no-good, and she's confident he's plotting against her."

"And what do you believe, Gracie?"

"Honestly, I don't know what to believe. Sometimes I think it's all his fault. Other times, I think he'd treat her differently if she'd show more kindness toward him. He knows she doesn't like him."

"I've only been here a couple of hours, but it seems to me it works both ways. I sense Ludie knows Zeke doesn't like her, either. Have you spoken to him about showing more kindness toward her?"

"Not less than a dozen times. He's a good man, but hard-headed for sure."

"Gracie, I had just arrived and was up here in your room, when Zeke opened the door and walked in. I'll have to tell you, it frightened me to see a strange man entering your bedroom."

"He was with me when I fainted, and brought me up the stairs. He should've knocked, but I suppose he didn't want to disturb me in case I was sleeping."

"Where does he live?"

"Uh . . . in the basement. He's the caretaker."

"The *caretaker?* Is his job to take care of you or the place?"

"I hope that's a joke, Veezie. If I remember correctly, you said you had a caretaker and a maid when you lived here at Nine Gables."

"Don't get your feathers ruffled. I'm asking, not accusing."

"I'm sorry. I guess I'm a little self-conscious. Worried about what people will say when they find out. Especially Daddy."

"Would you care to share what it is you're afraid they'll find out?"

"Zeke has asked me to marry him."

Veezie feigned surprise. "Marry him? Wow! Love at first sight, huh?"

Gracie's face distorted. "Love? I didn't say I loved him."

"You don't love him?"

"Of course not. But it's not as if I've led him on. Zeke knows I don't love him. He understands.. I loved Garth and I'll always love Garth."

"I don't get it. Why would you marry someone you don't love, Gracie? That doesn't make sense."

"Well being a young widow doesn't make sense, either, but it happened. Zeke loves me, and he won't take no for an answer, so why not? I have two choices. Either I can live out my life alone and lonely, or I can marry a man who loves me and wants to take care of me. Which would you choose, Veezie?"

"Ducky, you know my past. I've made some bad choices in my lifetime. I chose men who said they loved me, but they only wanted to use me. If I could live my life over, it wouldn't matter how many claimed they loved me, I wouldn't give myself to any man I didn't love. I've had to live with regrets, and although your father never brings up my past, I wonder if it doesn't cross his mind when he's holding me."

"But I know Zeke will be good to me."

"Gracie, Garth has only been dead seven months. You're still grieving. I'm afraid you'd be making a terrible mistake if you jumped into marriage this soon."

"It's too late."

"Too late? Are you saying you're already married?"

"No, but I gave him my word. He'd be crushed if I backed out now."

"Better to be crushed for a season than you be married for a lifetime to someone you don't love."

"Can we talk about something else? You've made it plain how you feel, and it's not that I don't understand what you're saying. But I can't break his heart. I won't."

Chapter Eighteen

Ludie was glad to find Uncle George at home. She pushed open the door and rushed in. “Uncle George, I’ve got some great news. You’re not gonna believe it.”

“Slow down, girlie, you’re talking too fast. I can’t hear that fast.”

“Gigi wants you to come to Nine Gables for Thanksgiving dinner.”

“Shug, I ain’t no cook. That was Beulah’s job. I reckon flapjacks and eggs is about the best I can do. I sho’ couldn’t put no Thanksgiving spread on a table. Did you tell her I cooked?”

“No. She don’t want you to cook. She wants you to come sit down at the table with the family. I told her you’re the best friend I ever had and that’s enough for her. Didn’t I tell you Gigi loves ever’body? She said she can’t wait to meet you.”

“Ludie, I know you mean well, but I can’t . . . it just ain’t right.”

“What ain’t right about it? I want you there and Gracie wants you there, and that’s all that matters. Please, please, Uncle George. Say you’ll go. You about the closest thing to family I ever had.”

"My, child, how you do go on. What makes you say such a crazy thing?"

"It's the truth. I didn't never know my mama or my granny, but you did. So you the only link I have to family. That almost makes us kin, don't it?"

George rubbed his eyes. "Means that much to ya for me to go, does it?"

"So you'll come?" She ran over and threw her arms around the old man. "Swell! I'll tell her to set an extra plate right side o' me."

"Lawsy, if that don't beat all. Yo' Miz Gigi must be one of the finest ladies I never did meet. She allowed you to bring me vittles when I was ailing, she took in all you orphans, and now for her to invite this wore out ol' colored man to come sit at her table—well, she must be mighty special."

"She's special all right. I'm so excited, Uncle George, I don't know if I can wait nine whole days."

****

Veezie moved her things in the room with Gracie, then went up in the attic and brought down a pink wicker bassinet. Her heart ached for her little Diamond and as hard as she tried not to think about it, she still wondered at times if she caused her baby's death.

That night, after everyone was in bed, Gracie whispered, "Veezie? You awake?"

"Yeah. What's wrong? You sick?"

"No. I've got to tell you something."

"I'm listening."

"I have a feeling Garth isn't dead."

"What did you say?"

"I sometimes wonder if Garth is really dead."

Veezie jerked straight up in the bed. "You aren't serious."

"Yes, I am."

"Gracie, honey. Why would you think such?"

"I've been having weird dreams. I talked to Brother Charlie about my dreams and I thought at the time what he said made sense. But now, I'm not so sure."

"Dreams!" Veezie giggled. "I'm glad you clarified. You won't believe what I thought you were saying. Trust me, I understand. I can't tell you how many times I've dreamed about my baby that died. It's always the same. I can see little Diamond's beautiful face, even though I refused to look at her before she died." Veezie's voice cracked. "You'll never know how I regret being so stubborn. I suppose it'll haunt me forever. If only I'd looked at her."

"I'm sorry, for your loss, Veezie, but you now have little Emerald. She's a doll."

"I do, Gracie, and I'm thankful, but I'm not sure you understand. As much as I love Emerald, the love I have in my heart for Diamond will live forever. It's irreplaceable."

"Veezie, I'm sorry I sounded callous. You're right. Love is irreplaceable and never dies. Tell me all about your dreams, then I'll share mine."

"Well, I'm nursing Diamond and when I wake up, I expect to

feel her tiny body against mine. It's such a letdown to realize she isn't there. Hasn't happened as much since Emerald was born, and I'm not sure if I'm sad or glad. So, you see, Gracie, I can relate. I know how real dreams can seem."

Gracie's lip trembled. "I thought you understood, but you don't. I knew you wouldn't believe me. Doesn't matter. I still believe Garth's alive."

Veezie's heart sank. Were they really having this conversation? "Then help me believe, Gracie. Tell me why you think he's alive."

"I can't explain. It's just a strong feeling I can't shake. It's like I know, that I know, that I know. The only thing I don't know, is *how* I know."

Veezie's mind shot back to the devastating time in her life when she lost her baby and sank into a catatonic stupor. She feared she was losing her mind. Now, she feared for Gracie. Was Garth's death driving poor Gracie insane? "I'd like to hear more. Do you dream he comes home from the war—or that he never leaves?"

"Nothing like that. In my dreams I'm walking and I hear him calling. I turn around and I see him, dressed in white from top to bottom. It seems strange he's wearing white. It would make sense if he'd joined the navy, instead of the army. He looks so handsome, though, and he runs toward me, yelling, 'Wait for me, Gracie. Wait for me.'" She shrugged. "Ah, but then I wake up. Always in the same place in my dream. But unlike your dreams, where you're left feeling depressed, I'm left with the hope I'll see my husband again." She giggled. "So what d'ya make of that, Miss Dream Interpreter?"

Veezie's throat tightened. "Well, I don't claim to be a dream interpreter, but if I were to attempt to interpret, I'd say you're having this dream because of deep-seated doubts about your forthcoming marriage to Zeke."

"Seriously? That's funny. Do you read palms, too?"

"You're poking fun, but think about it, Gracie. In your heart, you know Garth wouldn't want you to live out the remainder of your life with a man you don't love. I'd say your subconscious is telling you to wait for love."

Gracie reached over and turned on the bedside lamp. "You really think so?"

"I believe it with all my heart, Gracie."

"But why is he always in white and not in uniform?"

Veezie paused. "When you think of angels, what do you think of?"

"Wings and a halo?"

"Okay, but what are they wearing?"

"A white robe."

"Exactly. So, if Garth was killed, where did he go?"

"Heaven."

"Yes. So your subconscious places him in a white robe because in your heart, you know he's dead."

"Makes sense, I guess. Brother Charlie said its God's way of reminding me that believers never die. Oh, Veezie, Garth seems so real in my dreams."

"Gracie, do you really think Garth would want you to make the mistake of a lifetime, simply because you don't want to hurt Zeke's feelings? If you answer honestly, I believe you'll agree if Garth could speak to you, he most assuredly would be saying, 'Wait, Gracie.' But he wouldn't be saying wait for him, since he can't come to you, but he'd tell you to wait for true love to come again."

Gracie shook her head. "Love will *never* come to me again."

"It came twice to your father."

"Did it?"

"You wonder if he really loves me?"

"No, I can see in his face how crazy he is about you. But I sometimes wonder if he really loved my mother. If he had, he couldn't love you as passionately as he does."

"That's where you're wrong, Gracie. Shep Jackson loved your mother with his whole heart, body and soul. He loved her as much as any man has ever loved a woman. But I also know he loves me just as much, but in a different way. He has two daughters. He loves you both in different ways because you're both different. But it doesn't mean his love for one of you lessens the love he has for the other. And the same holds true with his love for me and Jenny. Enough talk for tonight. We'd better get to sleep. Switch out the light. You need your rest."

Chapter Nineteen

Saturday morning, Ludie helped Veezie make breakfast, then took a tray upstairs to Gracie.

"How you feeling, Gigi?"

"Better than I've felt in weeks, sweetie. I feel well enough to put up the crate of apples I bought at the market, last Wednesday."

Veezie stood in the doorway. "You'll do no such thing. I made your daddy a promise that I'd make sure you stayed in bed. Ludie and I will have those apples canned and lining the pantry before nightfall, so stop worrying."

A wide grin spread across Ludie's face. "You're gonna let me help? I've never put up apples."

"I hadn't either when I was your age."

"Can we do it now?"

Gracie winked. "Veezie, I think you've made a friend."

"Yes, Ludie and I hit it off from the start. I think we're cut from the same cloth."

Ludie's brow creased. "Huh?"

"Veezie means you two are very much alike, and I agree."

"For real? Oh, Veezie, I hope I'm just like you when I grow

up."

"Well, that's the nicest compliment I've ever received. I wish I'd been more like you when I was a teenager."

"No, you don't. I ain't so good. But I got reason now to wanna be better."

"I wasn't so good either, Ludie, until I found *my* reason for wanting to better myself. Now, why don't we let Gracie eat her breakfast and you and I get started on those apples."

They were peeling apples at the table when Ludie said, "Veezie, I've got a secret."

"Ooh, I love secrets. Can you share yours?"

"No, it's a surprise. For you!"

"For me?"

"Yeah. I think you're gonna be happy."

"I'm already happy, Ludie."

"I know, but this is gonna be a good surprise."

"And when do I get it?"

"Thanksgiving."

"Well, I can hardly wait." She screwed the ring on the last jar. "We'll let these jars cool and put them in the pantry later. You were a big help."

"Thanks. If that's all you need me for, I'm gonna run see if my friend is home. I won't stay long."

"Tell me about this friend of yours. He must be very special."

"He is for sure. But if I tell you, it'll ruin my surprise."

"Fair enough. I wouldn't want that to happen."

"Veezie, would it be alright if I carried him a jar of apples?"

"That would make a fine gift and I'm sure he'd appreciate it."

Ludie pulled off her sweater and wrapped it around a warm jar, before hurrying out the door.

When Veezie looked out the window and saw Zeke grab Ludie's sleeve, she stepped on the porch and hid behind a column.

He said, "Where you think you're going, girlie?"

Veezie's muscles tightened as she listened for Ludie's response.

"To see my friend."

"You ain't going nowhere. Get yo'self back in the house."

"But Veezie said I could go."

"Veezie's not in charge of you. I am."

Veezie peeked from behind the column, in time to see Ludie jerk from his grip.

"No, you ain't. I'd run away if you was in charge of me."

He drew his arm back as if he were about to smack her. "I said get back in the house. Get the mop and bucket and mop up the floors in the conference room, before I give you a lickin' like you ain't never had."

Veezie watched the child cower under the threat.

"The conference room? Nobody never goes in there."

"Maybe it's because the floors are dirty. Now, stop gabbing and do what I tell you."

Veezie stepped out and walked toward them. “Ludie, I thought you’d be gone by now. Why are you still here?”

“Zeke said—”

He stuttered. “I . . . I asked her to stick around. Thought she might help lighten your load.”

“She’s already been a big help. Be back in time to set the table, Ludie.”

“Yes ma’am.” She cut her eyes at Zeke and took off running through the woods.

Uncle George was outside chopping wood. “Hey, sugar.”

“I brung you something.”

“Law, child, I told you to stop sneaking stuff over here. You gonna get us both in trouble.”

“Didn’t sneak it. I asked for it.”

“Well, now that’s different.”

She held up the jar. “It’s canned apples, and I helped.”

“Is that a fact? My soul, if them don’t look jest like some Beulah woulda put up. I’ll enjoy these for sure. Thank your Miz Gigi for me, ya hear?”

“I’ll be sure to, Uncle George. And I’ll have a special surprise for you when you get there. It’s gonna be the best Thanksgiving of my whole life.”

“Well now, if it makes you *that* happy, young’un, it’s jest likely to be the best Thanksgiving I ever had, myself.”

Chapter Twenty

Saturday night, Gracie closed her eyes and hoped for a dream encounter with her precious husband. Logic told her Brother Charlie and Veezie were right and Garth was dead. Even so, there was something comforting about having him appear in her dreams.

At four in the morning, she awoke, hyperventilating. With the corner of the sheet, she wiped her clammy forehead and thrust her left hand over her runaway heart.

Veezie opened her eyes and turned on the light. "What's wrong, Gracie? You're white as a ghost."

When there was no answer, Veezie grasped Gracie's hand. "Should I call Flint?"

"No."

"Are you in pain?"

"No."

"I'm worried about you, honey. I think the doc needs to be alerted."

"I'm fine." Gracie's eyes watered as she squeezed Veezie's hand. "Oh, Veezie, it was great."

"What?"

"The talk we had just now."

She let out a long breath. "No, honey, I've been asleep. You must've dreamed it, but we'll talk all day tomorrow, if you like." She turned out the light. "Go back to sleep."

"No, I mean Garth and I talked. It was wonderful. I told him about the baby and he said he's coming home. Veezie, he says he thinks we'll have a little girl and he wants to name her Mercy. That's a swell name for a little girl, don't you think?"

"Gracie, it was just a sweet dream."

"But it was so real, Veezie. He asked me how I was doing, and I told him about you coming to stay with me. He said he was glad." She clasped her hands over her heart and giggled. "His dimples sank deep into his cheeks and he told me he loved me. He said, "Gracie, don't ever forget who you belong to. And then, I said, "I belong to you, Garth. I always will." He said, "No, you belong to God, and I'm just the caretaker. Then I cried and told him he couldn't take care of me because he wasn't here."

"Gracie, I've heard your daddy preach that God speaks to us in various ways, and He often spoke through dreams in the Bible. Maybe that's what's happening. What if God wants you to understand that you're about to marry the wrong caretaker?"

Gracie was determined not to let Veezie put a damper on such a wonderful experience, whether real or imaginary. "You know what he said when I cried and told him he couldn't take care of me because he wasn't here? He said, 'Hold on, my darling, I'm coming home.' Veezie, what if God is telling me Garth's not dead?

Isn't that just as easy to believe? The last thing he said before I woke up was, 'I'm so thankful for God's Grace and Mercy.' Veezie, maybe he meant it literally, but I believe he was referring to me and our baby girl."

Veezie's eyes watered, "Oh, Gracie. You can't allow yourself to continue with this fantasy. It isn't healthy. He's not coming back. He can't. You know it in your head, but now you have to convince your heart. Garth is dead."

"I thought so too, until I talked to him."

Veezie found it difficult to go back to sleep. She'd promised to take the children to her home church in Goose Hollow, yet her concern for Gracie now caused her to question the decision to leave, even for a couple of hours. "Gracie, are you sure you don't need me to stay? You didn't get much rest last night. I'd feel much better if I were here with you."

"Are you kidding? I feel wonderful, and the children are looking forward to seeing Brother Charlie again. He made a real impression on them, especially Maddie. It would break her heart if she didn't get to go. Now, scoot before you're late."

Veezie dredged up old memories—both good and bad—as she drove the children to Goose Hollow. She was excited to be going to her old home church for an opportunity to hear Brother Charlie preach once again. This time, with ears to hear.

He wouldn't likely be preaching many more sermons at his age.

Maddie thanked her repeatedly for taking them to church.

"He was really a preacher when you was a little girl?" Tanner asked.

"Yes, and I was much younger than you when I first heard him preach."

"Jeepers! He must be a hunnerd years old by now."

Veezie smiled. "You may not have missed it by far, Tanner. I thought he was a very old man even back then."

From the time she stepped inside the vestibule, Veezie felt at home again. Brother Charlie was even frailer than she expected, and needed help getting up the steps to the pulpit. The way his hands shook, she suspected he might have palsy, but when he spotted her in the congregation, he commenced to cry. Two deacons rushed up, thinking he was ill, but the old man motioned them away. "These are happy tears, folks. I just looked out over the crowd and saw someone who means the world to me. Some of you will remember little Veezie O'Steen who lived down the road a piece. She's the older sister to Jim, Lucas and Callie, who were adopted by Flint and Harper several years ago."

Veezie felt a blush on her face when people turned to stare.

"Stand up, honey and let the folks get a good look at you."

She looked at smiling faces and stood. "Thank you, Brother Charlie. It's a pleasure to be back."

"I hope you won't mind if I brag on you a bit. You can sit back down, 'cause this may take a while. A lot of these folks will remember the skinny little ragamuffin who used to come to church in overalls and brogans, until she turned about seventeen or eighteen, I reckon it was, and then she got her a red dress."

He threw his head back and gave a hearty chuckle. "Remember the one I'm talkin' about, sugar?"

Veezie smiled and nodded.

"My stars, I never wanted to burn nothing so bad in all my life as I wanted to burn that skimpy little dress. I can't tell you the times I went inside that ol' juke they called The Silver Slipper and pulled that young'un out and dared her to ever go back in. But go back, she did. Some of you who remember what I'm talking about are wondering if this could possibly be the same girl. Well, it is . . and it ain't." His voice took on a more solemn tone. "Folks, this is a prime example of what happens when God gets a hold of you. This beautiful young woman you see sitting there is now married to a fine preacher man and she's the mama to that sweet little angel sleeping in her arms. I'm told she's also the pianist in her husband's church at Mt. Pleasant. If the baby wasn't asleep, I'd ask her to come play the Doxology for us to begin our worship service this morning."

Veezie handed the baby to Ludie and stood. "I'd be honored to play, Brother Charlie."

The congregation applauded as she walked down the aisle.

****

Zeke was relieved to have Veezie out of the house. The woman made him nervous. Maybe it was his imagination, but it seemed

Gracie was pulling away as if she might be having second thoughts. All she needed was a little reassurance and he was ready to supply it.

He walked up to her room and sat on the edge of the bed.

She turned over and opened her eyes. "Zeke, I've told you not to come up here when we're alone. It doesn't look right."

"Don't be ridiculous. We're alone."

"Still, I'd rather you not make it a habit."

"Whatever you say, darling. But I had to see you without that nosey woman breathing over my shoulder." He leaned over and kissed her forehead. "Gracie, you've made me the happiest man alive. Do we really have to wait until the baby comes to get married? Why don't you let me call the judge and see if he'll come next week and perform the ceremony?"

Her face distorted. "Out of the question. If there's a wedding, my daddy will perform the ceremony, and it's too soon to spring this on him."

"For crying out loud, Gracie. *If?* You act as if you're a teenager awaiting his permission."

"Maybe it's not Daddy who needs time. Maybe it's me, Zeke. I've been having some unsettling dreams. "

He rolled his eyes. "Sounds to me as if you've been eating bologna sandwiches before bedtime. Whenever I have a weird dream, I can usually attribute it to what I had for supper. Anytime you have one of your nightmares, all you have to do is call me, sweetheart, and I'll come running." He traced her lips with his finger. "I'll do my best to make you forget all about those nasty old dreams."

"Maybe I don't want to forget them."

He gave her shoulder a little squeeze. "Ooh, they're that good, huh? I've had a few of those, myself. After we get married, we'll make those dreams come true."

"You're not hearing me, Zeke. I'm not sure I can marry you."

He jerked his arm back. "What are you saying? What reason would you have for changing your mind? It's that woman, Veezie, isn't it? She's jealous. Don't you get it? I haven't told you this, but she's been giving me the come-on. You won't believe the way she flirts when you're not around."

"You're right, Zeke, I don't believe it. I'm not saying you're lying, but I will say you're reading something into it that isn't there, if you think she's flirting. Besides, Veezie has nothing to do with my wanting to wait."

"Then what, Gracie? You need me. You know you do. So why wait, when I could be taking care of you, the way a husband takes care of his wife."

She licked her dry lips and muttered. "It's the dreams."

"Honey, that's crazy. Dreams aren't real. Life is real. You need me and I need you, and that's a reality. You promised to marry me. I couldn't go on living if you changed your mind."

"Don't say that, Zeke. It isn't fair to put that kind of pressure on me."

"Well, it isn't fair for you to lead me on by letting me kiss you and making plans to marry, and then suddenly say because of some stupid dreams you've changed your mind. How could you do that to me?"

"I didn't say I wouldn't. I said I'm not sure. The dreams began several weeks ago, but they're coming almost every night now, and I'm confused." She covered her face and sobbed.

"Okay, honey, I'm sorry I got upset. I know what's going on here. This isn't about the dreams, although you believe in your heart it is. When a woman's pregnant, she tends to build things up in her mind. That's all this is. You're making a mountain out of a mole hill." His face split into a craggy smile. "Why, I remember some of the wild ideas Lucy had before the twins were born. Oh, boy, some of the stupid notions she got in her head almost pulled us apart. We laughed at the craziness after the boys were born when she realized how silly she'd acted."

"Are you saying I'm acting silly?"

"Well, aren't you? You're quick to jump to conclusions. Like now. I was talking about Lucy's actions, and immediately you became defensive. And just because you're having some nightmares, you're wanting to call off our marriage. Does that make sense? It's the pregnancy, honey, causing you to overreact to situations. If it makes you feel better, we'll wait until the baby is born as we originally planned. I don't want you making any rash decisions while your hormones are playing havoc with your thinking. It's only about eight weeks away. Sounds like a lifetime to me right now, but you're worth waiting for."

After church, Veezie introduced the children to her friend, Harper, her husband, Dr. Flint McCall and Veezie's biological siblings, whom the McCalls adopted several years earlier. It was good seeing the kids again. At times, Veezie questioned if she did the right thing when she gave up her rights as the children's guardian.

However, seeing them now, she had no doubt her decision was the right one. She wasn't married at the time, had no source of income and not mature enough to raise three children. It was plain to see Harper and Flint had done a great job.

Her nineteen-year-old brother, Jim told her he'd be leaving for New Orleans in January to attend a theological seminary. Her younger brother Lucas seemed quite taken with Belle, and not bothered at all that he was doing all the talking. He held her hand and walked her around the church grounds and they sat down at the picnic tables under the trees, where the church held the annual dinner on the grounds. Veezie kept glancing their way, and from what she observed, Belle seemed as taken with Lucas as he was with her. If anyone could get a word out of her, Lucas would be the one to do it. Callie and Maddie played hopscotch as they waited for everyone to finish congratulating Veezie. Emerald giggled at the teenage girl playing peek-a-boo. Toby, Tanner and two other boys near the same age drew a circle in the sand and pulled marbles from their pocket.

Brother Charlie glanced their way, and yelled, "Remember boys, no playing for keeps."

"We know, preacher," they said in unison, although their tone indicated they weren't thrilled with Brother Charlie's rules.

Ludie was very quiet and stayed close by Veezie's side.

The younger children all went to sleep in the car on the way home.

Ludie said, "Veezie, did you really do them things the preacher said you done when you was growing up?"

"I'm afraid I did those and worse, Ludie, but I'm not proud of it."

"But Brother Charlie said God got a hold of you. Is that right?"

"Yep. He surely did, and turned my life around."

"So I reckon after you got religion you couldn't go back to them places the preacher talked about."

"It wasn't that I couldn't go back. I didn't want to anymore. When God changed my heart, He changed my wants."

"I wonder if He'll ever get a hold of me and change my wants."

"Ludie, I believe with all my heart God's already begun a work in you and what He begins, He finishes. You're a very special young lady. God's given you a servant's heart."

"Then He can take it back. I ain't gonna be nobody's servant and have people bossing me around all the time. I wanna be a nurse."

"Honey, there's a big difference in being a servant and being a slave. No one should have to be a slave, but a servant is someone who chooses to serve others. Doctors, nurses, firemen, teachers, and people who open orphanages all do what they do because they want to be of service to others."

"You mean like Gigi?"

"Yes, Gigi has a servant's heart. It's true some people will take advantage of an humble servant and begin to make demands on them. That's very wrong. But when I said you have a servant's heart, I simply meant you're happiest when you're doing for others. Gracie told me about your friend, and how you'd choose to go hungry in order to take him your food when he was sick. And the fact you want to be a nurse and help others is proof of your servant's heart."

"I never knew servants were so special."

"Ludie, everyone is special in the sight of the Lord. Don't ever forget that."

"Not ever'body. I'll bet I know somebody who's not so special in God's sight. Zeke Thorne. Ugh!"

Veezie decided to let it rest.

Chapter Twenty-One

For years, Ezekiel Thorne had been selling himself short, feeling inferior because he dropped out of school in sixth grade. No more. He was smart and had proved it. So what if he could barely write his name or didn't know how to talk proper?

Some folks use book learning to get where they want to go, but Zeke relied on a clever, conniving brain to get what he wanted. And never had he wanted anything more than he wanted Gracie Graham. He shoved his shoulders back and walked into Dr. Buchanan's office Tuesday morning.

He thrust out his hand. "Doc, I appreciate you going to Nine Gables to give Gracie the blood test. I wouldn't have asked if she coulda got outta bed, but in her condition, it was the only way."

The doctor appeared reluctant to shake hands. "Maybe it isn't any of my business, Zeke, but I didn't understand why you told Mrs. Graham I was making house calls for Dr. McCall. It took me by surprise and I must tell you, it made me a bit uncomfortable that you'd twist the truth and include me. Or why you chose not to have your blood test taken, when I could've done them both at your house at the same time. Am I being paranoid, or did you involve me in some sort of underhanded shenanigan?"

"I reckon it might seem peculiar, but the truth is, it's a surprise."

"Excuse me if I sound confused. Gracie doesn't *know* she's getting married?"

"Of course, she knows. She just don't know it'll be so soon. She thinks we're gonna have to wait until after the baby comes to get married. With her being pregnant, she didn't suspect a thing when you drew her blood. But don't ya see? If you woulda took mine at the same time, she would've guessed what I'm up to and it would've spoiled my surprise. Everything's all set. I'm gonna swing by the court house to pick up the marriage license after I leave here."

"Well, I suppose that explains why she thought I was referring to her pregnancy when I offered my congratulations."

"Exactly. I was scared you was about to let the cat out of the bag, but she didn't suspect a thing. I plan to surprise everyone at the Thanksgiving table."

"But why call me? Why didn't you enlist the services of her personal physician?"

"Couldn't. Her doctor is a close friend of the family and he'll be coming to Nine Gables for Thanksgiving dinner. He might've given it away, if I'd asked him to do the blood tests. I wanted to surprise everybody, not just Gracie."

"And I suppose you've lined up someone to conduct the

ceremony?"

"Of course. Her father's a preacher and since he'll be here Thanksgiving, he'll be able to marry us. I ain't left out nothing, doc."

"Well, it's evident you really love her, but marriage is a very serious step. Maybe it's none of my business, but the short time I was around her, I felt she was still grieving the loss of her husband."

"Aw, it's the pregnancy. You're a doc. Shoot, you know how women get when they're expecting. They ain't capable of making rational decisions. One minute they're up, the next they're down. I can't wait to see her face when I tell her I've taken care of everything. She just has to say, 'I do,' and it's done."

A crooked little grin crept across the doctor's face. "And what if she doesn't?"

"Are you kidding? She'll be tickled out of her gourd. My Gracie loves surprises."

****

School let out Tuesday at lunch for Thanksgiving Holidays. On the way home, Ludie cut through the woods and could smell Uncle George's barbecue a half-mile away. She spotted him standing over a brick pit.

"Hey, Uncle George. That's a mighty big piece o' meat to be eating all by yourself."

"Ain't for me, sugar. Mr. Oliver Weinberger brung it over for me to cook. Says he's pitching a shindig at his house on

Thanksgiving day. Why ain't you in school, young'un?"

"It let out early. I've had something weighin' on my mind all day long and I gotta get some answers."

"What kinda answers you be lookin' for, child?"

"Well, the day after tomorrow is Thanksgiving, and it's a time when family gets together. Ain't that so?"

"I reckon you right. But some folks ain't got no family, so they jest have to make do. Like me and you."

"But I got a feeling I do have family and you know where to find 'em."

"You be wrong, sugar. I don't know where to find her."

"*Her?* I knew it." She jerked on his shirttail. "Please, Uncle George, tell me what you know."

He hung his head. "Law, child, you won't leave well enough alone. Ain't it enough you got a roof over yo' head, plenty of food to eat and a woman who takes care of you like you wuz her own?"

"No, it ain't enough. I wanna know all about my granny and my mama. I wanna know ever'thing you know, Uncle George, and I got a feeling you know a lot."

"I declare, if you ain't stubborn as all git out. Go on in the cabin, and ol' Uncle George'll be in d'rectly."

He ambled in with a load of wood and let it tumble out beside the fireplace. After adding an extra log, he wedged in a short piece of kindling, then as if he had all the time in the world, stirred the live embers. Ludie sat on the floor, facing the open pit, chewing her nails. Maybe he'd forgotten . . . or changed his mind.

The old man looked tired, but Ludie knew he'd never admit to it. He pulled up a straight-back chair and held his weathered hands in front of him, turning them slowly to warm. She'd never seen him looking so somber. She waited, hoping she wouldn't need to prompt him, but the minutes drug as she waited.

With his elbows resting on the arms of the chair, his hands cupped around his face, he said, "Law, chile, I don't know where to start?"

"Start at the beginning. The day I was born."

"Nah, that's just the middle, sugar. I gotta take you back further than that for you to understand." His voice softened. "Back when I first fell in love with yo' granny."

Ludie's jaw dropped. "You what?"

The fire blazed, sending out occasional sparks, crackling and popping onto the brick hearth. With the tip of his worn brogan, George kicked a glowing cinder back into the fire pit. "You sure you want to hear this? There ain't no goin' back, once I let the cat outta the bag."

She nodded, unable to speak.

"Well, I was a young man and me and my older sister, Cleo, we worked on a Plantation in Goat Hill called Gladstone. We wuz both born in the quarters back of the Big House. The owner was a big man around town. His name was Gideon P. Gladstone III, and ever'body around knew him as Mr. Gid. Now, Mr. Gid, he had him two beautiful daughters. One was named Miz Alamanda and the other was Miz Delia."

Ludie tried to catch her breath. “So my granny was rich?”

“Richest woman I ever knowed. Not just ‘cause her ol’ man owned near ‘bout all of Goat Hill. That woman was rich in kindness and love.”

“Tell me about her, Uncle George. What was she like?”

His eyes glistened. “Like an angel, she was. She’d slip out to the cotton fields, lugging a big jug of sweet tea with ice in it. Ooh, doggie, that jug was a purty sight to us field hands. Ain’t nothing never tasted as good as sweet iced tea when you hot and sweaty from picking cotton in the blazing sun. But the jug o’ tea wadn’t the only thing I was eyeing. Miz Delia had the greenest eyes you ever did see. Looked like the ocean waters at Pensacola beach, but I don’t reckon you ever had the pleasure of seein’ the ocean.”

Ludie opened wide orbs. “I got green eyes.”

He chuckled. “Well, I be, sugar, if it ain’t a fact. You sho’ do.”

“What color hair did she have?”

“Why, her hair was soft and yellow like new corn silk and skin like peaches and cream. And, Lawsy, when she’d come waltzing in them fields, looking like an angel and yet acting like she wadn’t no better’n us pickers, it was a sight to behold.” He rubbed his hands over his wrinkled face.

“Don’t stop, Uncle George. When you say you fell in love, I don’t reckon you’d be talking about the romantic kind. You mean you admired her for being so kind. Ain’t that so?”

He buried his face in his gnarled hands. “Oh, sugar, I never shoulda started this conversation. You ain’t likely to understand.”

Ludie popped a hand over her mouth. "Oh m'goodness, Uncle George. You *are* talking about the romantic kind of love, ain't you? I see it in your face. Whoa! How in the world did that happen—you being a black man and my granny being a rich white woman? I'll bet that set some teeth on edge."

"Well, sugar, neither me nor Delia planned it. It jest sorta happened. Us falling in love, I mean. Oh, Lawzie, how I loved that woman." His voice quaked. "And she loved me as much as any woman ever loved a man and that's the honest to goodness truth. But we didn't try to fool ourselves. We had enough sense to know it'd come to no good end."

"So that's when you moved from Goat Hill to Flat Creek?"

"No. I reckon it shoulda been, but it weren't. We was two crazy kids in love, but we had sense enough to know we couldn't go to the Court House and get the papers to get married."

Ludie nodded. "I know. Colored folks and white folks can't marry. That's a sin, ain't it?"

"A sin? I reckon the sin was the lies we had to tell."

"Well, even if it ain't a sin, it's against the law. Right?"

"Yep. And that was the crux of the problem. Me and Delia decided we loved each other too much to ever want to be with anybody else. So one night, she slipped down to the quarters, and knocked on the door. I won't never forget it as long as I live." Uncle George stopped and his eyes lit up. "Cleo opened the door and Delia stood there holding one of them train cases in one hand. In the other hand, she had a Bible and she shoved it at Cleo and said, 'I come to marry yo' brother." His gold tooth sparkled in the light of the fire when he let out another chuckle. "That woman was a sight, I tell ya."

"So what happened? She didn't have no papers, did she?"

"Hold on, sugar. I'm getting there."

"Sorry."

"Well, my pappy was sitting there eatin' a bowl of grits, and I recollect jest like it was yesterday. He put down his fork and said, 'Girl, are you tetched in the head? You git yo'self outta here as fast as you can trot. You gonna get my son lynched with that kind of foolishness.'

"But then I stepped up and said, 'I'd rather die than live without her, pappy.' And that's when my mammy stepped up and said, 'Orin,'—that was my pappy—she said, 'Orin,' either you marry these two young'uns or I'll do it myself. So he took the Bible from Cleo, and me and Delia stood there in front of a pot-bellied stove and Pappy said a few words from the Good Book, and then told us to lay our hands on the Bible and swear our love for one another. We did."

"You ain't making this story up are ya, Uncle George? You funnin' with me?"

"It's the Gospel truth, sugar."

"So you saying you . . . you married my *granny*?"

"Well, not in the eyes of the law, but we believed we was married in the eyes of God, being how we swore on the Bible."

"And then what happened?"

"Well, my folks lit out to my grandpappy's cabin that night, so me and Delia could have us a honeymoon. Pappy didn't like it, but my mammy made him go."

"Didn't her mama and daddy wonder why she didn't come home that night?"

"Nah, she covered that before she left. Made like she was gonna stay overnight with a girlfriend." Uncle George stood and stretched. "You need to run on home, sugar. I gotta go back outside and tend to the barbecue."

"I'll wait. Ain't no way I could leave now."

****

When he arrived back at Nine Gables, Zeke went upstairs and knocked on Gracie's door. "Veezie, I don't reckon you'd mind leaving us alone for a few minutes. I'd like some time with my bride-to-be."

Veezie glanced at Gracie, who nodded. "It's okay."

"Zeke, I'm glad you came. We need to talk. It's about the dreams."

"I've been having dreams, too, honey. And them dreams are about to come true."

When his lips trailed from her cheek to her mouth, she turned her head. "You don't understand. Veezie thinks maybe God's trying to send me a message through my dreams. What do you think, Zeke?"

"I think she's nuts, so don't pay her no mind. Me and you got some plans to make. I know we can't take a honeymoon until after the baby is born, sweetheart, but as soon as you're on your feet, we'll get Veezie to come back and stay with the kids for a week in the spring to give us a chance to get away. I ain't crazy about her, but the kids seem to take to her, and it won't be like leaving 'em with a stranger. We'll take off and go to Birmingham—stay in one of them fancy hotels and maybe tour Vulcan. I always wanted to do that."

"What if he's not dead?"

"Gracie, you ain't been listening to a word I've said. What in tarnation you talking about? Who ain't dead?"

"Garth."

Zeke smirked. "You ain't serious."

"I'm very serious."

"For crying out loud, Gracie. I know you think the man was a saint, but I really don't think you can count on a resurrection. The army don't send uniformed officers to deliver one of them telegrams about the death of a soldier, unless they've got a body."

"It was a closed casket. What if he's *not* really dead?"

"Hogwash!" His teeth gnashed together. "Gracie, you told me about meeting the plane and seeing them lift the casket off with the flag draped over it. You've talked about his funeral. The man's dead. Dead as a doornail. Don't go getting loopy on me."

"I know it's hard to believe, Zeke, and I can't explain it—but when he visits me in my dreams, he's as real as if he were here in the flesh."

Fiery darts—or at least the ghastly impression of such—shot

from his beady eyes. She stiffened, bracing for his response.

"Gracie, how do you think it makes me feel to hear you dream about another man? After tomorrow, I don't want to ever hear that man's name again. You gotta bury the past, and Garth Graham is your past."

"But he's also linked to my future, Zeke. A part of him lives inside me. He's the father of my baby."

"Not after we're married, darling. I'll be the one your baby calls 'Daddy.'"

Gracie flinched, but why argue over something that would never happen.

"I hope we have a girl, because I've already thought of a name for her. Ida Mae Thorne. That was my mama's name. But if we have a boy, he'll be called Luther after my daddy."

"No, Zeke. She'll be called Mercy. Mercy Graham."

"Mercy?" He held his head back and cackled, as if she'd purposely told a joke to lighten the mood. "You can't be serious. Whoever heard of naming a kid Mercy? Honey, I've been set on naming a little girl after my mama, even before the birth of the twins. I was downright positive Lucy was having girls and I was gonna name them Ida Mae and Ima Faye. But when they turned out to be boys, I went ahead and let Lucy name 'em whatever she wanted, though I regretted it later. Her old man's name was Tobe Tanner, so she come up with Toby and Tanner. Frankly, I didn't like the names, since me and Tobe never did gee-haw. Didn't seem right to name my boys after a man I couldn't stand. But shug, I'll make the same deal with you I made with Lucy. If it's a boy, you name him—but if it's a girl, I get to pick her name."

Gracie's teeth gnashed together. "No! This is my baby, Zeke and I'll be the one to name it."

He bent down and kissed her. "Oh, sweetheart, I didn't mean to upset you. You know how much I love you, don't you?"

She swallowed hard. "I know you do. I'm sorry if I sounded snippy."

"Me too. Besides, we have weeks left before we gotta come up with a name. I'm sure time will take care of everything. "

Chapter Twenty-Two

Uncle George trudged back inside, "Shug, take that poker over yonder and stir the fire while I put on a pot of coffee."

Ludie pushed a log toward the back of the pit and quickly stirred the live embers with the iron rod, eager to hear the rest of the story. "So after you and granny married, did anybody find out what y'all done?" She chewed her nails, conjuring up all the patience she could muster, while the old man moseyed over to the coffee grinder and tossed in a handful of beans. After grinding the beans, she waited for him to pump water into the pot. She'd almost forgotten her question when he glanced down at her and mumbled, "I'm still here, ain't I?" A tear glistened against his dark face.

"You are, but she's not. I Suwannee, Uncle George, this is like pulling hen's teeth. Tell me the rest."

"Well, my sweet Delia, she—" He paused and shook his head slowly.

"Ain't no way you can stop, now, Uncle George. I got a right to know. She what? What was you about to say?"

"Sugar, she come up pregnant." He rubbed his gnarled hand

across his stubby chin.

"Whoa! That must've broke your heart. Whose baby was it?"

His face distorted. "Why it was mine, sugar. Delia wadn't never with no other man 'sides me and that's a fact."

Ludie slapped her hand over her mouth. "Oh, my stars, I reckon when she told you she was thataway, you had to haul buggy to keep from getting lynched."

"Nah, it didn't go down like that. Her pappy threatened to disown her if she didn't tell, but weren't no way she was gonna fess up, knowing what'd happen to me. Mr. Gid couldn't have folks knowing his daughter done got herself pregnant."

"So he disowned her?"

"No, I 'spect he wanted to, but then folks would talk. So, he sent her away to New Orleans to a boarding house for unmarried girls. He told her to leave the young'un and when she come back home, she was to tell folks she'd been off to one o' them finishing schools."

"Did she?"

He hung his head. "Yeah, she did."

"That's sad. So she didn't get to see her baby?"

Lifting his head, his gaze shifted from the floor to the rafters, as if the long-ago memory was tacked to the ceiling. "She saw her all right, although it wadn't her who brung the baby home. My sister, Cleo showed up at Gladstone with a baby in her arms, a day after Delia got back. Cleo told ever'body she'd gone off to get her grand young'un and she was gonna raise her."

"This is confusing. How did Cleo get the baby?"

"Delia had sent her money to take a train to New Orleans, but they rode separate trains back so when Mr. Gid picked up his daughter, they wouldn't be together." His lip quivered. "Ah, I tell you the truth, when I saw that young'un in Cleo's arms, I thought she was the purtiest little creature I ever did see. Her skin weren't black like mine and it weren't white like Delia's. It was more like a tad o' coffee with a heap o' cream." He reached in his back pocket and pulled out a handkerchief and wiped his face. "Our baby had the biggest green eyes. Just like her mama. Looked like jewels, they did."

"So what didja name her?"

"Comfort. Her name was Comfort, 'cause she brought comfort to our souls, just knowing we was gonna be able to keep our baby and wouldn't nobody know. I Suwannee, ain't never been two people prouder of a young'un than me and Delia was of that little green-eyed baby girl."

"So Mr. Gid didn't never know?"

"Nope. Never did. Cleo took Comfort to the shanty where we lived with Mammy, Pappy, and ten-year-old Dodie, our baby sister. Us grownups had to go to work at Gladstone ever'day, but little Dodie tended our baby good as any grown up ever could. Delia sneaked off to the cabin ever' chance she got. She had it all worked out. She was gonna sneak out o' the big house soon as everybody was asleep, and nurse little Comfort at twelve o'clock at night, then again at four in the morning and be back in her own bed before anybody woke up and missed her. Cleo pumped Delia's milk behind closed doors at Gladstone during the day for Dodie."

"So did anybody ever find out Comfort was your and Delia's baby?"

"Nah, never did."

"Whew! That's good, right?"

"Well, t'would seem so, but sugar, things don't always turn out like we plan 'em. Delia got an infection and died when Comfort wadn't but three weeks old."

Ludie ran over and threw her arms around the old man and cried with him. "Oh, Uncle George, that's the saddest story I ever heard. If . . . if my granny died . . . and she just had one baby, then—"

The old man scowled. "I warned you not to meddle. Didn't I tell you not knowing was sometimes better than knowing? But you wouldn't be satisfied, and now they ain't no going back."

"Uncle George! You're my grandpa, ain't ya'?"

He clinched his eyes shut. "Law, what have I gone and done?"

"But I'm white."

"You is, sugar, and as far as anybody gonna ever know, you gonna stay white. That's why you can't never tell nobody. You understand?"

"No. I don't understand. I wanted a grandpa and now I got me one."

"But can't nobody know, Ludie. Nobody. Listen to me, girl. Roots don't matter, it's the blossom what counts, and you're blossoming into a fine lady, so for both our sakes, let the roots stay where they belong. Buried." He pulled out a handkerchief and wiped beads of perspiration from his brow. "I Suwannee, I never shoulda told you."

"I'm glad you did. I wanna know more."

He squeezed her arm. "Promise you won't tell. Promise me."

She crisscrossed her hands across her chest. "Promise and hope to die. Now tell me the rest."

"Shesh yo' mouth, young'un. That kinda promise sounds like swearing to me. You don't swear, do ya' Ludie?"

"Maybe I have once or twice. But if you say it ain't right, then I won't never do it no more. Promise and hope to—" She giggled. "Just foolin' with ya, Uncle George. Now, tell me what happened after my granny died."

"Well, I was near 'bout crazy I was hurting so bad. I couldn't stay there at Gladstone with all the memories. So I upped and left and got me a job working here at Nine Gables, where I met Beulah."

"But what about your baby?"

"I left her with Cleo. Wadn't no way I could take care of a young'un, me working daylight 'til dawn. Cleo was done attached to her, and Dodie was good with her, so I knew our little Comfort would be in good hands. I went to see her at the Gladstone Plantation ever' chance I got, and by the time she got your age, I knew that young'un was plowin' in somebody else's field, and it tore me up inside."

"Whatcha mean?"

"Mr. Gid had a granddaughter about the same age as Comfort. Miz Lizzie was Miz Alamanda's daughter. She was a real looker and quite the socialite. Seemed to have ever'thng going for her. Drove around in a new automobile, had fine clothes, a slew of boyfriends and lots of parties. Comfort couldn't stand being on the outside, looking in when she knew she was ever bit as pretty and smart as Miz Lizzie. I 'spect the thing that hurt her most was when she heard talk among some of the servants, who figured out the truth. So when Comfort learned she was Mr. Gid's flesh and blood—that her mama and Miz Lizzie's mama was sisters—well, I think she decided if she passed for white, she could have all the things Miz Lizzie had."

"So did she tell Mr. Gid she was his granddaughter?"

"Nah, she knew it woulda got us all in trouble. Cleo wrote me later that Comfort started sneaking off over near Samson and hanging out in some ol' dance hall, where she'd meet fellows who didn't know she was colored. Wadn't no surprise when she wound up getting herself pregnant. If I was a bettin' man, I'd wager the sorry ol' rascal was some traveling salesmen she never saw agin after that night. Po' little Comfort was just trying too hard to find her a man to take her away from the kind of life me and Cleo had."

"I was that baby, wadn't I, Uncle George?"

"Yep, sugar, I reckon you had a right to know. You is that baby."

"Why didn't my mama want me? Was it 'cause I'm white?"

"Nah, sugar. Comfort was almost light as you is. She delivered you all by herself, then wrapped you up and left you on the Mayor's doorsteps. It come out in the paper about a foundling left on the Mayor's steps. A few folks wanted to believe it was his young'un, but he denied it."

"So how did you find out it was the same baby?"

"With nowhere to go, Comfort went back to Gladstone and told Cleo what she'd done. I heard talk that the mayor sent the baby to one of them foundling houses. Cleo said if I'd go git you, she'd raise you."

"So why didn't you, Uncle George?"

"When the time come, I couldn't do it to you, sugar, knowing the kind o' life you'd be facing. The woman came to the door holding you, and I Suwannee yo' little round face was as white as any Easter lily. Seeing them green, green eyes, and heart-shaped lips like my Delia's, wadn't no doubt the young'un in the woman's arms was Comfort's. I made like I wuz looking for work, and left without you. Hardest thing I ever done."

"So, who named me?"

"Your mama done that, sugar. They found a note pinned to yo' blanket, with the words, Eliza Clementine. She named you after Miz Lizzie. Her name was Eliza, too, and I reckon yo' mama wanted ever'thing that belonged to Miz Lizzie, even took her name and gave it to you."

"But Eliza ain't my name."

"Yeah, sugar, that's yo' *rightful* name."

“Then who named me Ludie.”

“That’s yo’ nickle name, shug. I reckon the first foundling home they put you in started calling you that and it stuck.”

“You sayin’ I got me two real names?”

“Yep. That was yo’ mama’s doings. Gave you what’s called a middle name. Clementine.”

“I wonder who she got that name from.”

Uncle George reared his head back and belted out the words to a song. “Oh my darling, oh my darling, oh my darling, Clementine. You are lost and gone forever, dreadful sorry, Clementine.”

“So there’s a song named after me?”

“Well, might be t’other way around.” His eyes squinted into tiny slits. “I’ve always thought it coulda been Comfort’s way of saying she was dreadful sorry, having to give you up.”

“If they didn’t know who my daddy was, how did they know my last name was ‘Doe’?”

“I reckon they just made up sump’n, sugar, since ever’body gotta have a last name. Kinda nice though. Don’t reckon they’s nothing purtier than a baby deer.”

Chapter Twenty-Three

Thanksgiving Day

Zeke took a long look at himself in the mirror and shifted his pose from left to right. Not bad looking, cleaned up, although there'd never been a reason to put forth the effort when Lucy was alive. She was a good woman, yet homely with no class. They were on a dead-end road together, but things were changing now that he'd met his beautiful, refined Gracie.

So what if he didn't have a high school education—what difference did it make? He'd been studying the way men of distinction walked, talked and dressed. Though he still had a few things to learn, he wasn't the same man he was when he arrived, and he'd done it all for her. Gracie Graham was a woman any man would be proud to have on his arm. She was worth changing for.

Zeke had done his dead-level best to make this a Thanksgiving Gracie would remember forever. In addition to having her father and stepmother there, he'd invited a few of her dearest friends—Dr. Flint McCall, his wife Harper, and their two youngest children, Lucas and Callie. Though Zeke hadn't intended to issue an invitation to Brother Charlie, he couldn't say no when Harper suggested the old gent could ride with them. Once he and Gracie tied the knot, he'd wean her away from these meddling people.

Harper and Veezie busied themselves in the kitchen, preparing all the traditional Southern dishes. Beulah's sweet potato casserole with pecan topping went on the table first. Then came the butterbeans, collard greens, cornbread dressing, creamed potatoes, deviled eggs, potato salad, cranberry salad and crispy cornbread made from Pollard's freshly ground meal. And if that wasn't enough to tempt the palate, the tantalizing aroma coming from the turkey in the oven was enough to make one's mouth water.

The weather couldn't have been nicer if Zeke had special ordered it. Cool enough for a light jacket and the countryside looked as if an artist had slung his brush and splashed the landscape with color. Not that the live oaks and pines ever changed from season to season, but the red poison sumac and golden wild flowers scattered across the fields hinted of a change about to take place. Zeke took one last side-glance in the mirror, and whispered, "Yes, indeed. Changes are coming, Gracie, my darling."

He went upstairs, bent down to kiss Gracie, then sat on the edge of the bed. "Sugar, the doc said I could carry you downstairs, but he don't want you staying up too long and tiring yourself out. I got a real surprise for you, but I'm gonna wait 'til after dinner. That is, if I can keep it to myself that long."

"I'll be glad to get out of this bed. I was afraid I'd have to stay up here and miss all the fun. Is everyone here?"

"Everyone except your ol' man. . . uh, your father. I'll be leaving shortly to pick him up at the bus station. You gotta promise me you'll stay on the couch and won't move until I get back."

"You worry too much, Zeke, but you're very sweet. I appreciate the way you want to take care of me."

"I love you, doll face. I couldn't stand it if anything happened to you or our baby."

Gracie cringed every time Zeke referred to the baby as his. She supposed she should be proud he was willing to love and care for her baby as if it were his own. *But it's not his own.*

When Zeke laid her on the couch downstairs, Toby, Tanner, Maddie Claire and Belle swarmed around her as if they hadn't seen her in months. The twins were still excited over the turkey shoot they attended with their father, the previous day. Toby said, "I almost won the prize, Gigi. I came about an inch from hitting the bull's eye. Mr. Bullard won the turkey, but the turkey Veezie's cooking is bigger than the one he took home."

"Way bigger," Tanner said. "Maybe fifty pounds bigger."

She hid her smile with her hand. "Well, I'd say that's a mighty big turkey. We should have plenty to eat. But where's Ludie?"

"She's sitting outside on the swing, waiting for her friend to get here."

Veezie sent the children out on the veranda with a sack full of pine cones, construction paper, scissors and glue to make turkeys to hold the place cards.

Ludie was put in charge of the decorations, but she couldn't stay in one place long enough to supervise. She'd jump off the porch, peek around the corner of the house, then amble back up the steps long enough to give minor instructions, then off the porch again. What if he changed his mind? She knew he wasn't in favor of coming and was only doing it to please her. But he *had* to come. She'd promised Veezie she had a surprise for her. Ludie could hardly wait to see both Uncle George's face and Veezie's when they'd spy one another for the first time in years. Veezie spoke of Beulah and George as if they were her family. Goose bumps ran down her arms, imagining the hugs that would take place, and it was all because of her. *Where are you Uncle George?*

When the children finished making the turkeys, Ludie ran into the kitchen. "Veezie, you mind if I run down to see my friend?"

"I thought you invited him to come here."

"I did, but it's almost time to sit down and he ain't here. I wanna go get him."

"I don't think that's a good idea, Ludie."

"Why not?"

"He must have a good reason, if he's decided not to come. You shouldn't pressure him."

Harper walked over and knelt beside Gracie on the couch. "It was so sweet seeing the kids swarming around you this morning. It's evident they love you very much."

"And I love them. They're good kids. But where's Ludie?"

Harper frowned. "Poor kid's been outside pacing all morning. Seems she invited her little friend and he hasn't shown up. Who is he?"

"I have no idea, but from what I've gathered, I take it he's a sickly child and probably poor. Ludie seems to have a problem trusting adults, so I let her share what she's comfortable sharing and try not to ask too many questions. I feel I'm slowly earning her trust. "

"Do you know where he lives?"

"Not exactly. She cuts through the woods to go to his house, so he probably lives on the other side of Juniper Square in one of those little shotgun houses."

"That's quite a walk. Must be four or five miles."

"She's a tough little girl. I'm so proud of her. Would you mind asking her to come in? I'd like to talk to her."

Ludie ran inside, fell to her knees beside the couch and with her head buried in Gracie's lap, she burst into tears. "He promised he'd come. He promised."

Gracie gently raked her fingers through Ludie's curls and whispered, "Sweetheart, I understand. It hurts when someone promises to come and he doesn't show. It's okay to cry."

The front door swung opened and Gracie could hear her father's deep voice booming, "Happy Thanksgiving."

Veezie threw down the dishrag and ran to greet her husband. They strolled arm-in-arm into the parlor where Gracie lay on the sofa. Ludie ran to dry her tears.

Shep Jackson leaned over and kissed his daughter. “Hello, sweetheart.” He straightened and eyed her round belly. His lip quivered.

“Please don’t cry, Daddy. I know you worry about me, but I’ll be okay.” She reached up and touched his damp cheek.

“Sweetheart, you’re so brave, but I know what it’s like to lose half your heart. I’ve always wanted to ‘fix’ things for you, but bringing back your beloved is something I can’t fix.”

“Daddy, it hurts, and I’ll always have a hole in my heart—but Garth left me a gift—a part of himself. How wonderful is that?” She rubbed her hand across her belly. “Your little grandbaby is gonna be just fine . . . and so will I. With both Flint and Zeke taking such good care of me, what can go wrong?”

His lip split into a craggy smile. “You think I’m bawling because I’m worried? Shucks no. I’m bawling because I just realized I’m old enough to be a Grandpa.” He bent down and kissed her once more. “Kidding, of course. I can hardly wait to spoil him.”

“You mean her?” Gracie giggled.

“Oh, so you’ve put in your order, have you? Well, I can’t blame you. But I know for a fact that little girls are thieves. They’ll steal your heart.”

Harper yelled from the kitchen, “The turkey’s coming out of the oven. Time to gather at the table.”

When Shep reached down to pick up Gracie, Zeke stepped

forward. “Excuse me, preacher. I’ll get her.”

Shep scooped her up in his arms. “I’m her father.”

Zeke blurted, “And I’m . . .” He glanced at Gracie, then stomped over to the head of the table and waited for all to be seated.

Ludie spoke up. “Zeke, that’s Brother Charlie’s place.”

His eyes narrowed into tiny slits. “Ludie, for cryin’ out loud, it don’t matter where nobody sits. Besides, you kids need to wait and eat at the second table, after the adults finish. Now, run outside and play until you’re called.”

“But it does matter, and Harper said I’m old enough to sit at the grown-up table. The names are on the turkey tails. They’re called place cards, ain’t they Veezie?” She pointed across the table. “Zeke, your place is over yonder next to Dr. Flint.”

Without waiting for Veezie’s response, he huffed. “I know what place cards are. I just don’t see no sense in ‘em. Folks oughta be able to sit where they wanna sit. But I ain’t one to squabble. I’ll sit anywhere. It’s fine with me.” He stomped over to the other side of the table and plonked down.

Gracie could sense Ludie’s pain and knew it had nothing to do with Zeke or place cards. The empty place at the table, set for her friend, was a huge disappointment.

But Gracie’s heart went out to Zeke, also. Poor fellow. Surely, he could feel the animosity in the room. It was only because these dear friends didn’t understand him. He’d gone to such lengths to make this a special day for her, and now he appeared embarrassed that he'd chosen to sit at the head of the table. If only they knew him the way she did, they'd understand his heart was always in the right place, although he often lacked tact in knowing how to handle a situation.

Led by Ludie, Brother Charlie took his place at the head. "Why don't we all hold hands while I ask God's blessings on our food."

Soon, the laughter began again. Gracie assumed the initial tension she felt in the room was more her imagination than a reality. She understood her father would be slow to accept Zeke, but she recalled his reluctance to accept Garth in the beginning, and yet he learned to love him like a son. She was confident it would only be a short while before her daddy and Zeke would become fast friends.

After the meal, Harper and Veezie cleared the plates, preparing to bring in the pumpkin and pecan pies.

Zeke shoved his chair back, stood and tapped his fork on the side of his tea glass. "Ladies, if you don't mind, please wait. I have something I'd like to say."

The room grew quiet.

"This is a very special day. Truly a day to give thanks."

Heads nodded in agreement and Gracie's father led the applause.

Zeke pushed his palms forward, silencing the crowd. "Thank you." He sucked in a lungful of air, and slowly exhaled. "It's with great pleasure I can stand before you today and announce that Gracie Jackson Graham has made me the happiest man alive by accepting my proposal of marriage. And Shep . . ." he paused. "I hope you'll allow me to call you Shep, now that we're gonna be family. We'd be mighty pleased if you'd perform the ceremony, here at Nine Gables, this coming Sunday. I realize that's quick and you'll have to make arrangements for someone to preach in your place, but it'd mean a lot to Gracie to have you do the honor. And naturally, whatever makes my little woman happy, makes me happy."

Gracie's eyes squinted. "But—"

He walked over and rested his hands on her shoulders. "I know what you're thinking, sugar, but don't you worry about a thing. It's all taken care of." He bent down and kissed her forehead before walking back to his chair. "Shep, I know you'll rest easier, knowing I'll be upstairs with your daughter during the night, instead of two flights of stairs between us. Now, I'll be able to take care of her, all day and all night. Makes me giddy thinking about it."

The room grew quiet. Very quiet.

Gracie glanced around at the expressions. "Daddy, would you please carry me upstairs. I'm feeling tired."

Zeke said, "Honey, I could do that for you. I'm sure no one at this table would consider it improper for me to lay you in your bed, under the circumstances. After all, I'm the one who brought you down here, and after next week—" He slid his chair back.

"Thank you, Zeke, but Daddy will carry me up."

The color drained from her father's face. He stood, picked his daughter up in his arms and carried her to her room.

After laying her in bed, he sat down beside her. "Gracie, I don't know how to say this, other than to blurt it out. I can't do it. I can't marry you to that man. I don't feel he's right for you."

Gracie glared out the window.

"Did you hear what I said?"

"I heard you, Daddy. Thank you for bringing me to my room and getting me settled in bed. Now, would you please tell Zeke I'm tired and want to take a nap, but to come wake me up in a couple of hours."

"I'll come back and wake you myself. It's not right for him to be up here alone with you. You're not married—*yet.*"

"Daddy, I don't mean to sound disrespectful, but I'm not your little girl anymore and I'm capable of making my own decisions, good or bad. Now, would you please tell Zeke to let me sleep for a while, then I need him to come stay with me?"

Chapter Twenty-Four

Ludie's lip poked out in a pout. "I enjoyed my lunch. May I be excused?"

Zeke said, "Ludie, I'd like you to stay at the table until we've had dessert. Harper and Veezie went to a lot of trouble to prepare those scrumptious pecan and pumpkin pies."

The only sound in the eerie room came from silverware clanging on china plates. Zeke seemed to be the only one in a gay mood. "You ladies sure outdid yourselves with the meal. I can hardly wait to taste the pies. Just before I left to pick up Shep, an old hobo showed up at the back door. I don't know if it was the aroma of the turkey, the sweet potato casserole or the pecans roasting in the oven that lured him here, or a combination of all three. Couldn't blame him for wanting to bum a plate. It was all just as good as it smells."

Harper said, "A hobo, looking for food? How sad to be alone on Thanksgiving. I hope you fixed him a plate. We certainly have more than enough to share."

"You ladies were still cooking and I didn't want to bother you. Besides, once you give in to these beggars, they'll be on your doorstep every day with a hand held out."

Ludie shoved her plate aside and jumped up. "That was Uncle George. I know it was. You're a mean man, Zeke Thorne. A real mean man."

Zeke said, "Go to your room, Ludie. That kind of behavior will not be tolerated in this house. I'll be up later to talk with you."

"I hate you."

Harper said, "Wait! Ludie, are you saying the friend you've been going to see is your uncle?"

"No. He just told me to call him that. He's my . . . he's my friend."

Zeke said, "She's pitching a fit over nothing. It was no friend of hers. The man who came to the door was an old colored man. He must've been eighty if he was a day. Ludie, I think you owe everyone at this table an apology."

Ludie pushed away from the table, and ran out of the house.

Zeke said, "I'll tend to her later. The girl's got some real emotional problems. She's been meeting somebody down in the woods in an old cabin. After Gracie and I marry, I'm gonna—"

He stopped when he spotted Shep standing at the foot of the stairs. "So is my little woman tucked in bed? I could tell she was getting tired."

Shep glared. "She said don't bother her for a couple of hours."

"Is that all she said?"

He mumbled. "She said . . . she said, in a couple of hours for you to wake her."

Harper whispered to Veezie. "I'm glad Gracie didn't see Ludie's outburst. She was awfully upset. Maybe we should go after her."

"Let me go. I think I know exactly where she went. Shep, honey, would you like to go with me?"

"Not unless you need me. I have some praying to do."

Veezie ran all the way to the cottage. The door was open and she could see Ludie sitting on the floor with her head leaning against George's leg, as his gnarled hands gently stroked her curls.

"Hush, pretty baby. Ain't no need for tears."

"But Uncle George, I never had a family Thanksgiving dinner, and me and you was about to have our first until he spoiled it. I hate him. I ain't never going back there. I'm gonna live with you."

George glanced at the figure standing in the doorway and blinked. "Why, I'll be. Is that really you Veezie? Nobody told me you'd be a'coming. Stop standing there and come on in, sugar. It's been coon ages since I seen you and Brother Shep. Pull you up a chair."

Ludie's eyes widened. "I didn't tell, Uncle George. I promise. I don't know how she found us."

"No need to get upset, sugar. I 'spect Miz Veezie knew right off where to find you the minute you said yo' friend's name was Uncle George. Now get off that cold floor and let me take a gander at Miz Veezie. Law, what a site you are, girlie. You a real lady. Yes'm, a real lady. My Beulah woulda been so proud to see you now. How ya' been, sugar?"

The minute he stood, Veezie ran and wrapped her arms around the old man. "I miss you, George. I thought you were in Detroit."

Ludie said, "He was, 'til he got word I was—" Her face paled. "I meant to say, until it got too cold for him up north. Ain't that right, Uncle George?"

"It was sho' nuff cold, alright. No doubt about it. And this ol' rheumatism flares up in cold weather."

Veezie said, "George, I'm so sorry about the mix-up at lunch. Zeke didn't know."

Ludie grunted. "Still didn't give him no right to turn Uncle George away. Ain't his house. Not yet, no how. Ain't mine neither, 'cause I ain't never goin' back."

George shook his finger. "Now, we ain't gonna have none of that kinda talk, Ludie. Miz Gracie's been good to you. She'll take care of you. And I'll be close by, so you can come visit."

"But I don't wanna visit. I wanna live with you, Uncle George."

Veezie jerked an old wool blanket from off the cot, and made a pallet on the floor. "Come here, Ludie, and sit down with me. Let's talk."

"About what?"

"About you. There's no way the state will allow you to live with Uncle George."

"They won't know."

"Yes, honey, they will. And they'll come and snatch you away and they could send you off somewhere and you might never see Uncle George or Gracie again. Is that what you want?"

"No. I just want Zeke to leave us alone."

"But I'm afraid he isn't going anywhere, so the best thing for you to do is to learn to get along with him."

Veezie felt her words had gotten through, when Ludie said, "I reckon what you say makes sense. I'll go back, but why don't you stay and visit with Uncle George? I know how he's missed you. He was gonna be your surprise from me and you was gonna be his surprise. Turns out, I was the one who got surprised."

George said, "Ludie, seems to me you acting mighty strange. You okay, sugar?"

"I'm fine, Uncle George. I just remembered I didn't get none of that pecan pie."

Veezie said, "Tell Harper I'll be there shortly to help her with the dishes."

"She'll have help. You just enjoy the visit." She ran over and hugged the old man. "Bye, Uncle George. I love you."

"I love you, too, sugar. You doin' the right thing by going back. Ever'thing's gonna be alright. You'll see."

"Sure, it will. Bye, Veezie."

"Bye, kid. See you in a bit." She tried to dismiss the uneasy queasiness. Was she feeling apprehensive because she could see herself in the child? "She's a pistol ball, isn't she, George?"

"Yes'm, she sho' is. She's that and more."

Veezie blew out a long breath of air. "I just hope no one ever buys her a red dress."

George lifted a shoulder. "I ain't following you."

"Just thinking out loud, George about a time someone bought me a red dress and it was the beginning of a road I had no business traveling."

"But you turned out right well, and I 'spect our little Ludie will turn out good, too."

"Sure she will. I'm just rambling. There's nothing to be concerned about." She whispered under her breath, "I hope."

Ludie picked up a long stick, then ran through the woods as fast as her long, skinny legs would carry her. When she reached Nine Gables, she sneaked up the back staircase to her room. She grabbed a dress, a blouse, a pair of dungarees, and two pair of step-ins, then tied her nightgown around them. Using the arms of the gown as ties, she knotted the bundle and tied it to the stick, the way she'd seen hobos toting their garments.

On tiptoes, she ran her hand around the top shelf in the closet until she felt a small coin purse containing money she'd made cleaning blackboards and washing dishes in the lunchroom—money saved to buy Christmas gifts. Her heart hammered at the sound of footsteps on the stairs. She crammed the purse in her pocket and snuck out the back way. If she ran, she could catch a bus and be out of town before anyone would miss her.

Chapter Twenty-Five

Walter Reed Hospital
November 3, 1945

"Sergeant Kelly, the nurse tells me you're beginning to remember bits and pieces of your past. I'd like for you to share with me all you can remember."

"Well, to begin with, doc, as I told the nurse, I don't believe my name is Kelly."

"Oh? Then, what do you think it is?"

"I'm . . . I'm not sure. But Sergeant Kelly doesn't sound right."

"I'm not surprised. Things have been pretty mixed up for you since coming out of the coma, haven't they?"

He nodded. "You have no idea."

"Well, you're doing much better, now, and it's my opinion that in time, everything will begin to make sense again."

"And is it true, the war's ended?"

"That's right, soldier, and you slept right through the excitement. Japan surrendered on the second day of September."

"How long have I been here?"

Dr. Martin picked up the chart hanging at the foot of the metal hospital bed, and flipped through several pages. "You were brought in, back in April. You were one of the lucky ones."

"Lucky?" He pointed toward his legs. "You call this lucky? I can't walk, I don't know who I am and I don't know where home is. What's so great about that?"

"You're alive. Four of the soldiers brought in with you, died."

"Maybe they were the lucky ones."

"You'll feel differently when your parents get here. Your mother was ecstatic when I told her on the phone you were awake. When you get back home in familiar surroundings, the memories will begin to return. I'll send a nurse in here to help you dress. Your uniform was in no shape to wear again, but your mother sent you some clothes to wear home."

"I don't want a woman helping me dress. I can do it myself."

"Are you sure?"

"Yes, I'm sure. There may be some things I don't remember, but dressing doesn't happen to be one of them."

After struggling with legs that failed to cooperate, the soldier in 217 rang for a nurse.

Without a word, he handed her his pants.

"Norm . . ." Her voice quaked. "I'm going to miss you."

"You've been swell, Martha. I appreciate your taking care of me these past months, even if I wasn't aware of it at the time."

The door opened and Martha whispered, "They're here."

A slender built man and a stout lady with her hair in a bun tiptoed in. The woman's smile lit up her face. "Hello, son."

He squinted. "I'm sorry. I don't know you."

Martha grasped the woman's hand and led her closer to the bed. "Norm, this is your mother."

"No. You're mistaken. I've never seen these people."

Martha put her arm around the weeping woman. "The doctor doesn't expect the amnesia to be lasting. Already, he's beginning to remember bits and pieces of his past. He remembers the war, but he insists his name isn't Kelly."

The man's lip quivered. "He's right. He's not our son."

The woman screamed. "Why are you saying that, Robert? A mother knows her own son." She leaned over the bed and laid her head on the soldier's chest. "My baby. My precious baby."

The door swung open and Dr. Martin rushed in. "I could hear the commotion on the other end of the hall. What's going on?"

Robert pulled his wife away from the bed. "Doctor, there's been a big mistake. This patient is not our son."

The woman sobbed. "Robert, admit it. You've never loved him from the day we brought him home from the adoption agency. You blamed me for not being able to bear you a child."

"Honey, don't do this. You know better."

The nurse said, "Mrs. Kelly, would you mind walking down the hall with me?"

"Thank you, nurse, I appreciate the wonderful care you've given Norm, and I don't wish to appear ungrateful—but I need to help my son get ready to go home."

"The doctor isn't quite ready to discharge him yet, so why don't you and I go to the cafeteria for a cup of coffee. After seven months, I feel as if we're close friends. Your love for him is heartwarming. I'd like to hear what Norm was like as a little boy."

"I suppose I could use a cup of coffee. Thank you." Her moistened eyes lit up. "He was the cutest little tyke. And so smart. Why, he could say his alphabet when he was three-years-old."

Robert waited for his wife to exit, then motioned for the doctor to walk with him outside the room. "Doctor Martin, I know you're confused and truthfully, I'm a bit confused myself. Not about our son, but I'm befuzzled about how to handle the situation."

"*You're* befuzzled? I can't begin to tell you how confused *I* am. You and your wife visited this soldier regularly during the months he was in a coma. I was impressed by the love you both showed. Now, that it's time to take him home, you suddenly decide he doesn't belong to you? What kind of parents are you?"

The man stood stoic. "I understand your frustration. I'll try to explain. When the hospital first called, I walked in here, expecting to see my son. Instead, I saw a stranger. Even with the bruises and his head bandaged, I knew he wasn't Norm. I think in her heart, my wife knew too, but she's in denial. Don't you get it? If he isn't Norm, it means Norm is dead." His voice trembled. "Doc he was our only child, and well, I think Mama just couldn't bear to admit he was gone. So her mind played cruel tricks. At first, I tried to convince her our boy was gone, but she became hysterical."

The doctor's face distorted. "Forgive me for not being sympathetic, but it seems to me you contributed to your wife's delusions by going along with her. Do you see what you've done?"

"Maybe it was wrong, but I honestly didn't believe the soldier would ever come out of the coma, and if it helped mama to believe Norm was still alive, then I felt it wasn't hurting anyone. So, I continued to bring her to visit. As unethical as it may sound to you, I love my wife and I did it for her."

"And you planned to wait until time to take him home, and then break her heart? You're right. It does sound unethical to me. Your wife deserved to know the truth, regardless of how painful."

Robert dropped his gaze. "You still don't understand, do you, doc? When the hospital called and said he was well enough to be discharged, but he still didn't have his memory, I was willing to take him home and care for him, since he didn't know who he was and no one else had shown up to claim him. Not just for mama's sake, but for our son. It would've been what Norm would've wanted. This soldier may not know who he is, but he apparently knows who he's not and he's emphatic that he doesn't want to go home with us. Please, doc. Help him find his family."

The doctor nodded. "I still have unanswered questions, but I suppose your heart was in the right place." He threw up his hand, seeing the nurse and Mrs. Kelly coming down the hall. He waited, then opened the door to Room 217 and the four entered together.

Norm said, "Mr. Kelly, I apologize for being sharp. I

understand you and your wife have been good to visit me these past months, and I don't mean to sound ungrateful, but—"

The doctor interrupted. "I think he understands what you're trying to say, soldier. Be patient while we try to help both you and the Kelly's, find answers to your questions." He reached down and lifted the dog tag from the man's chest. "Nurse, was this soldier's dog tag removed at any time?"

Her eyes squinted. "It's highly unlikely, Dr. Martin, but I can't say for a certainty. Several soldiers were brought in at the same time, the night he was admitted—most with burns over their bodies. I suppose it's possible it was momentarily removed to keep the metal from adhering to the raw skin, but I would assume once the wounds were bandaged, the dog tag would've been immediately placed back on the soldier."

"Did you attend this patient the night he was brought in?"

"No, sir, so I can only vouch that he was wearing the dog tag the next day, on third shift."

"So it's possible it could've been carelessly switched with Norman Kelly's?"

Nurse Martha glanced at the soldier and answered slowly. "I suppose it's possible."

The doctor rubbed the back of his neck. "I don't know what to say, Mr. Kelly. This should never have happened."

"I'm not here to place blame, doctor, but I need to know what happened to our son's body. I couldn't ask before, since my wife wanted so desperately to believe the soldier in 217 was our

Norman. But now, we need to know what happened to our son."

"I understand. I'm furious such incompetence happened in this hospital, and I intend to get to the bottom of this inexcusable situation. Follow me, sir. I promise you, we'll find your son."

After checking through the files, the doctor shook his head. "It seems eleven soldiers were brought in the night your son was admitted. Four bodies were shipped out on April 17th. I'll have Nurse Martha check the files on the soldiers who were shipped home to see if all four bodies were positively identified by their loved ones."

The nurse's gaze met with the doctor's. She shook her head and muttered. "I'm so sorry. I've already checked . . . and, uh, the soldiers were . . . well, according to the files, because of the nature of the wounds, the families were advised not to open the caskets. The dog tags were used for confirmation purposes. Her eyes watered.

The doctor's head lowered. "Mr. Kelly, I promise you and your wife I'll—"

"No need for words, doc. I hold no animosity toward you or this hospital. As traumatic as it is, I know the mix-up wasn't intentional." After walking out the door, he whispered, "Will you do me a favor?"

"I'll be happy to."

"Here's two hundred dollars. Please give it to the soldier in 217. Tell him it's from Norman. The *real* Norman."

****

After lunch, Dr. Martin walked in room 217. "I'm on my way home, but I wanted to stop by and give you something, Private Graham."

"What did you call me?"

"Private Garth Graham. I believe that's your name."

"And I believe you're wrong."

"Oh? Then what do you think it is?"

"Though I never once believed the Kelly's were my parents, ironically, their son and I happen to share the same first name. My name's Norman." He clasped his hands behind his head.

"You sure about that?"

He grimaced. "You know I'm not sure about anything. But it feels right."

The doctor checked the bandages. "I think I can explain. You've been here seven months. Your nurse, Miss Martha Walker, talked to you constantly while you were in a coma, always addressing you by the name we believed to be yours. It's undetermined how much a comatose patient may hear at times. I think it was her constant repetition that's made the name familiar."

"So who am I, doctor?"

"We aren't sure, but we won't stop until we know." He walked toward the door, then turned and placed an envelope on the bedside table. "I almost forgot to leave this."

"What is it?"

"It's a thank-you gift from Sergeant Norman Kelly for giving his mother a few extra months of happiness, believing her son was alive."

On his way out, the doctor held the door open for the nurse, who walked in holding a tray.

Her eyes lit up. "Hungry, Norm?"

"You believe that's my name, too, don't you?"

She shrugged. "Not really, but after all these months, I'll find it difficult to call you by any other name."

"Martha, tell me, honestly. Do you really think I'm Private Garth Graham?"

"I hope not."

"Why? Is there something wrong with him I haven't been told?"

She pulled up the bedside tray table and sat his food in front of him. Her head lowered. "I don't want to believe it because it appears Garth Graham had a wife. Oh, Norm, you must have sensed it by now. I've fallen in love with you."

He reached for the nurse's hand and gave it a little squeeze. "You've been swell, Martha."

"But you don't love me, do you? Oh, Norm. I wouldn't have allowed myself to get so close, if I'd thought there was a possibility you could be married. I adored the people I believed to be your parents, and they told me you were single. I began to fantasize you'd get your memory back and would love me as much as I've learned to love you. Mrs. Kelly was so devoted to you, and Mr. Kelly was devoted to her. I wanted to be part of a family like that." She bit her quivering lip. "Oh, why couldn't it be true?"

"I'm so sorry. Please don't cry. You're beautiful, you're smart and you're the most compassionate person I've ever known." He bit the inside of his cheek. "Well, since I don't remember many people in my past, I'm confident that's a true statement, even if I can't verify it. Any man would be crazy not to fall in love with you."

Her lip quivered. "Don't you get it? I don't want *any* man. I want you, Norm."

"Martha, if you truly care for me, help me find the truth. Please. I'm beginning to remember bits and pieces, but my life is like a jigsaw puzzle with all the corners missing."

"I don't know how much help I can be, but give me the pieces you remember and together we'll see what we can come up with."

"So you'll help me?"

"I don't know how much help I can be, but I'll try. Tell me what we have to go on."

"There are two special girls in my life, although I don't know how I know that. I dream about them almost every night. Grace is always running toward me, but I wake up before we can embrace. I think she's my wife, Martha, but I can't be sure. Maybe Mercy is my sister, although I can't seem to bring her into focus. But I have a feeling they're trying to reach me."

Martha's eyes lit up. "Norm, I've just had a thought. Do you not see something a bit peculiar with those names? *Grace*? And *Mercy*?"

"Peculiar? Not at all. I think they're beautiful names, but I don't know why I expected you to understand. Forget I mentioned it."

"Don't be so defensive. You asked for my opinion. Do you want to hear, or not?"

He shrugged. "Sorry. Go ahead."

"Well, the chaplain visited you often when you were in a coma, and he always ended his prayers with, 'Thank you, Lord, for your grace and mercy.' It's possible for someone in a coma to be semi-aware of their surroundings. People who have been in comas have reported being able to hear everything going on in the room around them. Your subconscious mind obviously picked up on those last two words of the chaplain's prayer."

"I'll admit it sounds plausible, yet I know in my heart Grace and Mercy are real. Grace's face, her voice, her body and even the fragrance of her perfume are so strong in my dreams. But Mercy has me baffled. I want to know how she fits into my life."

Martha's lip turned up in a crooked smile. "Maybe you were a bigamist."

So she thought it was all one big joke? He wanted to lash out, but was it her fault she found his story hard to believe?

The doctor walked back in with a box and sat down on the edge of the bed. "Soldier, I don't know what to say except I'm so sorry for the tragic mix-up. Let me tell you what we do know. There were a dozen soldiers brought in the night you were admitted. The remains of the men who died were sent to

Lynchburg, Virginia; Birmingham, Alabama; Pensacola, Florida; and Geneva, Alabama. Any of those towns ring a bell for you?"

"Should they?"

"Each soldier's belongings are deposited in a box when he's admitted. Those who don't make it are sent home along with their box. Each box in this ward is accounted for. The one I hold in my hand, I assume belongs to you, since Sergeant Kelly's parents have confirmed the contents are not their son's. I'd appreciate it if you'd take a look and see if anything looks familiar. Take your time. Pull out each article and hold it for a while. Try to remember."

He pulled out a small Bible and thumbed through the pages. The inscription inside was to "Garth from Brother Charlie."

The doctor waited.

"Doc, do you really think I might be this Garth fellow?"

"I do. But I'm hoping something in the box will set off a memory."

"This Bible . . . it says it's from my brother." His voice cracked. "It hurts to know I have a brother and I can't even remember him." He clenched his fists together and moaned. "Doc, help me. Please, can't you help me?"

"I may be wrong, but I figure the giver was a preacher."

"Hmm. I wonder." He shoved the box toward the doctor. "You may as well take this back. I can't remember."

"There's one more item in here I'd like you to see."

Chapter Twenty-Six

Ludie ran all the way to town, stopping only long enough to catch her breath. Her heart hammered when the only bus in sight pulled out of the station only seconds before she reached the door. She yelled, to her lung's capacity, though the humongous bus roared past. Two elderly men sat on a bench outside the station, playing checkers. She gripped her bindle and stammered. "Uh, excuse me sir, would either of you happen to know when the next bus leaves?"

"In the morning at nine-thirty," the skinny one answered.

The other one studied the board, then made his move. "Albert, you didn't ask her where she was a'going. How ya know what time the bus leaves, if you don't know the destination?"

"Looking at her, I got a feeling she don't care where it's going. Am I right, little lady?"

"Nevermind." She had no time to waste. Zeke would be looking for her and would surely find her before nine-thirty the following day. She shivered, imagining the new whelps he'd put on her legs if he found her. Nope. She had no time to wait for a bus. The train depot was a mile or so on the other side of town. It was probably a better idea, anyway. Trains go faster and she needed to get out of town as fast as possible.

Inside the train depot, she read the schedule posted on the wall and grimaced. Another train wouldn't be leaving until ten after seven. She'd have to hide out until then, just in case they missed her. She swallowed hard. Who would miss her? Nobody, that's who. Nobody cared about her. Not even Gigi. If she cared one iota for anyone other than herself, she wouldn't marry that creep.

Approaching the counter, she emptied her coin purse. "I want to buy a ticket to—" She glanced at the board to make sure she hadn't read it wrong.

"Speak up. Where to?"

"Uh, sorry. I'm on my way to Birmingham, Alabama. That would be the next train leaving the depot."

"That's right. What's in Birmingham, little lady?"

It was the way he said "little lady," that prompted her to spit out the first thing that came to mind. "I'm a mail-order bride. I'm on my way to meet my new husband."

"A mail-order bride? Say, how old are you?"

"Seventeen."

He raised a brow. "You don't look a day over sixteen."

Ludie tried to hide her smile. She'd take that.

****

Back at the cabin, George, stood and stoked the live embers in the fireplace.

Veezie swallowed the pain in her throat. “I’m so sorry for what happened at the Big House, today, George. That was rude of Zeke to send you away. I can’t imagine how humiliating it must’ve been.”

“Aw, sugar, ain’t no reason to fret yo’ pretty little head over sump’n that was my own fault. To tell the truth, I didn’t ‘spect nobody was gonna let me sit down at that dinner table. The onliest reason I went was ‘cause it seemed to mean so much to Ludie. I’d be willing to suffer any kind of humiliation for that young’un.” With a slight limp, he made his way back over to the straw-filled cot and sat on the edge.

“George, I can tell you’re very special to Ludie. Doesn’t surprise me. You and Beulah always did have a way with the down-and-out. I’m living proof.”

“Sweetpea, you was down when you inherited Nine Gables after Miz Ophelia died, but you wadn’t out, by no means. No sirree. You was a gutsy little thing and my Beulah, she loved a challenge.” He shook his head and chuckled. “To tell the truth, I don’t reckon she ever had a bigger challenge than you wuz. But, oh Lawsy, that woman woulda walked on hot coals for you.”

“You called me Sweetpea. No one’s called me that since Beulah died. It always made me feel loved to hear her say it. George, why don’t you come with me to Nine Gables? Harper will be thrilled to know you were Ludie’s secret pal. She’ll be excited to see you. You won’t have any problems from Zeke, I promise. I’ll personally see to it.”

"I appreciate the invite, shug, but I reckon I'll jest stay put. Tell Miz Harper if she has a minute, I'd be mighty pleased if she could slip off down here to see ol' George." His lip turned up slightly. "Law, it still baffles me how a mean ol' goat like Miz Ophelia coulda birthed such a sweet young'un."

Veezie rubbed her hand across her mouth. "When the will was read and I thought I was the birth daughter of a rich woman and was gonna inherit Nine Gables, it was like I'd died and gone to Heaven. Having grown up poor, I'll admit in the beginning I loved having all those nice things to enjoy. But you know, George, after I begin to hear of the kind of scheming woman Ophelia was, I was almost glad to learn the switch was faked and she wasn't my mama. I've held it against her for wanting to swap her own flesh and blood, but I suppose I have no right to criticize. I was willing to give my sweet little Diamond away to save my own reputation."

"Chile, nobody held that agin you. But now, Miz Ophelia was a horse of a different color. She couldn't stand for her high falutin friends to find out she mighta birthed a young'un what wadn't just right." His face twisted into a frown.

"You look peaked, George? You feeling sick?"

"Nah. Just thinking. Shug, you didn't hold it agin me and Beulah for going to the midwife and having her tell the truth—that she faked the switch, did you?"

"Not for a minute. Harper and I both understood why you had to tell the truth. Funny, how I thought inheriting the estate would make me happy. And yet, when Harper found she was written out of the will, she didn't seem to care. I couldn't understand at the time how she could be so calm. But I soon learned that real joy doesn't come from things."

The muscles in his face relaxed. "And you got joy, now, do ya' shug?"

"Oh, George, I have indescribable joy. Shep and I don't have a lot of material things, but I wouldn't swap my life with anyone or for anything."

She glanced at her watch. "My stars, I didn't mean to stay so long. I could talk to you for hours, but Shep will be sending the hounds out looking for me if I don't get back to the house."

"You made an old man happy by paying me a visit. Watch after Ludie for me, will ya? She ain't as old as you wuz when you moved into Nine Gables, but she's so much like you, I declare, you two coulda been sisters."

Veezie snickered and crinkled her nose. "You aren't the first to make the observation. Maybe we are. Who knows? My ol' man—Monroe O'Steen wasn't a faithful husband to my mama. No one wanted to believe me, but I knew the double life he was living. Wouldn't it be something if it turned out Ludie was my little sister?"

George smiled. "That'd be sump'n, alright."

Chapter Twenty-Seven

The soft voice outside Gracie's bedroom door caused her muscles to draw in a knot.

"It's me, hon. You awake?"

She swallowed the lump in her throat. How did her life become so complicated? "Come on in, Zeke."

"Your dad said you wanted to see me. To tell the truth, I'm surprised he gave me the message." He sat down on the edge of her bed and pecked her lightly on the forehead.

"Surprised? Why?"

"You serious? I don't mean to bad-mouth your ol' man, sugar, but he needs to back off and you gonna have to start standing up to him. You ain't his little girl no more. Maybe he'll realize that after we get married." The grin plastered on his face stretched from ear to ear. "I figured you wanted me up here to talk about our plans." He cackled. "I wouldn't take a plug nickel for the look on your face when I made the announcement at the dinner table. Shucks, I went to a lot of trouble to pull it off, but it went great, just like I planned. I really surprised you, didn't I?"

"Yes. We need to talk."

"Nothing to talk about, sugar. Everything's taken care of. Everything! Our blood tests, the license, the preacher—and more importantly, the bride and groom." He leaned his head back and cackled. "I had a hard time keeping the surprise from you, but I wanted this day to be one you'll remember always."

"Well, if that was your intent, you certainly succeeded. Zeke, I thought I'd made it clear. I need more time."

"Honey, I understand why you're hesitant. But it's like taking that first dip into the creek in early spring. At first, you're inclined to just poke your toe in. But you jerk it back because it doesn't feel comfortable. Too cold. Then someone tells you the best way is to jump in and it'll feel right. You aren't too sure, but you trust them and you dive in and discover they were right. It feels good. Jumping in was the best way."

"Zeke, we aren't discussing swimming."

"But the same principle applies. Gracie, I know you love me but you're afraid to admit it. I'm sure you're feeling uncomfortable with the idea of marrying again, and I understand. You're pregnant and your emotions see-saw. You're frightened of what it's gonna feel like. Trust me, darling, it's gonna be wonderful. That's why I handled things the way I did. It's time to stop getting cold feet and jump in. If it were up to me, we'd say our vows today, but we have to wait three days after getting the license." He leaned down and kissed her. "What's three days, when we'll have a lifetime together? Oh, darling, please share my excitement."

"Zeke, I can't marry you."

"Oh honey, sure you can. It's all settled. You're tired. It's been a big day for you. Need more cover? You look cold." He took the quilt lying at the foot of the bed and pulled it over her.

She shoved the quilt back. "No. I don't need anything, except for you to listen. We aren't getting married. We're not!"

"You don't mean that, Gracie. I love you and you love me. I know you do. You're afraid to admit it. After having lost one husband, I get it that you're scared something might happen to me, too, but ain't no need to fret. I'm not on the front lines, facing the enemy, sweetheart. I'll always be here for you."

"I'm sorry if I've ever given you reason to suspect I was in love with you, Zeke. I've told you from the beginning I was fond of you, but I never once said I loved you. You weren't listening."

He jumped up and with his hands locked back of his head, he closed his eyes. "I can't believe you're saying this, after all I've done for you. It's your ol' man, ain't it? Gracie, you're not a kid anymore, although he treats you like one. Don't let him meddle in your life. In *our* lives. At least I haven't crawled in the bed with you, the way *he* did with that little . . .. before he married Veezie. I know the kind of woman she was—and still is." His lip curled. "You can douse a leopard with red paint, but underneath he'll still be a spotted animal. Same holds true with a trollop. You can wipe off the war paint and put her on an old maid's outfit, but underneath the high collars and long skirts, she's still a trollop."

"I need you to leave, Zeke Thorne, and shut the door behind

you."

He fell on his knees beside her bed. "Oh, Gracie, you don't mean it. Please, hon, I need you. So you don't love me. You say you're fond of me. I'll take that until I can make you love me. We'll wait until after the baby is born the way we planned."

"I can't marry you, Zeke."

"Why? You need me. And I need you. You know it's true. I'm sorry I said what I did about your father and Veezie. Who am I to judge?"

"You ask why? Because it'd be wrong to marry you when every night I long for my husband to visit me in my dreams. You called Garth my 'first husband.' Garth Graham not only is my first husband, he's my last husband."

"I can make you forget him."

"Then that's reason enough not to marry you. I don't want to forget him."

His teeth clenched together. He paced the floor, then walked over to the door. "I'm beginning to realize you're doing me a big favor by not agreeing to marry me. You're a candidate for the loony bin. Those stupid dreams have you convinced a dead man is coming back. Well, he's not. He's a rotting corpse, Gracie."

"Zeke, pack your belongings and get out of this house."

"Fine. I'll be taking the boys with me. I don't want a crazy woman raising my kids."

The door slammed.

Chapter Twenty-Eight

"George? Our George? Unbelievable." Harper's jaw dropped. "How did you figure it out, Veezie?"

"When a cabin was mentioned, I thought of all the stories George told about living in the servant's shanty in the backwoods, before he and Beulah moved into the big house. So when Ludie called her friend Uncle George, I put it all together."

"I'm surprised he's still alive. How is he?"

"He looks swell for his age, although he moves very slowly. I sense he's in pain, but you know George. He never complains. He said to tell you he thinks of you often."

"Good ol' George. He's one-of-a-kind. I can understand why Ludie took to him. I don't guess anyone can resist his laidback charm."

Veezie winced. "Apparently Zeke could."

"Don't be too hard on him. There must be a half-dozen hobos a week who stop here looking for a bite to eat. How was he to know? Frankly, I feel we all owe Zeke an apology."

"Are you kidding? For what?"

"He went to a lot of trouble to make this a very special Thanksgiving. I can only imagine his anticipation as he waited eagerly for the right moment to make the announcement, and when he did, I'm afraid we were all quite rude. We acted as if he were sentencing her to the chain gang."

"I don't see a speck of difference."

"Veezie, you're being too hard on him. You know that's not true."

"Do I? I'd sooner be sentenced to Tutwiler prison than to be chained to the scoundrel for life."

The Grandfather clock in the antechamber chimed on the half-hour. Harper shrieked. "Oh m'goodness, Veezie, please tell me the clock is wrong. It can't be six-thirty already."

"I'm afraid it is. No one could possibly be starving as much food as we had for dinner, but I'll go call everyone to supper. Veezie walked into the Parlor, and found Brother Charlie asleep on the chaise lounge and her husband slouched over in the corner, reading a Bible." She glanced around the room. "Where's Flint?"

Shep said, "He'll be back shortly. He went to check on a patient who lives in the vicinity."

"On Thanksgiving?"

"Yes, on Thanksgiving," he grumbled. "Unfortunately diseases don't go into remission just because it's a holiday."

She eased down and sat in his lap. "Well, aren't you in a foul mood?"

He put his arms around her waist, and pulled her close. "Sorry

I snapped at you."

"What's wrong, honey?" She whispered.

His lip quivered. "What's not wrong? He's been up there all afternoon with my daughter. I raised her better than that. He has no business hanging out in her bedroom for hours."

"Darling, maybe we've been too quick to judge. Do I have to remind you that only a few years ago you were almost thrown out of the church because the milkman saw your car parked in front of Nine Gables when I lived here? It was understandable how Lum came to the conclusion that he did, but it wasn't the way it looked. Maybe we should trust Gracie's judgment."

"Veezie, the only reason I haven't been up there and jerked him out by the hair of his head is because I don't want to turn my daughter against me. She seems dead-set on marrying the louse and I know if I said what I feel like saying, I might lose her completely. But how could she do this to me?"

"Do what, Shep? What if she fell asleep and has no idea he's still sitting up there? After all, isn't that similar to our situation when Lum stirred up that stink? I had no idea you were in the room, when you accidentally fell asleep sitting by my bed. Nothing happened, yet there were people in Flat Creek Fellowship who were ready to string us up by our heels. Honey, you know as well as I, things aren't always as they appear."

"I know you're trying to help my feelings, sweetheart, but I'm afraid Gracie has been hood-winked by the lowdown character. I told her I won't marry them. She'll have to find someone else."

"You don't mean that, Shep."

"I mean it with all my heart. I refuse to have a part in helping her ruin her life."

"And what did she say to that?"

"Nothing. Made no difference to her. Her mind's made up, and I'm not ashamed to tell you the thought of her married to Zeke Thorne makes me sick."

"Honey, regardless of how you feel about the man Gracie has chosen, if you want to maintain a relationship with your daughter, you're gonna have to make an effort to get along with Zeke."

Harper walked into the dining room with the sliced cold turkey and placed it on the table while Veezie chipped away at a block of ice to go in the tea glasses.

Flint open the front door and yelled, "Am I too late for supper?"

His wife dried her hands on her apron and yelled, "Just in time. How's Mr. Culpepper?"

"About the same. Say, I'm starving."

"Starving? After all you ate for dinner?"

Harper walked into the parlor, kissed her husband, then said, "Shep, why don't you go upstairs and see if Gracie would like for you to bring her to the table?"

He shook his head. "Send someone else. I can't stomach seeing that louse up there in her bedroom."

"You mean Zeke? Didn't you know? He left."

"No. He's still up there. I've kept my eyes on the stairs and he hasn't come back down."

She shrugged. "Then I guess he went down the back way, but I know for a fact he's gone. Maddie Claire came in for a drink of water and said the twins left with their daddy. I looked out the window and his truck is gone and so are the boys."

Chapter Twenty-Nine

Shep ran up the stairs skipping every other one. He eased his daughter's bedroom door open and peeked in. She looked like his perception of an angel. Albeit, a sad angel. "You okay, baby?"

When he sat down on the edge of her bed, she threw her arms around his neck. "Oh, daddy. How could I have been so foolish?"

"Sweetheart, if there's one thing you aren't, it's foolish. What's the problem?"

"Zeke."

His heart hammered. Saying the wrong thing could drive a wedge through them. She was about to have his grandchild and Veezie was right. If he had to get along with Zeke, to protect his relationship with Gracie, then he had no choice but to hold his tongue—a tough feat without divine intervention. "Would you like to talk about it?"

"Daddy, he shouldn't have done it."

Shep gnawed the inside of his cheek, and waited for his daughter's explanation.

"He had no right to make the announcement at the dinner

table."

"Forgive me, honey, but I don't understand why you're so upset. I assume you love the guy, and want this as much as he does."

"Daddy, I told Zeke from the beginning I wasn't in love with him, and yet he was insistent that in time I'd learn to love him."

"And did you?" Shep swallowed hard, waiting for her answer.

"No. I realized shortly after I agreed to marry him that I couldn't and I told him, but he wouldn't listen. He had a doctor come do a blood test without telling me what it was for. Not only that, but he got the marriage license without my knowledge."

"It sounds as if you're saying he planned this whole shebang without your consent."

"That's exactly what I'm saying. After I began having the dreams, I knew there was no way I could ever marry Zeke. I'm in love with Garth and he's in love with me."

"Gracie, do you feel okay? You're acting peculiar."

"Daddy, please don't laugh, but I don't believe Garth's dead."

Tears filled his eyes. "Oh, honey. You're in denial. Garth can't come back. We went to his funeral. Don't you remember?"

She shrugged. "I don't want to talk about it. Let's go eat."

He scooped her up in his arms. "I'd almost forgotten the reason I came up here. I've suddenly developed an appetite."

Shep eased his daughter down in a chair and pushed her up to the supper table.

Veezie said, "What happened to Ze—"Shep gave her a stern look, causing her to leave the sentence hanging in mid-air.

"It's okay, Daddy. We might as well get it out in the open." Gracie tucked her napkin in the neck of her blouse. "Veezie, Zeke's gone."

"Should we hold supper for him?"

"No. What I mean is, he's *gone*. Really gone. For good."

"I don't understand. Are you saying the wedding is off?"

"Yes. He gathered his things and left shortly after taking me upstairs at noon."

"Oh, Gracie, I should've checked on you this afternoon. I had no idea. We all thought he was upstairs with you." She clamped her hand over her mouth. "Sorry. We don't have to talk about it."

"It's okay, I don't mind. Oh, Veezie, you should've seen his face when he stormed out of my room. He looked like a madman. I didn't know he had such a temper."

Flint and Shep exchanged befuddled glances when she giggled, showing no signs of remorse.

Shep said, "Honey, are you sure you're alright?"

"Alright? Daddy I don't know when I've been better. I have a lot to look forward to." She rubbed her belly. "Before Zeke left, he said he thought I was a candidate for the loony bin. Truth is, I was loony the night I let him kiss me. What was I thinking?" She glanced at her father and winced. "Oops! Sorry, Daddy."

Shep kept an eye on his daughter throughout the evening meal. He glanced Flint's way and frowned. Flint returned a slight nod, which Shep took as a sign the doctor understood his concern.

He'd never seen his daughter in such a state. She flitted from one subject to another, at times not finishing a sentence before starting a new one. Her hand gestures and animated expressions were so uncharacteristic, Shep was frightened. His soft-spoken, reserved Gracie had never been the giggly sort, and tonight she appeared giddy. Almost childlike. He watched as she downed two full plates of food.

She said, "The desserts look so good, I'm having trouble deciding between them, so I'll have a piece of both. Since you've all finished, Veezie would you mind calling the kids to the table?"

Flint pushed his chair back. "It's good Thanksgiving comes but once a year. It was just as good the second time around, but if I ate like this often, I wouldn't be able to fit through the door."

Shep agreed, then stood and motioned for Flint to follow him out to the veranda.

Pacing back and forth, Shep said, "Flint, I'm worried."

"Worried? Seriously? Frankly, I'd think you'd be relieved. I was happy to hear Gracie say the engagement was off. I'll have to tell you, Shep, I didn't feel good about that relationship. The fellow got under my skin the first time I met him."

"That's not it. I was thrilled to find out she wasn't marrying the chump. There's another problem."

"If you're referring to her sudden emotional turnaround, I think she's trying hard to keep from ruining Thanksgiving for all of us, so she's pretending everything's peachy. I have a feeling she'll have a long crying spell when we're gone."

"I wouldn't argue with your prognosis as a rule, doctor, but it's not her lack of tears that bothers me. Flint, she has it in her head Garth's coming back."

"What? Coming back? Surely, she's not serious."

"She's very serious. Claims he's alive."

"Whew! That *is* a problem. Shep, I don't know much about psychotherapy, but there's a doctor in Tuscaloosa, who specializes in it. Though it can be traced to the 1800's, it's still considered a rather new field. Not many doctors are equipped to treat problems having to do with the mind. I'd refer you, but Gracie would have to wait until after the baby is born to make a trip."

"If you're talking about sending her to Bryce's Hospital for the Insane, nothing doing. She's not crazy, Flint. She's just—" He bit his lip. "Well, I don't know what her problem is, but I don't want some quack messing with her head."

"Dr. Tomlin is no quack, I'll assure you, but I wasn't suggesting she be committed. My opinion is that she's going through denial and it's because she wants so much for Garth to see his baby. That being the case, those thoughts are likely to pass after the baby comes and she once again faces the truth. I wouldn't worry too much about it. I wouldn't turn it into a big deal. Arguing with her will cause stress she doesn't need."

"Thanks, Flint. I hope you're right." His body quivered. "It's getting chilly out here. Let's go back inside."

Veezie followed the sound of the giggles and found the children seated on the library floor with a board game. Her heart swelled, seeing her beautiful little sister, Callie, toss her head, slinging back long blonde ringlets. If she hadn't known before that the kids Harper and Flint adopted were her blood kin, there'd be no question now—now that Emerald was a carbon copy of Callie. She stooped down and said, "Looks like you girls are having fun."

Maddie said, "We're playing Uncle Wiggily and Belle's winning."

"Well, you need to wash up for supper. Where's Ludie?"

Shoulders lifted to a chorus of "dunno." Callie said, "I think she's mad about something. She ran out of the house at lunch and didn't eat her dessert. May I have hers if she doesn't want it tonight?"

Maddie shrugged. "She's probably at her friend's house. She goes there a lot."

Veezie shook her head. "No, she left to come home several hours ago. I'm sure she's in her room. Would you please run upstairs and tell her the adults are finished and it's time for you kids to eat?"

Harper and Veezie cleared the empty plates, and made room for the three girls to sit around the table, while Gracie finished the last bite of her pie.

Veezie said, "Maddie, did you call Ludie to supper?"

"She's not in her room. Maybe she's still at her friend's house."

Veezie swallowed hard. “Has anyone seen Ludie since noon?”

The nodding heads and peculiar glances confirmed her suspicions. Her lip trembled. “Oh no.”

Gracie screamed. “She’s run away, hasn’t she? She has. I know it. And it’s all my fault.”

Shep said, “Calm down, sweetheart. It isn’t good for you to upset yourself this way. She couldn’t have gone far. We’ll find her.”

“But Veezie said Ludie left the old man’s cabin around one-thirty this afternoon, saying she was coming back home. She wouldn’t have stayed out past dark, unless she didn’t intend to come back. Oh, Daddy, if anything happens to her, I’ll never forgive myself.”

“Honey, you can’t blame yourself. You had nothing to do with it.”

“Yes, I did. She tried to tell me Zeke was not who he pretended to be, but I wouldn’t listen. I’m sure when he announced we were going to get married, she made plans to leave. We’ve got to find her.”

Veezie said, “No, Gracie, if anyone is to blame, it would be me. I can’t believe I didn’t see this coming. I thought it peculiar the way Ludie’s attitude suddenly changed while we were at the cabin. One minute she was ranting about Zeke, then in a split second, he wasn’t so bad and she was ready to come back to Nine Gables. I should’ve known it was an act. Looking back, I now understand why she was so insistent I stay and visit with George.”

Flint said, "No one's to blame. And your father's right, Gracie. You can't afford to let this upset you. We'll find her."

"How can I not get upset, knowing she's wandering alone in the dark, scared and lonely? We have no idea where she went."

"The first place I think we should look is George's cabin."

"But you said she left there before you did."

"True, but since she has nowhere to go, she may be trying to convince George to let her move in with him."

"Do you really think so, Veezie? Oh, I hope you're right. Please, someone . . . go see if she's there and let her know Zeke's gone and there'll be no wedding."

Flint spoke up. "Harper and I will go. Veezie, you and Shep have a baby to tend to and besides, Gracie needs you. Try to keep her from stressing. If we aren't back before bedtime—"

Veezie nodded and ushered them out the door. "Don't worry, we'll take good care of Lucas and Callie."

"Thanks, but I haven't even asked where the cabin's located."

Harper grabbed him by the hand. "I know exactly where it is. I once lived here, remember?"

Chapter Thirty

The doctor pulled a weather-worn envelope from his jacket pocket and handed to the patient in 217. “Take a look. Housekeeping found this letter in Private Graham’s tattered uniform, and stuck it in a drawer. I was just made aware of it this morning.”

The soldier glanced at the name on the envelope, then let it fall on the bed. “Thanks, but I’ll pass. I’m not in the habit of reading another man’s mail.” The irony of his statement made him chuckle. “Funny, huh, doc? Truth is, I have no idea what my habits are. I can only hope I never stooped so low.”

“Sir, please. I can’t help you if you don’t work with me. Take a look at the return address. The first part of the town’s name is smudged. Something Creek, Alabama. We could get an Alabama map and trace all the towns located near creeks and hopefully, something will spark a memory for you.”

“I know you’re trying to help, doc, but how could I possibly recognize the name of a town when I have no recollection of ever having lived in Alabama?”

“Well, maybe this will help. The letter is signed, Gigi.”

"Oh? And that's supposed to mean something?"

"Yes. I assume she's your . . . Private Graham's wife."

"Or his friend? You have no way of knowing, do you?" Norm reached for the pitcher and poured a glass of water.

"Not yet. That's what we're trying to establish. The records indicate Private Graham's body was sent to a mortuary in Geneva, Alabama. However, it seems odd, since that isn't the return address on this letter."

"Simple, Sherlock. The Gigi dame wasn't his wife. They didn't live together." He placed the water glass back on the bedside table, then wiped his mouth with the back of his hand.

"That's one theory. But I'm sure you're aware of the flock of soldiers swarming to the altar in the last few hours before being deported. If the Private married recently, it's conceivable his address didn't have time to change before he was killed."

"And the other theory?"

The doctor's expression softened and his eyes twinkled. "Another possibility is that Private Graham's body never made it back to Alabama."

"What are you saying?"

"I'm saying he may now be lying in a hospital. In Room 217."

The envelope sailed to the floor, and Norm bellowed, "I've had enough of this. I'm telling you, I'm not that Graham fellow."

"Take it easy, soldier. I understand you're frustrated, but I'm only trying to help you find your way home." An uncomfortable silence settled over the stark white room. The doctor moseyed over to the window and stared out. “Looks like we might get another shower this afternoon. I suppose I can count on it, since my umbrella is in the car.”

Norm relaxed, convinced he’d won and the interrogation was over, at least for the time being. Then, tugged by guilt, he muttered what he hoped would be construed as an appropriate apology. “Doc, I’m sorry I had no right to be short with you. It’s not that I don’t appreciate your efforts, but sometimes I get the feeling I’m being coerced into accepting a life that belongs to someone else. All I want is to get my own life back.”

The doctor strolled back over and stood by the bed. “Maybe you’re right, soldier. Maybe you aren’t Private Graham. All I ask is you not be so quick to turn a deaf ear as we explore the possibilities.”

Frustrated that he’d opened the door once again to a subject he didn’t wish to discuss, Norm rolled his eyes. “I feel as if I’m being brainwashed to believe a lie, but go ahead. I’m listening.”

“That’s good enough for me.” He picked the envelope from off the floor and pulled out a letter. “The sender ends it with, ‘All my love, Your Gigi.’” He thrust the letter toward the patient. “Tell me, soldier—knowing you suffer from amnesia, how can we be sure this letter doesn’t belong to you?”

Attempting to appear cooperative, Norm reached for the letter, glared at the signature, then handed it back to the doctor. “Simple. My wife’s name is Grace. Not Gigi.”

The doctor’s lip curled. “Soldier, don’t you find it a bit

ludicrous that you'd know your wife's name, but not your own?"

Norm gnashed his teeth together to keep the angry thoughts from tumbling out, though his efforts were in vain. "Ludicrous, you say? Funny, you should use that word. Frankly, doctor, I find the whole situation ludicrous, but that revelation doesn't get us any closer to the truth, now does it? I can't explain how I know my wife's name is Grace, any more than I can explain why I don't know my own."

"If you're interested, I'll tell you what I think."

"Shoot."

"I think you dreamed her up."

The hairs on the back of Norm's neck bristled. "Not up but about."

The doctor's brows meshed together. "I'm not following you."

"You think I dreamed her up. I didn't dream her *up*, but I do dream *about* my sweet Grace. She's in my dreams every night." He gave a dismissive shrug. "Go ahead and laugh. I understand your skepticism, but I'm telling you, she's as real to me at night as you are standing here in my room today." His heart pounded. If there hadn't been ample evidence to declare him insane before now, Norm had just given the doctor a sufficient reason to put him away forever.

Relieved that the doctor refrained from either laughing or calling for restraints, Norm's muscles slowly relaxed. He was tired of the anger boiling inside him and the feeling to continuously be on the defensive. He needed someone to listen to him. If he couldn't trust his doctor, who could he trust?

The doctor's lips pursed. "Interesting. Perhaps we've just opened an important door."

"Seriously?"

"Absolutely. Dreams can sometimes unlock a lot of mysteries. Why don't we talk about what you and your wife discuss in those dreams and see what we can learn?"

"I'd like that. Mostly, we talk about someone named Mercy."

"Fascinating. So who is this Marcy?"

"Not Marcy. Mercy." He closed his eyes and tried to recall what it was he and Grace discussed to no avail. "It's so frustrating. Our conversations are crystal clear in the middle of the night, but as soon as I wake up, it's fuzzy. I can still picture Grace, but I can never pull Mercy into focus. I'm not even sure if she's an adult or a child."

"So you have no idea who she might be?"

"None. But I have a feeling we have a daughter."

"A daughter? Hmm . . . certainly every thought is worth considering. Agreed?"

"Absolutely."

"Then let's consider another option. Have you thought of the possibility you may have a wife in the States and . . . say, a girlfriend back in St. Lo, France?"

His back stiffened. "That's crazy."

"I'm not saying you do. Everything at this point is just a piece in a puzzle. If one piece doesn't fit, we'll try another angle, or choose a different piece until something clicks. I'm sure you're aware that 'merci' is French for 'thank you.' It's not uncommon for lonely soldiers to find them a cute little French girl for the price of a chocolate bar." He winked. "Maybe 'merci,' was a word your, shall we call her your secret interlude, repeated to you often? I agree it's far-fetched, but it's one theory for how a wife named Gigi and a side-line with a name like Merci, might transform into Grace and Mercy." He attempted to hide his smile. "Forgive me for saying so, but if my theory proves correct, I'd say you'll be in need of both grace *and* mercy, and lots of it when you get home."

Norm hadn't noticed the nurse standing near the door, but spun his head around when he heard her snicker. "I don't know why you people find this so amusing."

The doctor's smile faded to a frown. "Sorry, I meant no offense. I'm just trying to help you make sense of it all."

"Well, so far, you aren't succeeding. I suppose you also have an explanation for why I'd dream up a name like Grace if my wife's name is Gigi?"

"Not an explanation, but a possible theory. Are you interested in hearing?"

He shrugged. "Why not? I have nowhere to go."

"What if there was something weighing heavily on your mind at the time you were hit—possibly a disturbing letter from your wife, Gigi, concerning a grace period on a note due?"

Norm rolled his eyes. "I can't see how these fairytales are gonna help. My wife's name is Grace. Period. Get it?"

As if he hadn't heard a word, the doctor continued. "Just suppose you were lying on the ground, scared and bleeding, with your dead buddy next to you. What thoughts would be flitting through your head? I have an idea you'd be wondering what Gigi would do if you didn't make it? Would she lose the house? Maybe you were thinking, 'Can't die. Gotta help Gigi meet the grace period. Grace period—Gigi—grace period—Gigi, Grace. Gigi, Grace.' When you awoke from the coma, Grace could've been your final thought, and in your confused state, you called Gigi, Grace."

"You're really reaching, now, aren't you? That's absurd and you know it."

Martha poked a thermometer in his mouth and picked up his arm to check his pulse.

He grumbled, "Nurse, why do you keep cramming this confounded thing in my mouth?" His garbled words drew a smile from Martha, who made no attempt to answer. She withdrew the glass probe and scribbled something on a clipboard.

He muttered a quick apology, not so much for Martha's sake, who never took him too seriously, but to soothe the deep lines forming on the doctor's forehead. "Pay no attention to my rants. I know you want to help. But why is it, doc, I can remember how to put on my pants, comb my hair and brush my teeth, yet I can't remember who I am or who taught me how to do these simple tasks?"

"I understand your frustration, soldier, but be patient and I'm positive it'll get better in time. You're shell-shocked. Confusion is very common among soldiers who've been in combat, and especially after being in a prolonged comatose state." His lip curled in a slight smile. "I admit my measly attempt to come up with a theory defied logic, but the more we talk it out, the closer we're likely to come to finding the truth."

Martha said, "Pardon me for interrupting. I'm not sure if it's worth sharing, but I have my own thoughts about this illusive woman whom Norm refers to as Grace."

The doctor grinned. "Hey, let's hear it. It can't be any dumber than what I came up with."

"Don't count on it," Norm mumbled. "I've heard it, already."

Martha wrung her hands, and hesitated, but at the doctor's insistence, she forged ahead. "Doctor, I told Norm the chaplain visited him daily while he was in a coma and Pastor Mike always ended his prayers with, 'Thank you, Lord for your Grace and Mercy.'"

The doctor snapped his fingers. "Well, of course. That's it. Nurse, why didn't you mention it earlier?"

She dropped her head. "I wasn't sure it made sense."

"Why, it makes perfect sense. Don't you get it, soldier? Your subconscious picked up on the repetition of those two words, since it was the last thing you heard every day for months. Hey, I know you're still confused, but I believe we're closer to an answer than we've been thus far. Sleep on it, and tomorrow if you're ready, we'll make a phone call."

Minutes before time for a shift change, Norm rang for the nurse. "Martha, isn't it getting time for you to go home?"

"Actually, I'm off the clock now. I was about to leave. However, if you need me, I'll be happy to stay."

"Thanks. I do need you. I want you to help me get out of here."

"So you want to sit in the hall?"

"No. I'm leaving and I'll need a ride."

"What?" Her eyes widened. "I can't let you walk out of here, Norm. You haven't been discharged."

"What d'ya mean? Would I be leaving if I hadn't been discharged? Now, will you take me to the train depot or do I need to call a cab?"

She winced. "Norm, I don't know. I'd need to check with the doctor and he's left already."

"Go ahead. Call him. But don't take too long, because I have a train to catch and if we wait, I may have to stay in the depot all night. I don't think the doc would approve. Come on, Martha. You said you'd help me."

"Why did the doctor decide to discharge you? Did he make the call already? Do you know who you are?"

"Hey, slow down and stop worrying. I'll be fine. I'm sure the doctor will attempt to answer all your questions tomorrow."

"But where will you go? You can barely walk, even with crutches. You need help, Norm."

"I'm going home, wherever home is—home to Grace and Mercy. I'll crawl if I have to, but I'd be mighty grateful if you'd drive me to the depot. If you aren't willing to help me, just say so."

Martha sighed. "Of course, I'll help you."

Chapter Thirty-One

Wandering through the dense woods with no cabin in sight, Flint said, "Honey, are you sure we're going in the right direction? Seems to me we've been going in circles."

Harper shined the flashlight ahead. "It was easy to find in the daylight, but everything looks different at night." Then pointing, she squealed. "Look, Flint. I see it."

The dried leaves rustled under their feet as they hurried toward the cabin.

"Who's out there?" George yelled, peeking his head out the door.

"George, it's me, Harper."

He slung the door open. "Land sakes, chile, what you doing out here this time o' night? And who's with ya'?" He squinted. "That you, Doc?"

"It's me, George."

"Well, I Suwannee, it's good to see you two. Come on in and get outta the cold. I'll pull you up a chair."

"No need," Harper said. "George, is she here?"

"Veezie? No sugar, she left nigh an hour or two ago. I don't recollect exactly what time it was."

"I mean Ludie."

"Ludie?" His voice cracked. "No. No, Lawdy, please tell me Ludie ain't gone missin'."

"Don't fret, George. I'm sorry we had to upset you, but I was hoping we'd find her here."

"Hold on and I'll get my cane. I'm gonna find her. Po' little thing, I knew she was all tore up over . . . well, it don't make no never mind now. All that matters is we find her."

Harper said, "George, we know why she left. What Ludie doesn't know, is Zeke has moved out and there's not going to be a wedding. The best way you can help is to stay here and pray while Flint and I go looking for her."

Traipsing back through the woods to Nine Gables, Flint said, "Hon, I have no idea where to begin. You think like a girl. Where would you go if you were Ludie?"

She grimaced. "I'm afraid I was never as daring as Ludie. Perhaps we should ask Veezie. Those two are like two peas in a pod. Maybe she can give us something to go on."

Veezie met them at the door. "Did you find her?"

"Not yet, but we will," Harper said, trying to catch her breath.

"Check the bus station. Gracie said Ludie has a little money and I have a feeling she'll use it to get out of town."

Flint glanced at Harper and winked. "And where would you

go, Veezie, if you were thirteen and wanted to run away?"

"At thirteen I didn't consider consequences. I acted on impulse. So, I would've taken any money I could scrape up and bought a ticket leaving town. It wouldn't have mattered where I was going."

Harper grabbed Flint by the hand. "Let's go. Thanks, Veezie."

The man at the ticket counter was confident there'd not been a young girl boarding a bus all day. He insisted he would've remembered. Claimed he could count on one hand the tickets sold all day.

Outside the station, Flint put his arm around his wife and pulled her close. "Hey, don't look so glum. We're gonna find her. What about her friends? Maybe she's spending the night with a girlfriend."

Harper shook her head. "Not a chance. Gracie said she spent every spare minute at her friend's cabin, who turned out to be George, although Gracie wasn't aware who it was until tonight."

"Why don't we ride around town and ask anyone we see on the streets if they've seen her?"

When they rounded the corner, Harper yelled. "Stop. There's a man walking his dog. Let's ask him if he's seen her."

"About thirteen, you say?" He scratched his head. "Why you looking for her? She in some kinda trouble?"

Harper grabbed his sleeve. "Have you seen her or not?"

"Well, maybe I did . . . and maybe I didn't." He jerked his arm. "But I ain't gotta tell you nothing. You got no call to holler at me."

She closed her eyes and moaned. "You're right. I'm sorry. She's just a little girl, and we're worried about her. Please tell me if you've seen her."

"Well . . .I ain't too good at judging ages, but I was at the train depot earlier to pick up a package, and a girl I reckon to be about that age came in. Can't say if she stayed or not. I remember thinking she looked a mite scared. But don't go by me. Shucks, she coulda been twenty or twenty-five. At my age, ever'body looks like a kid."

Chapter Thirty-Two

Martha squeezed the steering wheel until her knuckles turned white. She stopped in front of the train depot.

Norm leaned over and pecked her on the cheek. "Thanks for the ride. You're a jewel."

Her lip quivered. "I don't know what to call you anymore."

"What's wrong with Norm?"

"Because it's not your name. We know that now."

He gave a light-hearted chuckle. "It beats, 'Hey you?'"

Tears rolled down both sides of her face. "Please let me help you."

"I know you mean well, but if I can't make it from the car to the train by myself, then I might as well lie down and die here on the sidewalk. I have to do this. Please, understand, Martha. I've got to find out who I am. Once I find my way home, I know everything will begin to fall into place."

"Will you let me hear from you?"

"You betcha. You've been swell. Take care, doll face. And thanks for everything." Norm opened the car door, and reached for his crutches. When he stood, he dropped a crutch and fell.

Martha jumped out, ran around and extended her hand.

His face scrunched into a frown. "Get back in the car. I don't need your help."

"Oh, Norm, please don't do this."

His voice quaked. "People are watching. You're embarrassing me. Just leave me be."

Her eyes welled with tears, seeing him struggle to maneuver the crutches.

He managed to stand and attempted a weak smile. "Stop worrying, nurse. Your patient has received his discharge papers."

"Do you have the list?"

"I do. Thank you for getting it for me."

"But if the families of those soldiers didn't open the caskets, what do you expect to find?"

"I expect to find out how many dog tags were switched. You and the doctor seem convinced Garth Graham's and Norman Kelly's were the only mistake made, but I'm confident there were others caught in the mix-up."

"Norm, I didn't remove the dog tags, but I can't fault the nurse who did. There were a dozen soldiers brought in the same night you were admitted. Most of them had severe burns on their bodies. I understand why a nurse might've felt the need to remove the tags if the metal was adhering to the raw skin until the wounds could be bandaged. But you act as if she threw them all in a pile with no regard to which soldier each belonged to. That's not what happened. I'm sure of it. We're trained professionals, but anyone can make a mistake, especially when faced with the chaos of that night. In spite of everyone's best efforts, we still lost four men. That's hard to take."

"I'm not placing blame on anyone. But somewhere an unknown soldier lies beneath a tombstone that has my name engraved on it. I have to know what that name is. When I find it, I'll be home. I figure since there were only four men who died the day we were brought to the hospital, and I know for sure the real Norman Kelly was one of them, I only have a few calls to make before finding where I belong. Mr. and Mrs. Kelly confirmed I'm not their son and the letter from a woman named Gigi is confirmation enough to convince me I'm not that Graham fellow. I'll stop in Virginia where Pvt. Nolan's body was sent. Nolan doesn't sound right, but how can I be sure? If I need to look further, I'll travel to Birmingham. If I have no luck there, I'll go on to Navarre Beach, Florida, near Pensacola, where Colonel Andrews was sent."

"Does Andrews sound familiar?"

He shrugged. "Not really. Norm is the only thing that sounds right to me, and we know that's not my name. Somewhere, Grace is waiting for me. I have to find her and let her know I kept my promise."

"Oh, Norm. Why wouldn't you go talk to Gigi Graham first, just to make sure? The return address had a double name, ending in the word 'Creek.' Shouldn't be hard to find, since I assume it's in the general vicinity of Geneva, Alabama where the body was shipped. I'm guessing the address on the envelope is a small community with no mortuary."

He shook his head. "You still don't get it, do you? I'm looking for Grace, not some grieving widow named Gigi."

When Martha heard the train approaching the depot, she threw her arms around his neck. "Take care, my friend. I pray you find the answers you're seeking."

His knees wobbled when he tried to lift his hand to wave goodbye.

****

Martha drove back to her apartment, crawled in bed and cried herself to sleep.

When she arrived at the hospital the following morning, the doctor met her in the corridor. "Martha, I don't know how to tell you this, but our patient in 217 has disappeared."

"Disappeared?" Her heart hammered. "I don't understand."

"Neither do I, but I went in his room early this morning to let him know we got a match on the fingerprints."

"Fingerprints? What fingerprints?"

"Didn't I mention I'd sent for a match? It's never been necessary since the dog tags are sufficient identification, but because they were removed, I sent in a request. We got it. Now, I have no idea how to contact him. Of all the hare-brained stunts, what was he thinking? The night nurse said he wasn't in his room when she got here, and she assumed he'd been discharged. Can you imagine? Discharged? I felt like discharging her for incompetency. She should've known better and given me a call."

"Uh . . . I don't know what to say."

"I'm sorry, Martha. I dreaded having to give you the news. I know you've grown quite fond of him. If only you'd been on the floor instead of that irresponsible nurse, it would never have happened."

She swallowed hard. "But . . . but I can understand why she would've thought he'd been discharged. The nurse knew you'd sent for the Kelly's to come get their son. However, she wasn't on duty when they came, so she would've had no way of knowing he didn't go home with them."

"I hadn't thought of that. I suppose I owe her an apology. I can't imagine he'll get far in the shape he's in, though. What a shame." He blew out a lungful of air. "Take a look at the results."

The doctor placed his hand on her shoulder. "You're white as a ghost, Martha. I can see this has been a shock to you. It wasn't what you expected, was it?"

She murmured. "No."

"I was stunned also, but it's a match. Why don't you take the day off? We can handle things for one day without you."

"Thank you, doctor. Maybe I will." How could she admit she drove Norm to the train depot? Why blame herself. He lied to her. When she questioned his leaving, he specifically told her that he'd been discharged. Or did he? She popped her hand against her forehead. No, he never lied. He simply said, "Would I be leaving if

I hadn't been discharged?" The answer was 'yes.' He would. And she had foolishly aided in his departure.

If the doctor had only mentioned fingerprinting, she was sure Norm would've stayed. And if only she'd known he wasn't discharged, she would never have helped him leave. All hindsight, and hindsight was of no value now that he was gone.

Oh, my precious Norm, will you ever find your way home?

Chapter Thirty-Three

After several milk runs along the way, Ludie was the only passenger to step off when the train pulled up to the depot in Birmingham, Alabama. Never had she felt so alone. Her heart pounded. If only she could buy another ticket and keep going, at least until daylight.

She walked inside and glanced around. There were only five people inside. A young couple who were so in love, they wouldn't have noticed if Frankenstein had stomped in, the elderly security guard napping at the ticket counter, a man sitting near the door with a newspaper covering his face—she assumed he was crippled, judging from the crutches near him—and a grungy-looking hobo lying on a slatted bench. Eyeing an empty bench across the room, she walked over and sat her bundle on one end to use as a pillow. If she could sleep the night away, things would look brighter in the morning. She thought of Uncle George and hoped he wouldn't worry. But he would. She knew he would. As soon as she could come up with a plan, she'd write and let him know she was okay. And she *would* come up with a plan.

Plenty of kids her age ran away. They made it okay. She would to, although tonight, when things seemed so scary, was no time to think about it. Tomorrow, she'd be able to think clearly and her situation would look much brighter. Now, all she wanted to do was close her eyes tight and shut out everything around her. She thought of how Mrs. Ward prayed about everything. But then God knew Mrs. Ward. She was about the finest Christian lady to be found anywhere. Ludie wasn't at all sure God would know a thirteen-year-old girl, especially a runaway orphan nobody wanted, and even if he did, what had she ever done for him? No reason he should want to help her.

Ludie awoke feeling something rubbing against her leg. Without opening her eyes, she swatted, then feeling flesh, she jerked her head up to see the hobo sitting beside her, grinning a toothless grin. "Get away from me, you creep. What do you think you're doing?"

"Be nice to me and I'll be nice to you."

She jumped up and ran across the room. Maybe it was time to try praying. Might not help, but it was worth a try. "God, can you hear me? I'm scared. I don't reckon I ever been so scared in my whole life. I ain't got no right to ask—" She tried to think of something spiritual to say, but all that came out was, "I'd be obliged, Lord, if you'd knock his lights out."

The hobo ran after her and grabbed her by the arm. He whispered, "You little wench, I could get you in a whole lot of trouble. Running away, ain't you? Didja know the cops lock up runaways? It's a fact. All I gotta do is go tell the guard and you'll be eating bread and water in jail for the next five years. Zat what you want? Huh?"

"You lying. They won't lock me up." She glanced around the room, hoping to see God show up.

"Okay, have it yo' way. I'm going up there and tell the guard. Want me to? Or you want to go with me? I'll call us a taxi and me and you'll get outta here, 'fore anybody misses you."

"Why are you doing this? I ain't never done nothing to you. Please don't tell nobody." She turned and the crippled man was standing beside her, with his crutches under his arms.

"What's going on?"

Ludie's pulse raced. If she told, would he turn her in? She'd almost rather be jailed for five years than leave with the creep.

The hobo said, "Mind yo' own business, crip. Me and the little lady having us a conversation."

"The conversation just ended. Get out of here and leave her alone."

"And who's gonna make me, crip?"

Ludie's throat tightened when the crutches dropped to the floor with a loud thud.

The man stood, unaided. "That would be me."

The hobo took the first punch and missed. Then the crippled man drew back and socked him in the nose, causing blood to squirt like a water pistol.

“Never mind, God,” she whispered. “I got me some help.”

When the crippled man leaned forward to pick up his crutches, he fell on his face. She picked up a crutch and proceeded to clobber the hobo with it. He yelled obscenities while blocking his face with both arms. Then she reached out a hand and helped the crippled fellow to his feet. He had such a kind face, she almost felt as if she knew him.

The ruckus woke the guard. “What’s going on over there?”

Planting her hands on her hips, Ludie blurted, “That hobo was messing with me and my uncle made him stop.”

“Uncle, my foot, you lying little wench,” the hobo yelled. “She’s a stinkin’ runaway and she tried to kill me with that crutch.”

The guard turned to the crippled man. “’Zat so, mister? She with you?”

The tall stranger leaned on one crutch. Glaring at the hobo, his face distorted. He mumbled, “Yeah. I reckon that’s right. The girl’s with me.”

Ludie threw her shoulders back and grinned. “I told you, so. Didn’t I tell you? Me and him, we like two peas in a pod.” She ran over and grabbed him by the hand and whispered, “Thanks, unc!”

The guard cocked his head and with a smirk, said, “You ain’t lying, are you, mister? She’s just a kid. You sure you ain’t pickin’ her up? She didn’t buy no ticket.”

Ludie thought it worth a try. “My uncle told me to meet him here. He’s gonna buy my ticket.”

The guard scratched his head. “So where you going?”

“Same place he’s going, naturally.”

Satisfied, the guard turned to the hobo. “Get outta here, you bum, and don’t let me catch you hanging around the depot again.”

Ludie sat down on the seat beside the crippled man, and feigned a smile at the guard, who didn’t appear completely convinced, but walked off without probing further.

She whispered. “Thanks for rescuing me from that creep. I was scared to death.”

“Yeah, well . . . I probably should’ve kept my mouth shut.”

“You couldn’t.”

“Sure, I could have. What makes you think I couldn’t?”

“Because you’re too nice.”

“That’s crazy. You don’t even know me. For all you know, you might’ve been safer with him.”

She shuddered. “Ain’t so, and you know it. Now, you gonna buy me that ticket or not?”

“Look, kid. You need to go home.”

“Ain’t got no home. I’m an orphan.”

“So where’ve you been living?”

“In an orphanage, but I can’t go back. Long story.”

“Well, you can’t go with me, and that’s that.”

“That’s too bad. I reckon we might both be in trouble if the cops find out you just picked me up here and left me.”

“Picked you up? Are you loco? That sounds like blackmail to me. You wouldn’t!”

"I wouldn't want to, that's for sure."

He ran his fingers through his hair and groaned. "Okay, so I'll buy you a ticket. Where you want to go?"

"Wherever you're going."

"Nothing doing. I can't have you tagging after me."

"You've gotta let me go, mister. Just until I can get far enough away they'll never find me.."

"Kiddo, for all you know, I could be a serial killer. You can't just take up with the first man who comes along."

"I didn't. You were second."

The man heaved a deep sigh. "Just because I rescued you from a bum is no sign you can trust me. Another bum would've done the same thing I did, if he wanted to get you to go with him. You're too trusting to be out on the streets alone."

"Well, ain't that the truth. And you couldn't leave a poor little penniless orphan to wander the streets—all alone—in hog-killing weather." She picked up her bindle stick and grinned. "So to be safe, I'll be stickin' with you."

"What makes you so sure you'll be safe with me?"

"You remind me of someone I once knew. He was a lot heavier than you. Well, not that he was fat, but he was bigger. Not skinny like you. And he didn't have a mustache, but he was good like you."

"I can tell you were fond of the man. Was he your father?"

Ludie pondered the question. Garth Graham was the closest thing to a father she'd ever had. Couldn't she choose? Her head bobbed up and down. “Yep. He was my daddy, alright. But he died.”

“That’s tough kid. I’m sorry. What about your mother? Is she dead, too?”

“Dunno. She put me on a doorstep when I was born. Ain’t never laid eyes on her.”

He was quiet for several minutes. “Okay, you win. I’ll take you with me, until I have a chance to figure out what to do with you.”

“Thank you.” She reached up and hugged his neck.

“Cut it out. I’m not doing you a favor. I should turn you in and let the authorities send you back to the orphanage.”

“You want them to arrest me?”

“No one is going to arrest you for running away. You might get a good lickin’ after going back, but I’m not convinced it wouldn’t be well deserved. But I guess if you’re going to pass yourself off as my niece, I should know you’re name.”

Ludie looked down at her feet. “Uh . . . uh, my name is, uh, Clementine. Pretty, ain’t it?”

“Are you making that up?”

“That’s my name. Hope to die if it ain’t so. Why don’t you believe me?”

His lips pursed. “That’s a peculiar question. It’s not as if I don’t have reason not to believe you. You paused before answering. I thought maybe you were trying to come up with a name.”

"Nope Clementine. That's me. What's yours?"

He sucked on his bottom lip.

"Now, who's pausing. You trying to think up something?"

"Of course not. My name's Norm."

"Norm what?"

"Just Norm. That's all you need to know."

She nodded and held out her hand. "Proud to make your acquaintance, Uncle Norm."

His eyes rolled. "Clementine is a mouthful. Mind if I call you 'Peanut?'"

"Whatever suits you."

Chapter Thirty-Four

Shep sat on the edge of his daughter's bed, and pulled a handkerchief from his pocket and dried her cheeks "Sweetheart, you need to get hold of yourself. I know how disturbing this has been, but you must think of yourself and the baby."

"Oh, Daddy, how can I be calm, when Ludie's been gone for days with no word? You heard the police. The chances of finding her now are almost nil."

He leaned down and kissed her forehead. "Honey, I'm sure she's fine. I guarantee you when her money runs out and she gets hungry enough, she'll come running back. You'll see."

"No. You're wrong, Daddy. She's not coming back."

"You can't know that."

"But I do. I know *her*. And why should she come home? Daddy, she loathed Zeke, and I'm beginning to believe she may have had more reason than I even suspected. She didn't stay long enough to find out I'm not marrying him." Gracie turned to her side, buried her face in her pillow and sobbed.

Shep stood when Flint walked in to take her blood pressure.

Gracie wiped her damp face with the sheet. “Flint, there was no need in your coming, today. I know you have other patients who need your attention, and if you have time to spare, I’d rather you spend it searching for Ludie, instead of hovering over me.”

He glanced over at Shep and frowned. Loosening the cuff from her arm, he said, “Gracie, I’ll have to tell you, I’m more concerned about your blood pressure than I am where a healthy teenager has voluntarily chosen to run off to. The police are chasing every lead. There’s nothing else we can do. You’ve got to get your pressure down, and stressing over Ludie isn’t helping.”

“You’re just like Daddy. Neither of you understand.”

Flint reached in his bag and pulled out a small pill box. “Shep, I’ll be on my way, but get her to take one of these every morning and one at night for the next three days. I’ll be back and check her pressure, after she’s finished the pills.”

Shep thrust out his hand. “Thanks, doc. I appreciate your coming.”

“Anytime. If you don’t mind, I’d like to make a few telephone calls downstairs before I leave.”

Shep picked up the water pitcher, filled a glass and handed to his daughter. “Okay, young lady. You heard the doctor. Stressing is not helping you, Ludie, or my grandbaby. So from henceforth, let’s concentrate on happy thoughts.”

“If only I could, Daddy. But I can’t quit thinking about her out there alone and lonely. I’m sure she’s scared to death.”

Her father squeezed her hand. "Honey, you're judging by how you might've felt at her age. Kids like her, who have been shifted from pillar to post—"

"Kids like her? What do you mean, kids like *her*? Daddy, there are no other kids like her. Ludie is one-of-a-kind. She's precious. I hope my little girl is just like her." Gracie let out a scream, grabbed her stomach and doubled over in pain.

Shep yelled, "Flint! Come quick! I think she's going into labor."

Gracie screamed and pulled at her hair. "No, I can't go into labor. It's not time. Please, help me, Daddy. Help me."

Chapter Thirty-Five

Norm walked up to the counter and bought Peanut a ticket to Pensacola, Florida. His stomach churned. What was he thinking, allowing a little waif to travel with him?

What if she was lying and had distraught parents searching for her? Would he be arrested for aiding a juvenile? What else could he do? He couldn't leave her in the train depot. She'd be a target for every vagrant who hopped off a train in Birmingham.

His next thought made him chuckle, as he debated whether the kid or the vagrant would face the biggest challenge. The girl had spunk, for sure. She was accustomed to taking care of herself. The way she clobbered that hobo was evidence enough that she wasn't raised by doting parents.

All the way to Pensacola, Peanut's mouth didn't close. "I ain't never seen the ocean before. Ain't it the most beautiful sight in the whole world? But then, I don't reckon I'd know, since I ain't seen much of the world. But I can't believe nothing else could be this pretty. You ever seen anything prettier? The sand is so white it looks like sugar, don't it? You ever been swimming, Uncle Norm?

I been swimming, but only in the creek."

"What creek do you swim in, Peanut?"

"Ha. You ain't tricking me. You just asking so you can send me back. But it ain't gonna work. I'll die before I'll live under the same roof with that creep."

"Is he really so bad?"

"He's worse. But I don't wanna talk about it. Where you from, Uncle Norm?"

"You can drop the 'Uncle Norm.' We got passed the security guard, but there's no need to keep up the pretense."

"I like it. Makes me feel all warm inside when I say it. Like we family, ya' know? I reckon if I was told I could make one wish and one only, I'd want to wish I was part of a family. But since that's impossible, I reckon I'd be stupid to waste my wish. So I'd just wish me and you could stay together for ever and ever. Wouldn't that be swell?"

Norm hid his smile with his hand. Poor kid. He almost wished he could make the dream come true for her. Were they both crazy? He didn't know who Peanut was, but even worse, he had no idea who he was.

After departing the train, she said, "Where to now?"

Norm saw a sign advertising cars for sale across the street. "We're gonna buy a vehicle."

"Jeepers Creepers, you got that kind of money?"

"I got enough to buy a used car, and it'll be better than riding a train, trying to get around in the different towns in a cab. Come on.

Let's go car shopping."

Norm walked over and kicked the tires on a 1925 Tin Lizzie. "Yep! This'll do fine."

"Shucks, we can probably walk faster than that heap can run."

"Stop griping. It's affordable. Get in while I pay the fellow."

****

Hearing the screams coming from Gracie's room, Flint rushed upstairs and took her by the hand as she thrashed in pain.

Shep paced the floor and yelled, "Can't you see she's in agony? Don't just stand there looking at her, for crying out loud. I can do that. You gotta help her, doc. What are you waiting for?"

When Gracie shrieked in an ear-splitting cry, Shep thrust his hands over his ears. "I can't stand to see her like this. Please, do something, Flint!"

Flint placed his hand on Shep's back, and ushered him out the door of the bedroom. "The first thing I'm gonna do for her is to get you out of there. You're almost as hysterical as she is. I'm not sure which one of you needs the ether the most. Go on downstairs, sit down and drink a cup of coffee, Shep. I need to examine her and find out if she's dilated."

Shep reached up and wiped the sweat from his brow. "I'm sorry for overreacting, but seeing her groaning in pain . . . well, she looked so much like her mother, just before . . . just before Jennie died."

Gracie screamed out in pain, and Flint rushed back into the

room and slammed the door behind him.

Shep poured him a cup of coffee, sat it on the table, then paced the kitchen floor, too nervous to drink it. His heart pounded when he heard Flint descending the stairs. Meeting him halfway, he said, "How is she, Flint?"

"Well, she's beginning to dilate, but I've given her something and we just need to pray this baby doesn't get in too big a hurry to get here. Gracie needs to hold on awhile longer." His gaze shifted to the floor.

Shep said, "You aren't telling me everything, are you? What's going on?"

"Shep, you need to prepare yourself for the worst and hope for the best. Some women are made to bear children. Some are not. We'll be fortunate if I can save one of them. Double blessed if I can save both. I won't lie to you, the situation is critical." He patted his friend on the shoulder, and left the house.

Shep fell prostrate on the cold kitchen floor and cried out. "Lord, I need . . . I need—" He pounded his fist on the floor and sobbed. "Oh, Father God, I've prayed for countless others and now that I stand in the need of prayer, I can't seem to find the words." The sobs ceased and Shep began humming a hymn. Soon the words were coming from his lips as he sang, "I need thee every hour, in joy or in pain; come quickly Lord, and abide, or my life is in vain." *Yes, Lord. I do need thee every hour. And especially an hour such as this.*

He tiptoed upstairs and peeked in his daughter's room,

relieved to find her sleeping.

****

Norm stopped at a service station and bought a Gulf Coast map.

"What you trying to find, Uncle Norm?"

He mumbled, "Home."

"Jeepers, you live here near the beach? Can I live with you?" She paused and scratched her head. "You're teasing me again, aren't you? You wouldn't need a map to find your way home, so what you need a map for?"

He rustled the map and glared at her over the top of the crumpled paper. "Peanut, do your jaws ache?"

She opened her mouth wide a time or two, then shook her head. "No. Why would you think my jaws hurt?"

"Because that mouth never slows down. No more questions. I'll let you know when I find what I'm looking for."

She crossed her hands over her chest. "You don't have to get sore."

"I'm not sore, kid. I just need a little peace and quiet until I figure out what I'm going to say when I get to where I'm going." His breath quickened when his finger traced the address on the map. He'd been quite disappointed when he arrived in Lynchburg, Virginia, and a woman named Dottie opened the door. But now, he was almost glad she wasn't Grace. He loved the ocean. He sucked in the smell of the salty air. *I'm home. I'm sure of it.*

"Well, if you know where you're going, why don't you know if you'll find—" She huffed. "Never mind."

He grinned. It must've been difficult for her to stop jabbering for a few seconds, but now that he'd located his home on the map, he had to get his thoughts together. Would Grace be shocked to see him? What a silly thought. She'd be waiting for him. He knew it. How he knew it, he couldn't quite say.

Peanut crossed her arms across her chest and poked out her lip. "Jeepers, how long I gotta stay quiet?"

"What you need, kid?"

"Just wanted to know why you're laughing."

"I'm laughing because I'm alive."

She rolled her eyes. "Well, I reckon it'd be hard to do if you wuz dead. Still don't make no sense."

Chapter Thirty-Six

Norm pulled up in front of a small clapboard cottage on a bayou. What a great place to raise kids. They could fish in their own backyard.

Ludie said, “Well, ain’t you gonna get out?”

He nodded. “Yep. But I need you to stay in the car.”

“Why? I wanna get out.”

“Because I need to talk to someone. Alone.”

“I need to stretch my legs. Can I at least walk down and look at the water?”

He shrugged. “Sure. Just don’t get too close.”

“Jeepers, Uncle Norm, I’m thirteen. I’m not gonna fall in, if that’s what you’re afraid of.”

“That’s not what I’m afraid of. There are alligators in the bayou. Sometimes they crawl up on the land, and trust me, if you think you can outrun one, you’re wrong.”

She shivered. “On second thought, I’ll stay in the car.”

His pulse raced. If there was any doubt in his mind before, there was none now. How would he have known about the alligators, if this wasn't his home? "Reach in the back, Peanut, and hand me my crutches when I open the door. I may be in there for a spell, but I bought you a Little LuLu funny book. It's in the glove compartment. It should help you pass time while I'm gone."

"Swell, thanks." She grabbed the book and clutched it to her heart. "Take your time. I ain't never had my very own funny book."

Norm's throat tightened as he walked up the long walk. A boy appearing to be in his late teens answered the door.

The tall lanky kid said, "If you from a collection agency, you might as well leave now. Mama's not here, and even if she was, you'd be at the bottom of the list."

Norm swallowed hard. "You live here?"

The smart-alecky kid leaned his head out the door and pretended to look at the house number. "Yep, I'm at the right house."

"What's your name?"

"Dalton Andrews. What's yours?"

"Uh . . . Norm. Does someone name Grace live at this address?"

"Nah, you got the wrong house. Nobody lives here but me and Mama."

"Was your father . . . uh, I don't know how to ask this—"

"My ol' man's dead. Killed in the war. Say, did you know him?"

"We were in the war together. I was wounded the day he was

killed. Tell your Mother I came by and offered my condolences."

"She's walking up the sidewalk now. You can tell her yourself."

Norm turned to see a woman almost twice his age behind him. "Good afternoon, ma'am. My name is . . . well, I was telling your son I was wounded the day your husband was killed. I offer my condolences." His voice broke.

"Thank you, soldier. That means a lot." Her voice quacked. "Charles was a good man." She handed him a handkerchief and reached in her pocketbook for another. "Won't you come in?"

"No, thank you. I have . . . I have another stop to make. I hope my visit didn't upset you."

"On the contrary. Any friend of Charles' is a friend of mine. Come back any time."

He reached in his wallet and pulled out a few bills. "It isn't much, but—"

She pushed his hand away. "Keep your money. Our prayers were answered today. I've just come from the Post Office and a check I've been waiting for came in the mail." She stood on her tiptoes and kissed him on the cheek. "God bless you, soldier."

Norm drove through several small towns in Alabama. Some looked vaguely familiar, others he was certain he was seeing for the first time in his life. Driving past the Court House in Geneva, he slowed and glared up at the huge clock atop the impressive building.

"Whatcha stopping for?"

“Just trying to remember.” He scratched his head. “I do believe I’ve been here before.”

Her nose crinkled. “You don’t remember?”

He didn’t respond.

“I’ve been here lots of times. I used to live near here in a foster home, ‘til Mr. Ward died and Mrs. Ward moved away.”

“Did you like it?”

“It was okay. They were good to me. There’s a flowing well near here and it fills up a big swimming pool. In the summer, the Wards took us to Lake Geneva almost every Saturday. I asked you once, do like to swim, Norm?”

“Probably.”

She snickered. “You’re the funniest man. You don’t know if you’ve been here and you’re not sure you like to swim. You’re kidding, right?”

He grinned. “If it makes you laugh, that’s all that matters.”

She nodded, knowingly. “I knew you were pulling my leg.”

Ludie had no idea what Norm was searching for, but if he didn’t want to talk, she could abide by that. There were plenty of times she didn’t want to answer questions from nosey folks. She always stayed in the car, out of the way, when he went knocking on doors. As long as he let her go along for the ride, she’d wait until he was ready to tell her.

She gathered he was a religious man, though she didn’t pry. He always asked God’s blessings over their food and got on his knees every night and prayed. He even prayed in his sleep, but all she could ever make out were a couple of words like grace and mercy.

They traveled a lot of country roads, sometimes sleeping in the car, sometimes lying on a couple of old army blankets under the stars. Occasionally, they'd stay in a motel room and get to sleep on real beds, although most of the time it felt as if she was sleeping on the slats, the mattresses were so thin. Didn't matter. She was with Uncle Norm. All was right in her world. If only she could help lift the burden he seemed to be carrying, so he could be as happy as she was. He stopped at several houses along the way, though he never told her why—a log cabin near Holmes Creek, a big farm house at Sandy Creek, and a little shanty near Double Bridges Creek. Whatever he was looking for, he didn't find, or if he did, he didn't tell her.

"Where d'ya suppose we'll be on Christmas morning, Norm?"

"Not sure. According to the map, there's another community nearby called Flat Creek, I'd like to check out."

Chapter Thirty-Seven

"Flat Creek? No! I ain't going back. Who told you?"

"Good grief, Ludie, what's wrong with you? Who told me what?" The look on her face answered his question. "That's where the orphanage is, isn't it? Hey, Peanut, I didn't know. I promise. I'm looking for someone, and there's a possibility there may be a woman there who can help me find the information I'm seeking. But it's time you and I had a talk about your situation."

"You're gonna make me go back. That's why we're going to Flat Creek, isn't it?"

"Peanut, you've been swell not to pry, but the truth is, somewhere, there's a woman waiting for me, and I don't know where to find her."

"So you think she may be in Flat Creek?"

"Not sure. But you can believe me when I say I had no idea the orphanage was located there. However, now that I know, we'll go in together and sit down for a little talk."

"You think I ran away because I'm bad, don't you? Well, maybe I am, but I ain't going back. I mean it, Norm. I'll run away again if you take me back."

"Calm down, kid. I'm a pretty good judge of character. After sizing up the place, if I deem it unfit, I'll find you a decent place to live, and that's a promise. But you can't keep running all over the country with me."

She sobbed. "Zeke can fool you. You'll believe him. You'll think I'm making it all up."

"Zeke?"

"Yeah, that's the creep Gigi married."

"Did you say, Gigi?" He swallowed hard.

"Yeah."

"You're saying the woman who runs the orphanage recently remarried and her name is Gigi?"

"Yeah. What's wrong, Norm? You look funny. You know her?"

His breathing slowed. If this Gigi was his wife, then he had to face the truth—the doctor had been right and Grace was a figment of his dreams.

His teeth ground together. What decent widow would be remarrying so soon after burying her husband? Not the kind of woman he would've chosen. The bitter taste of bile rose to his throat. What if he really was Garth Graham and married to this Gigi woman? He hoped not. Oh, how he hoped not. His heart pounded at the possibility he'd been chasing a dream.

Rubbing his temples, he attempted to rub out the paranoid thoughts. Grace was real. Of course, she was. When he awoke from his dreams, he could see her face, hear her voice, smell her perfume, feel her in his arms. He *knew* her. If only he knew where to find her. He wiped sweat from his forehead. He'd prayed for God to show him what to do with this little runaway, but he'd also prayed for God to lead him back home. God led him here—to the orphanage—for Peanut's sake and not his. A strange coincidence, but that's all it was. "Sure. That's it."

"You talkin' to me?"

"No, kiddo. To be honest, I'm not sure who I'm talking to."

Driving into Flat Creek, Norm said, "Peanut, you'll need to show me how to get to the orphanage."

"But Uncle Norm—"

"I know what you're about to say, but I need to talk to the people who run the place. You have to trust me. I just want what's best for you."

Her bottom lip trembled. "Ever'body always thinks they know what's best for me, but nobody knows. I know what's gonna happen. You're gonna dump me and forget all about me."

"You're wrong. Even if I do feel it's for your best to grow up in the orphanage, you'll always have a special place in my heart. I could never forget you." Norm came to a crossroads. "Which way?"

Without speaking, she pointed to the left. After driving three or four miles down the road, she yelled, "Stop. Please stop."

Norm slammed on brakes. "What's wrong?"

"That little dirt road we just passed. Before you take me to Nine Gables, I need to do something. Please?"

"What's down there?"

"You keep asking me to trust you. Can't you trust me, just once?"

Norm shifted to reverse, backed up, and drove down a narrow path that looked as if it hadn't been traveled in years, and ended in front of an old shanty. "We must've taken the wrong road, Peanut. Nothing here."

Her face lit up. "That's what you think. Let's go inside." She jumped out, opened the door on the driver's side and pulled on his arm. "This is where Uncle George lives. I want you to meet him."

"You have an uncle? Well, why didn't you say so, kiddo? I would've brought you here earlier. But if the orphanage was as bad as you say, why didn't you come live with him?"

"Can't. People talk."

"What d'ya mean? Why would anyone talk about you moving in with a relative? Is he a criminal?"

She laughed out loud. "Uncle George? 'Course not. I reckon he's about the most honest, sweetest man who ever lived." She shrugged. "It's complicated."

He grabbed his crutches, but she was already steps ahead of him. She ran to the door and beat on it. "Uncle George? It's me. Let me in."

When no one answered, she opened the door and ran in. "No, no, no," she screamed. "He's . . . he's dead."

"You don't know that, sweetheart. Maybe he moved out. After, all this place is too drafty for anyone to live in."

"No. Somebody done come and took away his stuff. His clothes are missing. He's dead. I know it. He wouldn't have left. It's all my fault. I should've stayed to take care of him. He wasn't well and he depended on me." She threw herself across the old cot in the corner of the room and squalled, as if her shattered heart could never heal.

"I'm sorry, kiddo. I really am. Maybe we should go."

"Go? No. Please, not yet. Please?"

He reached over and wiped her face with his handkerchief. "I'm sorry about your uncle. I wish I could've met him."

She snubbed and sat up on the edge of the bed. "You would've liked him and he would've liked you." She glanced at a calendar hanging on the wall. "He must've died shortly after I left. The November page hasn't been torn off."

"You can't blame yourself, sweetie. You've said he was old and sickly. I'm sure you brought him a lot of joy while he was alive, just as you've brought joy into my life."

Her eyes widened. "You mean that? I brought joy to *you*?"

"Of course, I mean it. I love you, you crazy little munchkin."

She suddenly pounced up from the bed and threw her arms around him. "Oh, I love you, too, Uncle Norm."

When he attempted to pry her arms from around his neck, she held tighter. "Uncle Norm, what's the date?"

"December 23rd."

"That's what I thought. It's almost Christmas."

"Yep, a couple of days from now."

"Do we have to leave tomorrow? Can we stay here two nights? I want it to just be me and you on Christmas, here at Uncle George's. Please don't take me back to the orphanage until after we have Christmas together."

How could he deny her such a simple request? Truth be known, his heart was feeling as heavy as hers. He'd miss the little urchin. But logic told him he had no choice but to take her back where she belonged. A place where she'd be cared for. "It's a deal, kid. Two nights, but two only."

"Swell! And I have a terrific idea for Christmas morning. You play like you're giving me a present, and I'll play like I'm giving you one, too. I'll try to think of something real nice. Something I'd get you if I had the money, and you do the same. It'll be almost as good as if it was real."

"But it won't be real."

"Don't matter. It'll be fun to see what you'd give me if you *could* splurge."

"It doesn't take much to make you happy, does it?"

"Will you do it? *Please*? Will you play-like you giving me a present?"

"Yeah, kid. I'll do it. When do we exchange these make-believe gifts?"

"When we first wake up on Christmas morning. I'll give you a box and I'll put something in it to represent what I wish it was.

You can shake it, and make guesses. I've always wanted to have a box I could shake at Christmas. You ever done that? Shake a box and try to guess, I mean?"

He nodded. It was easier than admitting he didn't know.

"Of course, it won't sound like what it really is, but we'll guess anyway. And when you give up, then you open it and I'll tell you what's in that box that was thought up special, just for you."

"I think I understand."

"You give me a box and I'll shake it. But I know I'll never guess. So, then I'll open it and you tell me what it is. Won't that be fun?"

"I suppose. But what if we can't find a box big enough for the make-believe present to fit in?"

Her shoulders lifted. "It's just play-like. We'll pretend the box is as big as we want it to be."

"You're one-of-a-kind, kid."

She'd been told before there was none like her, but the way Norm said it brought a smile. He made it sound like something to be proud of.

Chapter Thirty-Eight

Veezie sat at the window in Gracie's bedroom, waiting for the mailman. Saying goodbye to Shep after Thanksgiving had been difficult, but they both understood he had an obligation to his church, and the separation would only be for a short spell. He'd return to Nine Gables for Christmas, then leave again and come back as soon as the baby arrived.

"The mail truck's here," she squealed and ran down the stairs and out the door, hoping to have a letter from her husband.

When she entered the bedroom, Gracie said, "I gather by the long face you didn't get any mail."

Veezie's brow scrunched into a frown. "No. I mean yes. No. No!"

"What's wrong, Vee?"

The wrinkles in her forehead deepened. "It can't be."

"Veezie, you're scaring me. Is something wrong with Daddy? Honey, if he needs you, please go to him. I'll be fine."

She plopped down in a nearby chair. "It's not from Shep."

"What's going on?"

"I'm not sure. Gracie, the return address is from Monroe O'Steen."

"Isn't that your father? But I thought he was dead."

"So did everyone else . . . everyone but me. I never believed the scoundrel died."

"Well, aren't you gonna read it?"

Veezie leaned her head back and closed her eyes as she held tightly to the unopened envelope. "I don't know. I can't imagine he'll have anything to say that I want to hear. He hasn't made any attempt to contact me in all these years, so why would he write me now?"

"How did he know where to locate you?"

"He didn't. He addressed it to me at Goose Hollow, and the Post Office there sent it to my address at Mt. Pleasant. I suppose Shep gave this forwarding address."

Gracie said, "Vee, I'm so sorry you had such a sad life. I can't understand why some of us are born with wonderful, loving parents who provide for our needs, and others, like you, have to suffer throughout childhood. But I'm grateful God chose to put you with my daddy. No one could possibly love you more."

A half-hearted smile slid across Veezie's lips. "You're right. Shep does love me, and that makes up for all the grief of my past." She sat up straight in the chair, and ripped the end from the envelope. "I might as well see what excuses dear ol' dad has to offer. After all, 'I can do all things, through Christ, who strengtheneth me.' There's no way Monroe O'Steen can hurt me anymore."

She unfolded the letter, written on lined paper and read aloud: *"Dear Veezie,*

After the way I treated your mama and you young'uns, I have no right to ask anything of you."

She rolled her eyes. "I knew it. He wants something. Well, where was he when I needed him?" She held the letter for several minutes before continuing.

"I have no excuses to offer for the way I treated my family. I was good at fooling everyone at church, pretending to be some sort of saint. I heard your mama died, and I reckon you have every reason to believe I'm the one who put her in the grave, from the grief I caused her. You'd be right to think such. I told myself if I went to church enough, I could fool everybody, but there were three of us who were never fooled. Me, you and God.

I know you won't believe this, but I really did love your mama, but when I was drunk, I did things to her no man has a right to do to any woman. I finally got so tired of trying to live a double life, I packed up a bag and told your mama I was gonna look for a job, but the truth is, I couldn't stay sober long enough to work. I regretted leaving, but I was a mess and finally gave up trying to straighten out my life.

Then six months ago, I was on the streets of Pensacola, panhandling, needing enough money for the next drink, when a preacher stopped and placed a silver dollar in my tin cup. We talked for about three hours, and before he left, I prayed and asked God to forgive me for all the wrongs I've done to people and to help me change my wicked ways. I'd tried to change before, but found I couldn't do it on my own. With God's help, I haven't had a drink in six months.

I have no right to ask you to forgive me, but I needed to tell you that I'm sorry I was such a no-account daddy, and if I had it to do over again, things would be different. I loved your mama and all four of you kids. I just didn't know how much until I lost you.

Yours truly,
Monroe O'Steen
(I didn't sign "Daddy," because I lost the right to call myself that, the day I walked out on you.)"

Gracie said, "I declare, if that doesn't beat all. I'm sure you'd like to give him a piece of your mind."

Veezie folded the paper. "You'd think, wouldn't you? For years, I've hated the man. I hated him because of the lies and the way he put on a show at church with that holier-than-thou attitude, when I knew what he was really like."

Gracie smirked. "I can't believe he'd have the audacity to write, after all these years. If I were you, I wouldn't give him the satisfaction of knowing I read the letter."

"But you don't understand, Gracie. It's true, my father was a drunkard, a hypocrite, an abuser and an all-around scoundrel. He didn't provide for us, but this is a letter of repentance and my God is the God of second chances." She paused. "I choose to forgive my daddy."

"You what?"

"I said I choose to forgive him."

"Oh, Vee, how can you sit there and say you forgive the man? He doesn't deserve your forgiveness."

"You ask how? Only by God's grace. As I read Daddy's letter, I recalled several years ago as I stood before the church body at Flat Creek Fellowship, with a big red letter *S* around my neck. Feeling condemned for a sin I considered unforgiveable, I confessed to the church that the letter I wore, stood for sinner." Her voice cracked. "I'll never forget how Shep looked at me with tender eyes, then pulled out a pocket knife and cut the rope and the letter fell to the floor. Remember what he said next? 'Veezie', he said, 'You're wearing the wrong letter. God has drawn the letter *F* in blood and branded it on your heart. It can't be cut off, washed off or wished off. It's permanent.' I hung my head in shame, thinking he meant the *F* stood for fornicator. But he quickly said, 'No. The *F* stands for forgiven.' I can't explain the burden that was lifted, knowing that not only had God forgiven me, but your dad, the one person on this earth that mattered most to me, chose to forgive, when I didn't deserve his forgiveness. So don't you see, Gracie? My sins were no bigger, no less than my father's.

Not only has God forgiven my father, but I choose to forgive him, also. And I suddenly feel as if a ten-pound weight has been lifted from my shoulders." She clasped the letter to her heart and sobbed. "What a wonderful Christmas present."

Chapter Thirty-Nine

Christmas Eve

Norm's throat tightened when Peanut ran into the kitchen and threw her arms around his waist. He slid the iron skillet off the eye of the wood stove and feigned a frown. "Watch it kid, can't you see I'm cooking? You want to get splattered with hot grease?"

"Don't care if I do. This is gonna be the best Christmas of my whole life, and that ain't no lie. Nothing could make me sad today. Nothing!" She lifted a shoulder. "Well, maybe one thing, but I ain't gonna dwell on it."

Her best Christmas? Was she serious? Celebrating in an abandoned shanty with a stranger? No tree. No presents. He swallowed the pain. How did he allow himself to get so attached to the kid? He'd go talk with the people who ran the orphanage, but he had a feeling it was no better than the picture she'd painted. According to her, the chump moved in with this Gigi woman a few weeks after her husband's death, months before they married. This was not a suitable environment for a vulnerable kid like Peanut. But what if she made up the whole story, to keep from going back?

He had to know.

She watched Norm fork up half-a-dozen slices of thick, sizzling bacon. “Smells good. Where’d you get the vittles?”

“I spotted a store yesterday as we rode in. Drove over this morning and picked up a few things. Sit down and let’s eat.”

In between bites, Peanut said, “I miss Uncle George somethin’ awful, but I don’t think he’d take to me feeling sad while he’s being so happy. Do you?”

If he waited, she’d answer her own question. The kid had no problem carrying on a one-way conversation. He hid his smile when she didn’t slow down long enough to take the next breath.

“He’s happy, all right, ain’t no doubt about it. I ain’t never seen nobody who couldn’t wait to get to Heaven. It’s all he talked about. And if anybody could get a pass through them pearly gates, it’d be my Uncle George. That old man was good as gold.”

Norm took advantage of an opportunity to ask a question, when she gulped down a glass of milk. “Peanut, you said only one thing could take away your happiness today. Mind telling me what that would be?”

For the first time, she appeared to be at a loss for words. Perhaps he should’ve left well-enough alone.

Staring down at her empty plate, she muttered, “You gonna leave me at Nine Gables, ain’t you?”

“Nine Gables?”

“The orphanage.” She swiped the milk from her upper lip with the back of her hand. "I don't wanna talk about it. I reckon you'll do what you gotta do, and I'll do what I gotta do."

"And what does that mean?"

With a shrug, she stood and picked up the empty plates. She grabbed Uncle George's barbecue apron from off a nail near the sink, put it around her neck and pumped water into an aluminum dishpan.

When she dried the last dish, Norman walked over and lifted the apron over her head "You ready?"

Her lip poked out. "Now? But you promised. You said we could stay until after Christmas."

"And we will. But if we're celebrating Christmas here, we'll need a tree, won't we?"

She squealed. "You mean it?"

"Of course, I mean it. Come on. Time's wasting."

Norm found an axe in a shed out back and led the way through the woods. "When you find one you like, let me know and we'll cut it down."

Ludie stopped and scrutinized half-a-dozen before she spotted the perfect short-leafed pine. "What about this one, Uncle Norm? Isn't it beautiful?"

"About the most beautiful tree I've ever seen. You have a real eye, kiddo."

"Reckon it's big enough?"

"Oh, I think it's plenty big. If it were any larger, we wouldn't be able to get it in the house. Look around and see what you can find to tie on the branches, and we'll decorate it after I make a stand and get it in the house."

"Uncle Norm, you know what I wish? I wish you was my daddy."

His throat tightened. He leaned the axe against the tree and wrapped his arms around this child who had managed to steal his heart. "I'm sorry life has dealt you such a bad hand, kiddo, but wishing for something doesn't make it happen. If it did, neither one of us would be celebrating Christmas in a rundown shanty in the middle of the swamps."

Her lip quivered. "I would. I'm glad to be celebrating in Uncle George's cabin with you." Her eyes welled with tears. "But you wish you wadn't here with me, don't you?"

"It's not that, Peanut."

"Yes, it is. You can't wait to get rid of me. Well, you don't have to put up with me no longer. Go ahead. Take off and leave me. That's what everybody does."

"Seems to me you've done some leaving yourself. I'll wager the orphanage is in the same place you left it."

"You don't get it, do you? Gigi didn't give a flip about me or she would've listened when I tried to tell her the truth about Zeke. She chose him over me and he hates me. Ain't nobody never give a flip about me. Nobody except Uncle George."

"You're wrong, kid. I think you're pretty special." Hoping to get her mind off painful memories, Norm spotted a tin can lying on the ground. "Bring me that can."

"Whatcha gonna do?"

"You'll see." He pulled out his pocket knife and cut off the bottom. Then, he cut a section of vine, hanging from a tree. After running the vine through both ends, he laid the can on the ground and stomped the center. Holding both ends of the vine, he held it up. "What d'ya think? Our very first Christmas decoration."

"I think you're about the smartest man in the whole wide world, Uncle Norm. It's beautiful. This is gonna be a Christmas I won't never forget."

He lowered his gaze. "Neither will I, kid. Neither will I. We'd better head back to the cabin. It's getting colder." He picked the tree up by the trunk to drag through the woods.

"You go on. I'll be in d'rectly. I'm wanna look for more decorations."

Norm made a stand for the tree out of two old boards he found in the shed and set it up in the corner of the room.

Forty-five minutes later, Peanut ran in the house, shivering. She'd taken off her sweater and wrapped dozens of treasures she found in the woods, including pine cones, a pocket full of chinquapins, a few ripe persimmons, Spanish moss, three tin cans, a couple of small apothecary bottles and a long scuppernong vine. "This is all I could find."

"You did good, kid. The Spanish moss will add a nice touch. We'll pretend they're icicles."

After hanging all her treasures, she stepped back and gazed. "I

Suwannee, I ain't never seen a prettier tree. Just wish we had some real boxes to put under it."

"Well, go look in the shed. I picked up a couple while I was at the grocery store this morning."

She squealed. "For real?" She ran outside and came back in with two empty boxes. "I know exactly what I'm gonna give you. I thought about it all night long, last night." Holding both boxes, she said, "Which one you want?"

"I'm gonna need the big one, if that's alright with you."

"You serious? You already know what you gonna give me?"

"Well, of course, I do. I've been thinking about this, too, you know."

"Oh, Uncle Norm, I don't know if I can wait 'til tomorrow. You wanna let's open our presents now?"

"No way, kiddo. We're gonna wait until Christmas morning."

Ludie closed her eyes tight, but sleep wouldn't come. She tried to imagine what Uncle Norm would give her, if he had the money to buy something real. Not that it really mattered. Whatever he pretended to be in the box would be almost as good as it being real, just knowing he cared enough to play-like. In years past, she was lucky to get an apple or an orange for Christmas. The thought of opening a present—even an imaginary one—picked out just for her, was ten times more exciting than a piece of fruit. Maybe twenty times. No, a hundred-thousand times more fun. Never had she been so excited. She snuggled under Uncle George's moth-eaten wool blanket and eventually fell asleep.

Christmas morning, she sprang out of bed before daylight, and ran over to where Uncle Norm lay wrapped in an old quilt on the floor, in front of the fireplace. "Uncle Norm, wake up. Get up! It's Christmas."

He sat up and yawned. "Okay, okay. Turn your head, Peanut, while I put on my pants."

She picked up the largest box under the tree and shook it. Her heart pounded with excitement at the sound of something rattling inside.

Tucking his shirttail in, Norm said, "So, any idea what it might be?"

She giggled. "Uh . . . a new dress with metal buttons?"

Norm shook his head. "Nope." His throat tightened. So she wanted a new dress. How he wished he could buy her one, but the money was getting short and he had no idea when he'd have more. First, he had to know who he was. And so far, he hadn't made much progress.

She shook the box once more. "A box of candy?"

"Wrong again." The first thing he'd buy her, as soon as he found his answers would be a big box of chocolates. The kid deserved so much more than life had dealt her. If she was his . . . but she wasn't and pretending wouldn't make it so. He'd find out tomorrow who had guardianship, and if he wasn't satisfied with what he discovered, no way would he leave her with folks who wouldn't treat her right.

"I give up. Can I open it now?"

"Sure, kid. I hope you like it."

She tore open the box and dumped out four small nuts. A black walnut, a pecan, an acorn and a peanut.

Norm said, "This is the family I'd give you, if I could, Peanut! A mama, a daddy, you and a baby sister. You're one-of-a-kind, kid, and if I ever have a little girl, I hope she turns out to be just like you."

She crammed the nuts in her pocket, and ran out of the cabin, sobbing.

Wasn't this something she wanted? Maybe she was expecting something tangible. Had he misunderstood?

Norm stumbled through the woods until he heard her snubbing. She was sitting on the ground, leaning against a large hickory nut tree. He pulled off his jacket, handed it to her, then wrapped his arm around her. "Kiddo, I'm sorry I ruined your Christmas. I guess I'm not very good at picking out presents."

"You think I'm squalling because I was disappointed? Oh, Uncle Norm, I'm crying because you gave me the most wonderful present in the whole world."

He looked on the ground beside her. She had the nuts lined up. Five, not four.

A wide grin wrapped around her face, almost to the point of reaching her glistening eyes. "Wanna meet my family?" She pointed first to the walnut. "This is my daddy. His name is Norm."

"Honey, maybe you shouldn't—"

"Wait! I'm not through. And this pecan, well this is my mama. Her name is Gigi." Her eyes lit up. "Naturally, I'm the peanut, since you call me that, but I reckon you might as well know, I go by Ludie. And this acorn, well, this is my baby sister, but she doesn't have a name. Not yet, anyhow."

Norm's gut knotted as if he'd swallowed a pound of chinquepins. What had he done? Naming the nuts was the last thing he would've expected her to do. Should he reprimand her for making him her daddy? Did it matter? After all, it was a Christmas fantasy. Right? She was a bright kid. She understood it was make believe. Tomorrow everything would be back to normal, and he'd be Uncle Norm again. And the woman she was so crazy about would still be married to the man Peanut had such a dislike for. Didn't all kids fantasize the way they'd like things to be? Wasn't this what he wanted? To give her a family, even if it was make-believe and for only a day? Why not go along if it made her happy.

"I see you've added an extra one to our family. I guess you have a brother?"

"You know I don't have a brother. That's Grandpa George. I found him lying under the hickor' nut tree."

"You mean Uncle George, don't you?"

"Nope." She picked up the hickory nut and clutched the small nut to her heart. "He's my Grandpa."

Norm nodded. "Fine. I suppose every family should have a grandpa."

She laid Grandpa down and picked up the tiny acorn. "Since you're the daddy, you should name the baby. What's a good name, Daddy?"

Norm tried to blink away the tears and blurted the first thing that came to mind. "How about Mercy?"

"Mercy? Perfect. That's a great name." She held the acorn in her palm, as if cradling an infant. With her head cocked to the side, she whispered, "Hello, Mercy. I'm your big sister. Welcome to our happy family."

"Peanut, I'm freezing. Grab your family and let's head back to the cabin."

"*Our* family, Daddy." She opened both fists. The walnut and pecan were in one hand and the peanut, acorn and hickory nut in the other. "I won't ever, ever let us get separated." She dropped all five nuts in her pocket. "There! We belong together."

When they reached the cabin, Norm picked up a few pieces of firewood and carried inside. "I have a question. When you named your family, you called yourself Ludie. It's kinda cute, but why did you decide to change your name?"

"I didn't change it."

"So you were fibbing when you told me your name was Clementine?" He put three logs in the fireplace and leaned over to light a stick of kindling.

"No. Eliza Clementine is my rightful name. Ludie's what I've been called all my life."

"I see." He tousled her hair with his fingers. "You're quite a girl, little Miss Clementine."

She dismissed his words with a hearty head-shake. "No, Daddy. Clementine was a runaway orphan. I'm not an orphan no more. I got me a family. Since Grandpa George calls me Ludie, I reckon you should, too."

"I'm confused. So you had an Uncle George *and* you have a Grandpa George? You've never mentioned your grandpa. Where does he live?"

When Ludie ignored the question, Norm grinned. "I get it. Grandpa is make-believe. Right?"

She shrugged. "Maybe he is, maybe he ain't." She reached in her pocket and pulled out the tiny acorn. "Hello, little Mercy. I'm gonna help Mama take care of you. I'll feed you and I'll even change your diapers. We have the best family in the whole world." She walked over to the table and lined the nuts in a row.

Norm swallowed hard. He'd thought he was doing the right thing. Now, he wasn't so sure. Was she beginning to confuse fantasy with reality? What would it do to her when her "daddy" would walk away and leave her at the orphanage?

"Pea . . . Ludie, you do understand our family is make-believe. Just as there was no real gift in that box, those nuts are . . . well, they're just nuts."

Bright emerald eyes opened into giant spheres. "No, Daddy. These ain't just nuts. This is the family you wished for me. And it's the best family in the whole world."

"Sweetheart, I . . . I don't think you should call me Daddy.

Let's stick with Uncle Norm."

"Why?"

"Because I'm not your daddy."

Ludie crossed her arms and stuck her lips out in a pout. "You ain't my Uncle, either." Tears poured down her cheek. "Well, if you don't want me, I don't want you, either." She threw the nuts across the room and darted out the door.

Norm sucked in a deep breath. What had he done? Poor kid. For a few minutes, she was experiencing the best Christmas of her life, and with a few ill-placed words, he'd taken it all away from her.

He ran out the door and caught up with her as she ran down the road. "Hey, Ludie, your Mama told me to tell you the baby needs a bottle. Would you mind feeding her?"

Her face lit up like a neon sign. She threw her arms around him. "Tell her I'm coming. I'll change her diapers, too."

"Thank you, Ludie. We're so proud to have a big girl like you to help with our sweet little Mercy."

They walked back to the cabin, arm in arm.

Norm stared at his box under the tree. Whatever she'd chosen to put inside, he'd act as if it were exactly what he wanted. She had no way of knowing, since what he wanted possibly didn't exist.

****

At four-thirty, Christmas morning, Gracie shook Veezie. "Wake up. It's time."

"Time?" She wiped her eyes and yawned. "Time for what?"

Before Gracie could answer, Veezie popped up in bed and slung her feet off the side. "Oh m'goodness. It's *time*?" She sailed out of bed and grabbed her robe. "Hold on. I'll run down the hall and wake up your father and tell him to get Flint on the phone."

Gracie giggled. "Calm down, I feel fine."

"But you said . . ."

"I said it was time. I didn't say I was dying. My water just broke, but I'm not hurting."

Veezie reached in the chifferobe drawer and took out a fresh gown and threw it toward the bed. "Need help dressing?"

"No, I can handle it. Oh, Veezie, I'm so excited."

Veezie went running down the hall and within minutes, the house was abuzz. The kids were too busy opening gifts from Santa to pay attention to the excitement taking place upstairs.

Shep paced the floor until Flint arrived and then fell to his knees in the hallway, just outside his daughter's room, while the doctor examined her. "Please, Lord . . . please help my Gracie to deliver a healthy child." If only he could erase the image of Gracie's mother lying in a coffin, but the picture was embedded on his brain. A verse from Proverbs that he'd quoted so many times, came to mind. "Trust in the Lord with all thine heart and lean not to thine own understanding."

The doctor walked out a few minutes later. "Any coffee still on the stove downstairs?"

Shep grabbed him by the arm. "Flint, how is she? She's not due for another two or three weeks. Can you stop the contractions?"

"And why would I want to do that? You're about to become a grandpa, ol' man. Calm down. This could take hours. That baby may not come before nightfall. Now, how about you and I go see if there's coffee in the pot?"

Before he could object, another verse popped in his head. "What time I am afraid, I will trust in thee." *I am afraid, Lord, but I choose to trust you. I leave my sweet Gracie in your hands.* He sucked in a lungful of air. "Coffee sounds good. Let's go."

As they walked down the stairs, Shep thought he heard someone say, "I will never leave thee, nor forsake thee." He glared at Flint. "Did you say something?"

Flint shrugged. "Nope. You must be hearing things."

"Good."

"Shep, are you okay?"

"Never been better, except I'm starving. I wasn't hungry this morning, but maybe we can talk Veezie into making some of her famous pancakes and frying us up a few slabs of salt pork."

"Sounds good, but I thought you were anxious for us to get back to Gracie."

His smile was hard to hide. "It won't take long for us to eat. Besides, I'm not worried. I left her in good hands."

Chapter Forty

Ludie ran in and picked the nuts off the floor. She stuck four nuts in her pocket and with the acorn cradled in the palm of her hand, she pretended to be feeding a baby. Then tiptoeing over to the cot, she gently laid the acorn on the mattress. She whispered, "Now that Mercy's asleep, why don't you open your present, Daddy?"

Norm swallowed hard. A part of him wanted to explain that after today, she needed to go back to referring to him as Uncle Norm, yet he couldn't deny his heart swelled a little each time he heard her call him, "Daddy."

She handed Norm the box. He shook it and Ludie's joyous laughter sounded like a dozen tiny bells ringing at once. "Don't shake it so hard. It might break."

"Break? Hmm. A pair of spectacles?"

"No, silly. You don't need glasses. Guess again."

"Oh, I know. You bought me a new car and you're afraid I'll break the windshield." He loved to hear her laugh. Sounded like a dozen little bells ringing at once.

"A new car would've been a swell idea, but nope, that's not it.

Give up?"

"I think so. Can I open it now?"

"Sure. You wouldn't guess in a million years."

Norm reached in and pulled out a soda bottle. "This is what I've always wanted. How did you know?"

"You're being funny. You don't even know what it is. It's a Genie bottle."

"Ooh, my very own Genie. What a great gift, kiddo. Thanks. Now I can have anything I wish for."

"Not anything. You only get one wish. So what will it be?"

"Only one?" He had two things he wished for. He wanted to find Grace and he wanted Ludie to be happy. How could he choose? Would it not be selfish to put his own desire ahead of the child's? He laughed at himself, acting as if there was a Genie inside the soda bottle, waiting for him to choose between the two.

Her smile stretched from ear to ear. "You like it?"

"I love it."

"Well? Make a wish."

"I wish . . . " He paused.

"Go ahead, Daddy. Rub your hand over the top, while you wish. That's how you do it."

"Okay, don't rush me. This is very important, you know." He held the bottle in one hand and rubbed his hand over the top. Then with his head bowed, he prayed. "Lord, I thank you for bringing Ludie into my life. She's given me the best present in the whole world, because I needed a reminder that I have a heavenly father who isn't stuck inside a bottle, allowing me one request and one only. Father, I love Ludie, but you love her even more than I do. My prayer is that you'll make yourself known in a mighty way and confirm to her that whatever situation she finds herself in, she has a father—a real Father, who is looking out for her best interests. And Lord, if I'm seeking for someone who doesn't exist, then please fill the void in my heart, so I can stop striving and get on with my life. Humbly asking these requests in the name of your son, Jesus Christ, and thanking you in advance. Amen."

He reached over and hugged Ludie. "Thank you, sweetheart. I'll keep this bottle forever, and anytime I begin to feel hopeless, I'll have a reminder that as much fun as it may be to pretend we have a Genie in a bottle, the truth is, we often forget we have something even better. We have access to a God who invites us to come to Him as many times as we desire, to ask for anything we need."

She snuggled up under his arm and looking into his face, said, "I got you just what you wanted, didn't I?"

"Yes, you did. We're gonna be fine, Ludie. Yes ma'am, you and I are gonna be just fine. I don't know what's gonna happen, but I have a peace that whatever it is, God is working it out for our good. I hope you can believe it, too."

Her lip quivered. "If you believe it, then I can. I'm ready to go back to Nine Gables, Daddy, if you want to take me." Her voice cracked. "You won't forget me, will you?"

"Sweetheart, I could never forget you . . . But I don't think you should call—"

She reached up and covered his mouth with her hand. "I know you aren't my daddy. But it's still Christmas, right? I can pretend, can't I?"

"Sure kid." He winked. "Grab your mama and little sister. And don't forget Grandpa George. I think we're ready to go—now that God has gone before us."

Ludie threw her arms around Norm. "Daddy, I'm gonna miss you somethin' awful, but to tell the truth, I've missed Belle and Maddie Claire." She lifted a shoulder. "I reckon I've missed Toby and Tanner, too, even though they made me mad when they pulled on my pigtails and said they could outrun me."

"Could they?"

"Are you kidding? I'm much faster but they wouldn't race me because they knew I'd win.

Still, they're funny and I'll be glad to see 'em them again. But don't tell them I said so, or I'll deny it."

"So tell me about the girls. Which one is the youngest?"

"That'd be Maddie Claire. She's only six but smart as a whip. Why, she can clean a house better'n most grown women. She's sweet, too. I was pretty cantankerous when we first moved to Nine Gables, but she never got mad at me. She clung to me like kudzu. I couldn't get rid of her no matter how mean I was to her. I reckon she's about the sweetest little girl in the whole wide world. I can't wait to see her."

"And the other little girl is her sister. Right?"

"Yeah, that would be Belle. She's eight, but she doesn't talk."

"Oh? I suppose she's deaf?"

"No. She hears perfectly. She just doesn't talk."

"Doesn't, because she doesn't like to talk? Or can't?"

"Well, we know she can, because she said a word on the way home from school one day, but then when we tried to get her to say it so Gigi could hear her, she clammed up and wouldn't say it again."

"You sure she said a word, or maybe made a grunt that sounded like a word?"

"No." Ludie quickly crossed her hand over her heart. "I promise, she talked. She really did."

"So what did she say?"

"Puppy. And not once, but she said it again, clear as day. We all heard it. We were walking past Mr. Weinberger's house and there was a litter of puppies inside his gate and Belle squealed, 'Puppy, puppy.'" Ludie giggled. "We all jumped up and down and started hugging her, but then she stopped talking and looked scared. That was it. Never another word."

Norm stopped the car, and turned around in the middle of the dirt road.

"Why you turning around?" She pointed ahead. "Nine Gables is that-a-way."

"I just had an idea. It's Christmas day. Wouldn't you like to give the kids at the orphanage a Christmas present?"

She ginned. "Sure, that'd be swell! I'll give 'em my box." She rubbed her chin. "Hmm, let me think what I can pretend is in it."

He pulled up in front of an old country farmhouse and stopped. "I have an idea." He pointed to a sign nailed to a tree. "What d'ya think?"

Ludie's smile broadened as she read the two words. "Free Puppies."

Norm opened his door. "Come on, let's go take a look."

"Oh, Daddy. You're the best in the whole world. I wish you'd still be my daddy tomorrow."

They walked up on the porch and a farmer in overalls came to the door. "The puppies are back of the house. Go around and take your pick. Get the whole litter if you're a mind too," then slammed the door.

Ludie didn't hesitate before choosing the scrawniest of the bunch. She picked him up and cuddled him in her arms. "I'm gonna name him King."

"That's a fine name for a Christmas puppy, since this is a time when people all over the world come together to celebrate the birth of King Jesus. But I'm curious. What made you choose the runt? I figured you'd pick the solid black one."

"Why? Because he's the prettiest? He'll get picked for sure. I wanted the one no one else would want. I know what it feels like to be lined up in an orphanage and have married couples walk right past me to pick a younger, prettier little girl to take home with them. No one ever wanted me, either."

"Oh, honey, I hope you don't think that's why I'm taking you back to Nine Gables. If there was any other route, I'd take it, but there's not. Not yet, anyway. However, if I can find what I'm looking for, I promise, if it's at all possible, I'll be back to get you."

"You mean it, don't you?"

The old car bumped and chugged down the corduroy dirt road. Ludie pointed. "It's about two, maybe three miles ahead. Not so far on foot."

He reached over and pulled her close. "I'm sorry, kiddo. I really am. I don't want to leave you—and that's the truth—but I have to consider what's best for you. We both know that dropping out of school is not an option. You've already missed a lot. It'll be difficult to catch up. You understand, don't you?"

"I know. It ain't so much going back that makes me weepy. It's knowing I won't be able to run through the woods to visit Uncle George, when I get lonely." She pointed to a long driveway. "There it is. That's Nine Gables."

His eyes widened. "Jeepers. That huge castle is an orphanage?"

"I reckon you might call it a castle. It was a fine place to live until Zeke showed up."

"Ludie, give him a chance. Maybe he won't seem so bad, once you get to know him better."

"I'll try, but he doesn't like me and I know it."

"That's because he doesn't know you. Let him see the sweet

girl who lives inside you, and he'll have to love you. Remember how mean you said you were to Maddie Claire, but when you finally realized she really liked you, it made you change your mind about her? Why not give Zeke that same opportunity?"

"You really think it'll work?"

"With all my heart. He won't be able to resist loving you. I know for a fact that—"

Ludie suddenly squealed and pointed to two little girls playing in the front yard. "Look, there's Belle and Maddie Claire." Her bubbling laughter made Norm forget what he was about to say.

"They're playing house. I Suwannee, them two make the best play houses. See the apple crate? That's their stove, and the upside-down bucket is the table. They always keep pretty flowers on their table." Giant teardrops rolled down each side of her face, but Norm had a feeling they were happy tears.

"For a long time, I wouldn't play with them 'cause I thought I was too old, but Maddie Claire kept begging. Then one day, I gave in and played like I was having dinner with them. Seeing how happy it made them, I ate near 'bout everything they cooked, after that."

"You're a good kid.So what was on the menu?"

"They cooked chinaberries and made Indian cane salad. A lot."

"Chinaberries? And you ate them?"

"No, silly. It was just play like. You can't eat chinaberries, but the Indian cane is pretty good. It's sour, but I like sour."

"I suppose the boys pretended to be the daddies."

"Not really. Mostly they played ball. One time, Zeke caught 'em smoking rabbit tobacco and tanned their hides. Gigi tried to tell Zeke it wouldn't hurt 'em, but Zeke said 'today it's rabbit tobacco, tomorrow, it'll be cigarettes.' To be honest, I've smoked it myself, but I didn't see the fun in it."

The car hadn't come to a complete stop when Ludie jerked open the door and jumped out. Norm stayed in the car and watched.

The two little girls left their playhouse and ran with open arms. Maddie Claire, squealed, "It's Ludie. Where you been, Ludie? We've missed you, haven't we, Belle?"

Belle nodded and threw her arms around Ludie's waist.

Ludie said, "Where are the twins? I have a Christmas present for all of you."

"A present for *us*?"

"Yes, but we'll have to find Toby and Tanner."

"They don't live here no more."

"They don't? Where are they?"

Maddie Claire shrugged. "Dunno."

Ludie handed them the box, and Maddie sat it on the ground to open it.

Belle squealed with delight at the sound of a yelp coming from inside the box and grabbed the puppy in her arms.

Norm's throat tightened. "Thank you, Lord," he whispered. "You knew exactly what the child needed."

Maddie Claire and Ludie's infectious laughter caused Norm to laugh with them, though his eyes clouded with water.

Ludie said, "His name is King."

"King." Belle repeated, holding the pup close to her heart. Then, in slow, halting words, as if her words were playing out on a 33 1/3 vinyl record set at 78 RPM speed, she said, "Thank . . . you . . . Ludie . . .for the . . .puppy."

Maddie Claire squealed, "Belle, you talked. Don't stop. Say something else."

Belle lifted her shoulders and giggled. "Merry Christmas, everybody."

Chapter Forty-One

Norm slipped out of the car while the girls fussed over King. Was he doing the right thing? If so, why the knot in the pit of his stomach?

If this Zeke fellow had any thoughts of punishing Ludie, he'd have to do it over Norm's dead body. The kid had been through enough. He wanted to grab her, shove her in the car, drive away and never look back. Instead, he lumbered up the tall marble steps and rang the doorbell.

A tall, lanky black man opened the door. "Good afternoon, sir. Whom may I say is calling?"

"Uh . . ." He swallowed hard. "Just tell Mrs. . . . the lady of the house that Ludie has returned, and I'd like a word with her."

The old fellow stared over Norm's right shoulder, then rocked back on his feet.

Norm grabbed his arm. "You okay, sir?"

Norm heard Ludie squeal. She ran up the steps skipping every other one.

"Uncle George! I thought you wuz dead. She grabbed him around the waist in a hug. Whatcha doing here at Nine Gables?"

"We'll talk about me later, chile. Where in tarnation you been? I been worried slam crazy."

"I'm fine, now that I know you're alive." She threw her arms around him. "Oh, Uncle George, I didn't think I could go on living without you." She grabbed Norm by the hand. "Uncle George, this is my . . . my friend, Norm."

George tipped his head. "Nice to make your acquaintance, sir, and I sho' thank you for bringing my baby back home."

Norm thrust out his hand. "So you're Uncle George. I thought—well, never mind what I thought. All that matters is you're here, and from what Ludie's told me about you, I know I can trust you to take good care of her."

"I'll try my best. Yessir, I'll try my best. She's a mighty special young'un."

When the butler's voice cracked and his eyes watered, Norm had a strange feeling the bond between these two was stronger than either could admit. The old black man acted as if he could be her . . . *grandpa*? He recalled her exact words when she said, "You can call me Ludie, like my Grandpa George." Impossible.

Ludie held the old man tightly about his waist. "Oh, Uncle George. I dream up lots of stuff, but I ain't never dreamed up a Christmas good as this one. Now, tell me why you're here?"

"Why, sugar, I work here. Miz Harper and Doc came down to my place looking for ya, the day you went missing. You might recollect, it was real cold Thanksgiving Day, and the doc, well, he said it was too cold for me to stay in the shanty. So next thing I knew, they was back saying yo' Miz Gigi was beggin' for them to come get me and insistin' I move back into the basement where me and Beulah lived years ago."

"You mean . . . me and you gonna finally get to live together? For real?"

"It's the truth, sugar."

"Where's Gigi? Is she mad at me for leaving?"

"Oh, sugar, she ain't mad at you, but you gave her a fright, you did. I tried to tell her the Good Lord was watching over you, and you'd be comin' down that road in due time, but she kept sayin' it was all her fault. I Suwannee, po' little thing cried for days and days after you left."

"T'weren't her fault. I wanna see her, and tell her so. I spect I'll get a whoopin' from Zeke, but I don't care. I'll take it, long as I can be with you, Uncle George."

"Why, Mr. Zeke ain't no problem no more, chile, and Miz Gigi . . . well, she's upstairs. Just got through birthing a baby." His eyes widened. "It's good the little rascal finally got here or Pastor Shep woulda wore a hole in the linoleum, traipsing back and forth."

"The baby. I almost forgot. I want Gigi to meet Norm. Can we go up?"

Norm shook his head. "That's not a good idea, kiddo. She won't feel like company. Maybe I should come back later."

A man, standing at the top of the stairs with a stethoscope hung over his neck, looked down and shouted, "Impossible! It can't be." His eyes narrowed into tiny slits. "Is it . . . is it really you? But . . . but they said you were dead." He wiped his brow. "Unbelievable. Oh my soul, she tried to tell us. I can't wait to see her face when you walk in her room."

Norm couldn't tell if he was laughing or crying.

Ludie threw up her arm. "Hi, Doc. It's me alright, but I ain't dead."

"Not you, Ludie, although I'm thrilled to see you, both. What a surprise."

"Both?" Norm's knees weakened. *He recognizes me*. Could it be true? The woman upstairs who had just given birth to another man's baby was his wife? Well, not for long. If she hadn't been granted a divorce already, surely this would be grounds. But if it happened to be true, not only was he married to a two-timing woman, it also meant Doc Martin was right and Grace was a figment of his dreams. That would be the hardest part to accept.

"Come on up," the doctor yelled, leaning over the baluster. "This is like a dream come true." He let out a loud guffaw. "What am I saying? It *is* a dream come true. What a wonderful Christmas present this will be. She's doing fine and has given birth to a healthy baby girl. Her father's in the room with her."

Norm's throat tightened. So the father of the baby girl was in the room. *Well, of course, he'd be with her.* Whatever made him think he'd be speaking to Gigi alone?

Ludie snatched him by the hand and pulled him up the stairs. "Come on. You said you wanted to talk to her."

"True, but this isn't the proper time. Uh, not with the father in there. I'm sure they want to be alone."

The doctor grabbed Norm in a hearty bear hug. "Are you kidding? Trust me, he'll be as thrilled as she will. It couldn't be a better time."

Norm's feet felt as if they were glued to the floor. *There's no Grace. No Mercy. I'm married to a cold-hearted woman named Gigi who couldn't wait for my corpse to cool before remarrying.* His heart pounded at the thought. But why get so upset until he could know for sure? If by some wonderful chance this Gigi dame wasn't his wife, then her wretched affairs were no concern of his. But he considered Ludie his business, and before he left, he'd want assurances that this was a stable environment for an impressionable young girl.

Ludie ran ahead, leaving him to enter alone.

He crammed his hands in his pockets to stop the shakes and slowly eased through the partially open door. The laughter and merry voices in the room ceased the moment he stepped inside. Glares and dropped jaws made him want to grab Ludie and run.

Then, his gaze settled on the beautiful woman lying in bed with a tiny baby nestled next to her body. *That's Gigi?* He had to question how such a sweet-looking face could be guilty of the sinister acts he'd suspected. A horrid though entered his mind. Maybe *he* was the scoundrel. His throat closed and his stomach burned as if he'd swallowed a pound of DDT. He wanted to turn and run, but his legs failed to obey. "Excuse me, I don't know—"

Before he could complete his statement, the woman raised up in the bed, and with tears flowing like an uncapped well, held out open arms. "Oh, my darling, I told them you were coming home, but no one believed me."

The doctor, who had followed him into the room, bent over the bed. "I'll take the baby, Gracie."

She shook her head, indicating she wasn't ready to part with the beautiful little girl with a head full of black wavy hair.

Norm swallowed hard. *Did he say Gracie? Grace—Gracie!* At that moment, as if someone turned a key and released the locked memories, his heart hammered. *Yes! I remember. I do. My Gracie.* Swallowing the lump in his throat, he eased down on the edge of the bed and brushed a lock of hair from her forehead. With lips trembling, he pressed his face against hers and cried. "Oh, Gracie. It's you. It *is* you. Gracie. My Gracie."

"Yes, sweetheart, it's me." She stroked his cheek. "A wise old man once told me God can speak to us through various means. Through his Word, through angels or even through dreams. Now, I know it's true."

He whispered, "I believe." His lips slid across her damp cheek, finding her mouth.

Then as if a fire had been lit under his feet, he jumped up. "I had no right to do that. I forgot. Have a nice life, Gracie."

Gracie's eyes widened. "What's wrong, honey?"

Ludie said, "What's going on here? You two know each other?"

His voice cracked. "We did. Once upon a time. Before she gave herself to another man and had his baby." He turned on his heels and rushed toward the door.

"Garth, wait! How could you possibly believe this baby belongs to another man? She's yours, Garth. Yours and mine."

He stopped short, then slowly made his way back, his lips quivering. "Is it true?"

Ludie's eyes squinted as she scrutinized Norm's face. "What did she call you? You're Garth? For real? I thought I only imagined it, 'cause I wanted you to be him. You've lost a lot of weight." Her eyes squinted, as if trying to bring the Garth she once knew into focus. "Your hair's grown out . . . and, and you've got a mustache." With her head cocked to the side, she glared, then squealed, "You really are him. What happened to you?"

Garth draped his arm around her. "Hold on Ludie. We'll have a lifetime to talk about the past. First, I need to wrap my head around the here and now. This is all going way too fast for me. Let me get this straight. Gracie, are you saying we're still married?"

"Yes, yes, yes, my darling! And this is our daughter." She pulled the cover away from the baby. "Mercy, meet your daddy. Look, Garth. She even has the dimple in her chin, just like yours."

He threw his cap in the air and let out a whoop. "Mercy?"

She nodded. "Like it?"

"I love it."

Ludie's mouth gaped open. "But that's what you—" She shrugged. "Never mind. I'll never understand, even if you explain."

"Shh!" Gracie cupped her hand over her ear. "Listen! Am I imagining things or is that our wedding song I hear?"

Outside, carolers belted out the refrain to *Joy to the World . . . He rules the world with truth and grace . . . And wonders of His love.*

Garth fell to his knees beside the bed and bowed his head. "Oh, Father God, although the wonders of your miraculous love is too magnificent, too marvelous, too amazing for my finite mind to fully comprehend, I acknowledge that when I was weak, you were strong. Thank you, Father, for your bountiful *Grace* and *Mercy . . .* and thank you. Lord, for bringing me home to mine."

GRACIE'S SOUTHERN COOKBOOK

PORK CAKE: (*Mrs. J.A. Rodgers from, Geneva, Alabama, passed this recipe down to Mrs. Will Redd from Mt. Pleasant, who shared it with Veezie, who gave it to me.*) *Cream six eggs with two pounds of brown sugar. Add 1 ½ pounds ground fat pork, 5 cups flour, 2 lbs. raisins, 1 quart chopped nuts, 2 tsps. soda, and a teaspoon of each of the following: cinnamon, cloves and allspice. Add a pint of boiling water. Mix and bake at 350 degrees for about an hour and thirty minutes. Bake in two tube pans.*

FIG PRESERVES: *A peck of figs, ten pounds sugar, couple of sliced lemons and ½ box baking soda. Put figs in sink or very large pan. Sprinkle with soda and pour boiling water over them. Let stand fifteen minutes. Drain and wash through three or four washes. Alternate layers of figs and sugar until all is used. Add lemon slices. Begin to heat on very low until juice covers figs. Increase heat to medium and cook until syrup is thick or figs done. Scald jars and drain. Fill with hot figs and seal. NEVER STIR AND FIGS WILL REMAIN WHOLE*

FRIED CHICKEN: *Cut up a fryer, salt and pepper good, then put in paper sack with flour and shake til covered. Fry in hot, deep grease until brown and crispy. (If grease is too hot, it'll get done on the outside and won't be done on the inside, but if grease is not hot enough, it'll be soggy and not crispy.) So fry between hot and real hot. Take up on newspaper to soak up the grease.*

BEULAH'S SWEET POTATO CASSEROLE: *Bake 6 nice-size sweet taters in hot oven til done. Remove skins, put in a bowl and mash up good with a potato masher. Add one cup sugar, a teaspoon vanilla, two eggs, a half-cup sweet milk, and three sticks oleo margarine or 1 ½ pounds butter. Pour in greased baking dish. Now mix up the topping. One cup flour, one cup brown sugar, one stick oleo, one cup chopped pecans. Spread the topping over the potato mixture and bake at 350 degrees for at least thirty minutes or until brown and pecans have a chance to get good and roasted or it won't be crunchy on top.*

CHITTERLINGS: (Better known as Chit'lins) *Take a ten-pound bucket of cleaned chitlins, pour into large pot and cover with water. Add a cup of cider vinegar, some bay leaves, a couple of onions, two nice-sized, peeled and chopped Irish potatoes, a chopped Bell pepper, salt and pepper to your liking. Bring to a boil; turn heat to low and simmer about 3 hours or until chitlins are tender. Drain the water and serve with hot sauce. Yum!*

CHICKEN 'N DUMPLIN'S: *Cut up a fat hen and boil in salty water. When falling off the bone, take up and set aside. Now, to make the dumplins. Sift a couple of rounded cups of self-rising flour into a bowl. With your fist, waddle a hole in the center and pour in a cup of your broth. Knead it like you would biscuits, and roll out on floured newspaper with your rolling pin, thin as you can get it, and still be able to lift strips off the paper. Cut into strips (about one inch wide and two inches long). Sprinkle good with flour to keep from sticking together. Drop one at the time in broth, but don't stir or they'll be tough. Just use your fork to gently pull them apart if they appear to stick. Cook about twenty minutes or until tender.*

BOILED PEANUTS: *Wash green peanuts, put in pressure cooker and cover with water and salt. Put on lid and when valve begins to jiggle (or about 10 lbs. pressure) start timing and cook 15 minutes. Set off to cool.*

TURNIP GREENS: *Boil about a ¾ slab of fatback, (or any pork will do.) in about three quarts of water in a large Dutch oven. Boil about thirty minutes. While meat boils, take about 4-5 pounds of thoroughly washed greens and put in the pot with the meat. Water should just cover tops of the turnips. Add salt and pepper to your taste. Needs to be seasoned good with pork and plenty of salt. Cook til tender, about forty-five minutes.*

CORNBREAD: *A good two cups of Pollard corn meal, half-Tbls salt (Garth likes his cornbread salty) and about 1 1/2 cups water or more. That's all! If you gonna fry it, make it almost soupy so it'll have crispy edges, and fry patties in hot grease. If you gonna bake it, make it thick enough to form a pone, then place in an iron skillet with enough hot grease in the bottom to cover good. Lay the pones on the hot grease and dab a little grease on tops. Stick in a 450-500 degree oven and cook until brown and crispy. (In South Alabama, if made with eggs, it's called eggbread, not cornbread. Eggbread is what you use to make chicken/turkey dressing. Any true Southerner knows Pollard meal from South Alabama is the only corn meal to use to make real cornbread.)*

PECAN PIE: (*Gracie got this recipe from Miz Lottie*) *Beat three eggs slightly, add 1 cup sugar, 1 cup white corn syrup, 1 ½ cups whole pecans, 2 level Tbls. flour, 1 Tbls. vanilla, 1 stick oleo. Combine in bowl and stir well. Pour into 2 unbaked pie shells. Bake in 400 degree oven for ten minutes, then reduce heat to 350 degrees and bake 'til firm and pecans are good and roasted, about 40-45 minutes*

FRIED SQUIRREL: *Cut up a squirrel, salt, pepper and roll in flour. Fry in deep grease until brown. Fork up the pieces on newspaper. Then pour up the grease, leaving the brown flour crumbs in the bottom of the pan, add water and stir to make gravy. Bring to a boil. Then place squirrel back in the pan, cover, and cook on low heat until meat is good and tender when stuck with a fork.*

AUNT ALMA'S NINE-LAYER CHOCOLATE CAKE– *My Aunt Alma Miller's famous cake recipe, she sells in Enterprise.*

CAKE: *(Basic 1,2,3,4 cake recipe.) 1 c butter, 2 c sugar, 3 c flour, 4 eggs. Grease and flour nine 8 inch pans, and divide cake mix evenly. Spread with back of spoon. Bake about 11 minutes or 'til toothpick comes back clean. Remove from pan immediately. (Run knife around edges to release from pan.*

FILLING: *4 Cups sugar, 1 c hot water, 2/3 c cocoa, 2 sticks butter, 2 t. vanilla.*

Mix sugar and cocoa. Add boiling water and stir thoroughly. Add vanilla. Cream butter, then stir into mixture. Cook on medium heat, slightly boiling, for twenty to maybe thirty minutes (soft ball stage when dripped from spoon into a bowl of water) Don't stir or beat or it'll sugar. Cool in pan of water and spread when cool.

PEANUT BRITTLE: *1 ½ cups sugar, ½ c white corn syrup, ½ c water, 2 c raw peanuts, 1 t. soda, ¼ stick butter. Cook sugar, water and syrup 'til mixture spins a thread. Add peanuts and cook slowly 'til mix turns golden brown. Add butter, then soda, continue stirring while cooking. Pour onto buttered slab. Using two forks, spread mixture as thin as possible. When cold, break into pieces.*

AUTHOR'S NOTE: If you've enjoyed the Switched Series, I'd love to from you. My email address is kay@kaychandler.info. A review on Amazon is always much appreciated. Thank you for choosing my books. God Bless!